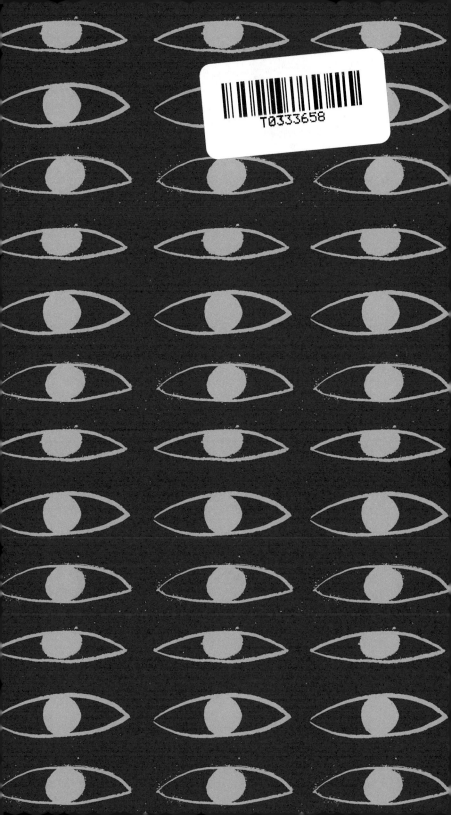

Bardskull

BARDSKULL

Martin Shaw

unbound

First published in 2023

Unbound
Level 1, Devonshire House, One Mayfair Place, London W1J 8AJ
www.unbound.com

Text design by PDQ Digital Media Solutions Ltd.

A CIP record for this book is available from the British Library

ISBN 978-1-78965-156-0 (hardback)
ISBN 978-1-78965-155-3 (ebook)

Printed in Great Britain by CPI Group (UK)

1 3 5 7 9 8 6 4 2

MIX
Paper | Supporting
responsible forestry
FSC
www.fsc.org
FSC® C171272

CONTENTS

The uproar in your hand I could never have predicted. Never corralled, sweet-talked or defended myself against. I walked out one summer morning and barely ceased till St George's Day of the next year. These three accounts come from a place, Holne Chase, on Dartmoor in the far west of Britain. At the end of this account I find I have fallen into a devastation of love.

It would be chicanery to tell you this has been crafted for your pleasure. It hasn't. It would be a fiction to tell you I have absolute purchase on the encounter. When I dare pick the book up it seems at times like an extended incantation, at others a series of battles. It often frightens me.

These are words from the rough, from the stomp. Things hurtled through me, old things. I am not the same.

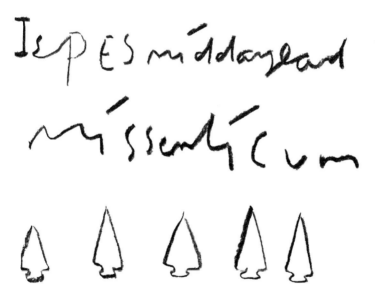

part one

bardskull

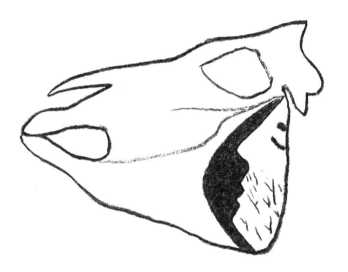

And I tell you this

The slaughterhouse of language did not begin here. It did not
begin in the cider bar of Newton Abbot where we fill our jaws with
smoky, flat, stultifying vats of the stuff. Tony of Scorriton says you
can't trust cider without some cow shit in it, scudding around at the
bottom of the glass. A mystery swirl, an incant of grass and gut, a
little gamble on health and safety.

Percentages are for blow-ins. Grockles.

No. We commit to distention. To the apple-madness. We fucking
commit. Bloaters all, alive in the moonlight, scampering about,
hitting things.

No. It wasn't us that killed the speech. The holy hoofprint of
the rough word still thwacks about in the gob of Dan from the
woodyard, fists like hams but nimble as a wren when cradling a
seedling. Words crackle around him like weird, wet light, and it's
your own theory-addled sickness if you can't see it.

Numbskull

Nanskull

Dadskull

Bardskull

When I was small and at the new big school I got pulled out of
class. I was in the wrong group. I was with the smarts and I was
not a smart. I was taken to the belly of the school to my people.
They smelt bad, like clothes left in the washer. There was a boy
permanently in the cupboard with his tiny, pale cock out, in case
someone – *anyone* – would come in and give it a tug.

This was the Numbskull I got put into. I crawled deep down into its fontanelle, and into the brainmuck, and not much was meant to happen thereafter. I was meant to stay there.
Never got more than 13% in maths. Percentages again.

Some great threat had been avoided, when I was plucked out of the room filled with light and windows.

Nanskull is in the forest round the cottage where I am I am I am going to tell you about secretive things that happen in it. It's a time for telling secrets.

Nanskull is my granny, Monica, walking the dog in the woods, fifty years before I ambled in. Monica's mind is adrift in death-woe. Of course it is. A husband is gone, first or second, I can't remember. Grief is a thing so deep even a white person can make a song-line from it. Granny's lines are spindle-thin now, like a frost about to meet the sun. I can only just make them out. But Nanskull is the first of us here. Before me, or Dad or anyone. So let's begin there. I see her on the night-lawn, coins spilling from each sleeve, telling us to *spend the fucking money*. You can't spend it over here, she says, no matter how much you tip.

Nanskull will speak to Numbskull across the owl court of my garden. I listen with the black ram in one hand, the knife in the other.

Here at the gate of the dead.

She speaks as deep as Tiresias, old Irish words.

Last night the dog was howling for you
The snipe was calling for you
Through the branches and bleak marsh.

You are the sorrowed secret of the woods
And may you be without mate

Till you find me again.

When I go to the well of loneliness
I sit quietly and comb through
All my trouble.

I behold the world but
I do not
Behold my man.

He has an amber look
To his hair.

Then Monica is gone into the woods again, calling for her dogs, calling for her son, calling for her husband.

When my dad is seventeen, she will die.

Dadskull is the skull of an almost-orphan. Night walker, pushing his hands out into the black, endlessly walking, since I was a little boy living near the sea waiting for him to come home so I could fall asleep. He is eating dark as he walks, body fattening with the calorific encounter of numinous night. It wasn't food that made him big, it was the dark. He is learning languages from ancient places to one day become a vicar but he will not become a vicar he will become a preacher, much better, jostling his curation of words out away from the Celtic west to the Saxon east.

Crowland

Yaxley

Whaplode

Maybe as far as Long Sutton

Dadskull is nested up in his solitary haunt throwing twigs at Holland, but in some way he is always glancing west. Teachers tried to make Dadskull kill words, and he manfully tried, but they erupt at the worst-possible fantastic times. He wears a badge that says I AM SPARTACUS. This is what makes him a wonder, a Hermian articulator of messages from his florid, unfashionable, magnificent dead. Dadskull is glancing west again.

❖

In the last century an old Indian man told me a secret. The kind from South Dakota not Delhi. He told me this thing. He told me myth could maintain the health of the world, but when we forget these very special stories everything goes a little crazy. He told me I had to keep remembering.

He said the old stories released a kind of oxygen. People would gather around the tales. And that I had to make a life from this. I never saw him again but I did what he said. I track these very special stories. They are like jaguar teeth in a Dorset copse, or tundra snow in Brighton, rare. Keep remembering.

But I do forget, of course I do. I can barely remember to feed the cats, let alone the earth. But enough of that. Enough of the excuses.

I am going to take a walk now, and you are going to come with me. We are headed to a place I am almost afraid to think about, a place I know well. We are going to walk the river and the forests around my cottage, here on the southern flank of Dartmoor. If I am lucky I am in the middle of my life and I am in an enjambment of loss and fatigue. So I go walkabout. See what comes.

When the Saxons stood on Dartmoor they gave a name to its original people.

Wealas
Foreigners

For hundreds of years afterwards Dartmoor people were called:

Wraytors
Strange Men

The moor makes odd, dark people with odd, dark, magical minds.

It is that kind of place. Barbaric. Better left well alone.

❖

I'm by the water

The current on the river Durius is low but fast-moving, there
is spray like beer froth every few yards, and rocks gesturing
pugnaciously below, rocks that look all the living world like rusty,
boozy barrels. I will squat like an escaped prisoner and slurp all that
darling ale up, all of it, every crazeling gobful. I will drink the whole
river up. All of it, the tributaries and snaky little streams too. I will
deny the salmon and the trout and the otter. I will block out the sun
for the swift and the toad.

I defy you to look at a river and not see your fast-escaping life.

At the same moment I am fetishising my dotage, I hear the wood
pigeon, the very oldest sound in my archival boom-box of memory.
As I am stretched on the rack of first sounds and last thoughts I am
sat at an old oak table gazing across the river at a lightning tree. It
is long and slim and white, as white as a larch, the shaman-tree of
Siberia. It is dignified and introverted amongst the old-growth oaks.

If you have a book called *River* by Ted Hughes this is where the cover
photo was taken. Right down a track at the bottom of my garden.

Ted fished because he wanted CONTACT

In darkness he wanted the tug of line, the prehistoric oomph of the hunt, to draw all blood-truth of the moor into his nervous system. Tyger, tyger, burning bright.

Lascaux erotics, the rest is just skittish chicken shit.

But in the cover photo you don't see the little oak table I sit at now.

This is the table I take women to when it is time for us to part. Not like Bluebeard, not macabre, just a man becoming less freakishly available. I don't want to nest anymore. That was another time.

So she and I will look at the slim white tree together, and she will say it or I will say it and it will end.

But today there is a man standing on the other side of the river, under the pale tree.

I think it's Mark, my old painting teacher, or maybe my grandfather Alec.

Regal, white-haired old guy.

I call over, smirk: *Are you an archetype?*

—STUPID.

You ever use that word again in my direction I will thin you right out.

That is depleted language, you stuttering little peasant. I will tell you what I am.

Listen hard, *Wealas*.

I am the Myrddin. Your Merlin.
Merlinus Sylvestris Merlinus Caledonius

That's me, waving at you there.
Well, the string-bean, barely fed
bit of you that can still see me.

You grub.
You are pixellated,
pathetically out of focus,
your prayers stay your side of the river.

Me, I had the old powers. I GLOWED.

I made mandate from dirt:
I hexed up wisdom and laws
from the thistle-grass of South Wales.

I just wrenched them out of the earth,
mucky clods of magic.
I was the shit-kicker.

This is not quite my patch, but near.
Wales.
Just a day's ride or a splash-bath from here.

To get to you, my blurry boy of the *Durius*, I swam
your *Bray*, your *Ashburn,* your *Meavy,*
your *Mardle,* your *Thrushel,* your *Lyd,*
your *Warfleet,* your *Torridge.*

Good rivers all, but wrung
me out, the amount of effluent
I drank sloughed off the fields.
I puked it up outside
Taunton services.

Rest of the time I was a horse thief.
Gallop gallop gallop
I stole apples from your garden.
All the time you were talking to your
dead granny, I stole your apples.

Make your head crooked so I can tell you things.

You should know I have a sister, one who is still loyal.
She follows my bone-white trail, my moon over the water; my
            dream-beckoning.
It is her time now.

This is who I am and what I did.
There is little still water on Dartmoor so

LET THE FLOW COMETH

I will go to every single miserable hump of hill in every stretch
of Broken Britain and ring every bloody underground bell until
Arthur, Bors, Galahad, the lot of them, rupture the soil and clean
the politics from this whole enclosure. My enclosure, the matter of
Britain.

And I ask you, Wealas,
Where's my sister?
This is meant to be her age.

And like that, he is gone.

♣

The bards underwent a frozening you see.

How we see them is not what they became. Whatever scrub or
bush you grew from, it infected your dialect, so if you had a gift for

jabber, your place couldn't help but speak through you. As natural to you as breasts or beard, cunt or cock.

Merlin is one of this earlier variety.

But the bardic schools started to bleach it out. They got you scrubbed and spanked and speaking in a fixed way, with fixed stars. Nothing like what we think: writhing *Astral Weeks*-esque nature-people wandering back from stone circles with their heads on fire.

Nope.

Maybe the Romans did it: that the schools needed to unify a strong, tribal voice against the sheer organisational chops of empire. But whatever happened, it didn't regroup. You could pluck verse from five hundred years apart and there's only a hint of inflection to tell them apart. Shoddy, boring.

A frozening.

Not an emerging, a bearing witness, a rupturing. That was from some earlier time, the time that Merlin knew about. My head hurts from talking to him.

I keep walking the river.

It was strange, watching the magus talk across the water. I mean he really was a shit-kicker.

Yes, he was Merlin, but it was pretty bloody clear this was not fucking Gandalf.

And I bet all his prophecies came true. They had that wretched tang of truth in them. Too much truth overwhelms. Never popular, prophets.

We are passing a place I like to swim, opposite the entrance to three old tin mines. Every tin mine has a dragon in it, say Dartmoor people, and I only really have the rocks to visit one of these regularly. I'm not looking that way now, I keep looking over to the river, and over to the other bank.

I bump into two men on my side, fishing.

One is a rumpus, a gurgle of champers; one is measured, enduring.

Dafydd and Finegas. A lover and a hermit.

And why are you not on the other side of the scrying bowl, the other side of the waters, like Merlin?

The one with toffee in his pockets and a bucket of booze at his thigh pipes up

—Dafydd, pleased to meet you. Dafydd ap Gwilym. It's a matter of station. Gradation. Me and Finegas, we lived. We lived like you do. Got caught up in poetry and women and the sauce, but Merlin was a god walking all along really. He's thin-skinned, like Jesus, and he belongs on the other side of the Durius.

But us, here, we are smaller players. We get time off, and when we do, we like to fish for poems.

—Finegas, pleased to meet you likewise. I spent seven years by the river Boyne, waiting for a poem to come in the shape of a salmon. But on the day it came, my servant cooked it, pricked his finger and took its juices into him. There was no malice in him, it was a thing that was meant. He was a good lad.

My servant had desires, but he always followed the deepest one: the search for wisdom. He would bed in under birch and by fawn, but he never stopped looking. So it was right he would be gifted.

[12]

He had given himself fully to the service of my hut: he carried water
and kept the fire; he cut dry rushes for the floor. He was taught the
rules of metre, the cunning scope of words, and the high calling for
a clean, brave mind.

Every day his questions continued to leap
from the green waves of his thinking:

'How does the salmon get wisdom into his flesh?'

Not hard to answer, I told him.

Overhanging a secret pool
there is a hazel tree.

Its ripe nuts drop from tree to pool,
and the salmon eats them.

Flushed, the boy spoke:

'Could we not just track the sacred hazel,
and eat them ourselves?'

Such a tree could be discovered only
by eating the nuts;

those very nuts that can only be found
by eating the salmon.

He writhed, then wrestled out his patience.
They must wait for the salmon.

This was the salmon I caught and he consumed.

When it was done, a great tranquility
swept into me.

It was quite a battle with that fish, I said.
'Did it give good account for its life?'

It did, but that is not the battle I speak of.

We cleaned up and made fire, drank tea, and under the stars the boy
became Finn MacCool.

We three sit breathing in a happy-sad way as salmon quietly pass
their rods.

Dafydd sups his cider and speaks

—I'm here because I'm on the run.
Even now, I'm on the run, and I died in the fourteenth century.
Lover man. Born in Ceredigion, gold on my fingers, booze in
my cup. In love with the Troubadours, I was, till the Black Death
noticed me and walked me out round the back of the barn.

Dafydd has the puff in him now, and starts to wave his arms like a
slow windmill, Finegas, twinkling, urges him on, and Dafydd starts
to recite. Oh the glory, the banging glory of the man in flight, even
without his harp he is alight.

I've caused hard anger to erupt,
Because I'm a thief of secret love.
She is the memory of high summer.

She glanced at me and me at her – we traded glances,
The foam-white girl shuddered into my heart,
Like a round arrow flies through a sheaf of dry stubble.

My breast, my care, my body,
It didn't stand a chance.

This girl is the gem of Wales.

And I will be a heart-wrecked Welshman
With not an acre to my name
If this gets out.

At this Finegas laughs and clumps his shoulder. Now they are
speaking in Gaelic and Welsh and I don't know what's going on.

To add up you speak in English
To speak of love you speak in Welsh
That's what I heard.

I reluctantly pick myself up and carry on walking. I can hear them
chat over my shoulder for several minutes, I turn back and they are
there, then not.

When they are not, the most woeful, unexpected sadness comes to
me and I cry a bit.

✤

tredan uriglast elþeodigra

Of those fearful of the unfamiliar

Do not look at the tree ridge where I look down on the man talking
across the river to the marvellous

Do not look

I look. I look at him.

glomen gied ond gumman snyttro

The wise man learns many songs and plays them on the harp

He would be one like that, I think.

✤

In the middle of watching stories I am being watched. There is something up there, on the ridge, looking at me. No, it's not what you think it is, it's not Death, at least not especially. No more than usual. But there's something up there. It seems to be talking to itself, but the words are mangled. I just can't make them out.

When I was Numbskull I always thought someone was watching me. This watcher would leap benignly from behind a bush and inform me I came from another family, far away, and I had to leave, immediately, for some kind of sea voyage. It was all terribly important, and both they and I would require cloaks to pull the adventure off.

Then you get older and you realise that no one's eyes are on you most of the time. You're not even in focus to the general public, just a kind of nervy blur. So finally, today, I am being witnessed. Isn't this what I've been waiting for? It doesn't seem so intoxicating now. This is not Jack in the Green, or Gerónimo, or a giggling Dalai Lama, this is some guy on a horse speaking backwards words to himself.

I don't have time for this.

One thing I have learnt in forty-eight years is that there are certain things we need to turn our head away from. And I turn my head away from you. We don't have to see everything that is out there to see. So I choose to not see you. You are a-blinded to me.

Horseman pass by.

The river is stiller now, and shallower. My friend Richard remembers a time when maybe only minutes would pass before a salmon made an appearance, a good seven pounder, but now they go out to sea and don't come back. The river is becoming an acid bath with so much crap sluicing off the fields.

I take a little fly, a little bait, and bury it like a totem in the sandy mud by the river. That the great, mysterious, disappearing salmon would return. Not so I could catch them, but so I could praise them. And in their absence, that's all I have left.

I sit. The family I was born into are getting older. We stand at the lip of the falls together, clinging. Every now and then one of us slips over, and we see them disappear into the vertical foam.

Little pine boxes sailing away.

The indignity that the world continues without us. The indignity.

In ancient Devon you lived to be remembered, that you so gutted life it had no choice but to ruefully remember you. You made it sore and resentful. You had it.

Can you so gut the world with your presence that you leave a scar?

Once that would have sounded romantic to me, now it sounds fucking awful.

The Dumnonian way is to be buried with wheels, to have a pit – a pit chucked full of treasure, a brocade of lovers saying weighty things about your generosity and a grief-party that lasts for years. No one sobers up, but bemoans the ludicrousness of continued existence in the absence of your wayward bloody sweetness.

I am walking and wondering if I still have the stomach for that.

Winter Nose
Spring Nose
Summer Nose
Autumn Nose

My summer nose is smelling autumn. Exactly in the middle of August, autumn is bustling in, five, six weeks early. There's more rain about to land in the next twenty hours than in a usual month. Only three weeks ago I stood gabbling in Watkins Books in Cecil Court off Charing Cross Road on the hottest recorded day in London's existence. Men were stripping to their pants on the Tube, babies shrieked, I had to buy a new set of clothes before my reading I was so drenched. Furnace.

And now I have to cut my summer nose off with a Stanley, and replace it with my autumn. Ahead of time, before it had its full use. It has not smelled enough suntan lotion, barbecue, sizzling hot sand, or the slippery, summering wet between a woman's legs. Not the woodsmoke just yet, I petition you, not the wet weather gear.

Spinney me a little more gooseberry, haywain love in the lowing afternoon. I know about the frosts, and the scurrying animal hedges and the spiderwebs of soon-come-September. I know about that. My heat is not this longing for summer bloom – that may indeed help. My heat is a combustible issue.

Splendiferous heat, not inferno, and with a dry, cool wind, I charm you into the valley, this secret valley, secret stretch of Durius.

Bards would have seen this stuff coming, surely? Read the change in the movement of horses, or the marbled leylines of glutinous fat displayed on a goat's guts. Had a full, twelve-month report on the first day of winter, delivered by a gangly arrangement of seaweed on a Tintagel rock. I think so. Definitely.

I am circling back on good Finegas, the hermit and his servant.

You see I have a story of that boy Finn when he was known as Deimne, before he was really, truly Finn.

Deimne had fallen in with young bards on the road. They spoke a glad chatter, and for such a wilded and lone boy as he it was a dizzying proposition to be amongst them. These sheltered him amongst their lively banter. These were lads with a plumage, a strut, a true north of verbosity, sixty thousand lines of verse to be battered into them before their study was done. They would have many florid turns of tongue for what the day presented.

Ah, but these were scholars not masters. In the high branches you can't always see the brown bear that comes to shake the tree.

From out of the bushes came a bandit who slaughtered the lot in a second.

The only one left standing was Deimne. When the robber man heard of Deimne's parentage he wept hard. The highwayman was right-hand man of his father, before the captain's slaughter and betrayal. His father was high man of the Fianna, warriors and poetic elite.

Some will tell you the robber they call Fiacull was the end of the boy's bardic education.

That is horseshit. It was a deepening. Fiacull was the dark-eyed teacher.

Fiacull took the boy to his home, a dismal swamp, not one japey-joke within it, and pummelled the ornamentation out of him. He showed him what complexity of eloquence could sound like.

He trained the boy to swim the swamp with a dagger between his teeth.

When the boy was ready he showed him his Spiteful Spear – the Birgha. This spear was wrapped in a cloak and tied down, so deadly was its aim. What it aimed at, it hit.

So to become a poet, you need to be tutored by a bandit as well as a hermit.

You carry the most woeful spear that everyone knows you have but you almost never use it.

That's what gives you your nose for autumn.

This was not a falling away from the path, this was the path.

It's that stink-spear that would save not just the boy's life, but the deep culture of Ireland, down the way a bit.

The rain is a-slosh now, the river gobbling, slobbering it all up. The silver sheet of vertical flicker against the gleaming clumps of holly.

I am surrounded by the vast, peaceful crying of the world, like a veil, a magical muffle. It is announcer of unique privacy, rivalled only by snow.

I am gleeful at this turn, sheltering under birch with berry-big slops onto my lap. Mulch me dear torrent. Sweep me up in your disclosure, corral me in your enclosure, fumigate my static, wash away my pixellated soul.

I am past the old sign that says HOTEL GUESTS GO NO FURTHER in red paint on white board, nailed high.

I do go further, I absolutely do go further, slipping on the shiny shingle, watching the river pick an even wackier time signature for its propulsion. I climb the bank, no little thing in the scudding bales of wind that have joined in the party. The bracken is high as a man, heather delicate and purple, young oaks looking scrubbed for baptism by wonderful wetness with an Arthurian fog creepy-crawly coming in. I am high above the river now, likely death-high if I fell, on an unsettling crag. I trip bad into a ridge of lichen and granite, instantly and utterly soaked. Every piece of wood or root I reach for crumbles in my hands. This is

EAGLE ROCK

I seem to have my hands full here. I gradually, agonisingly crawl out of the enjambment. Levi's stuck to me, smeared with delicious smelling muck. I flake out on the sodden grasses, too breathless to care about the wet, already so marked, mangled and mashed as I am.

An eagle is watching me.

At the very top of a tree at Eagle Rock *is* an eagle. Biggest I ever saw.

At the bottom of the tree is a sow.

The eagle is tearing rotten meat with its beak and claws

Then dropping it through the branches to the sow.

The sow is gnashing on the rancid flesh

In the rain, on Eagle Rock.

Ah, I know what this is here, this arrangement, this constellation. I know a little bit. This is like an old Welsh tale of a man who became an eagle and how his uncle sung him back to his original shape. So I sing the words:

Beside a river an old oak grows,
Sheltered from cold wind that blows
I know I do not tell a lie –
The man Llew rests there on high.

Cocking his head, the eagle
drops from the high branches to the middle.

There is an oak on an upland best,
Wet with rain an eagle nest,

May his hardships soon be o'er
And Llew restored to us once more.

Again the eagle drops down now to the lowest branches.

For the final time, I sing:

Grows an oak upon a steep
Where an eagle his home does keep;
If I do not speak falsely,
Llew will come on to my knee.

The eagle alights on my knee.

With a small cut of rowan branch,
I stroke the back of the eagle's head,
shape-lurching from bird back into Llew,
scrappily awake, deep flustered,
naked and blue-skinned on the August turf.

And I am scrappily awake and gasping at this impossibility.

Numbskull made me not an eagle but a sow, a grumbling sow.

That was the totem, down at the bottom of the school building.
They served us all rotten meat; choice cuts were for the top floor.
Our eyes grew smaller, piggy, red, distrustful, down in the dark. I sat
next to a boy who had fallen off the back of a motorbike when he
was between little school and big school. He got changed by it. And
fuck, we mocked him. We mocked him and mocked him and mocked
him. Would have taken fists, pinches and slaps to him, but he was too
gently big. And he, the best of us. That was a sin of mine, right there.

Llew had much bigger, weirder misfortune than my scraps.

He was a man under enchantment, in a complexity of enchantments actually. He fell in love with a woman created of flowers who fell in love with someone else and why shouldn't they, and then became an eagle when the woman of flowers and her new love tried to finish him off. And she became an owl that hoots in my woods, just to be clear.

But because I knew that little song he is an eagle no longer. And I think he will be taking a leaf out of Merlin's book when it comes to revenge. Conflict resolution has not hit mythology just yet, ho ho.

The sow is still here for some reason. Hasn't magicked itself off. Lots of acorn mush to slobber, and the last green cuts of meat scattered amongst the roots of the oak. I watch its fat, sleek shape munching, tense, in case it *poof!* disappears into the ether. But it doesn't. It watches me with titchy, dulled eyes, and waddles over the lumpy turf.

It knocks me out for an hour or so.

How much bad meat did I consume? When did I become sow? My leg is bleeding where the eagle laid his claw. Eagles have such great names:

Wind Witherer
Vedrfolnir
Drien
Aetos Dios

The old bards used to fancy themselves as eagles, something magnificent. That they would

GO TO THEIR DEATH WITH ABUNDANCE OF HONOURS

They would not 'become nothing', get cremated and scattered, hush-please-don't-make-a-fuss. No. They would electrify their people with the measure of their achievement, brand their village with white-gold rings and hunting dogs and fires that never went out. They would leave everyone plump and drunk, all the better, and their pomp, thwack and psychic liveliness lived always on as the secret word in continuing good fortune, their name the inner structure of the abundant, happy village spell.

But we have a visitor about to throw his helmet in the ring, blow the whole thing up.

Achilles, eagle supreme, standing talking to us right now, says it's all unutterable horseshit.

—Listen, tiny dicks.
Sooner live like a slave to a poor man than be King of the Dead. Your reputation will serve you not a jot down there.

Achilles, in this very specific, very particular moment, reminds me of my mum.

I know we are moving fast here. But this mad jumble is where I live. I abide in a place where a Greek hero will resemble my mother at the same moment magical sows from Welsh myth glower through the rain. So it is. This is that much-fetishised word, *imagination*. Maybe more than just imagination, maybe an imaginalia, a coven of ghost, animal, human and elemental thinking. There are so few handrails when we really get into the spirit-forest, so few. All the furies just bang into one another.

So back to Mother.

She would clink glasses with Achilles, and look askance at the ruin of Merlin. Abundance of honours is something utterly personal to her. Not dished out by general or headmaster, but in the quiet of the day by the holy maker, for things that no one else ever sees.

Sometimes people ask me if I have a conscience, and what does it look like?

I tell them it's five foot two, has white hair, a lovely face, great energy and a certainty of position. This conscience, forged in both the power of feminine voice and feminine silence, is distrustful of centralised power and too much officiousness. If Dadskull opened the road of Sun to me, Mumskull opened the road of Moon.

And she is pointing now, across the waters, at a woman on a horse. She's telling me to pay attention.

A woman comes canter, canter, canter. Gliding across the shallow river, a woman who can live on both banks. She rides a pale horse, large and formal, and is dressed in golden silk.

Rhiannon.

I slide down the bank like a breathy idiot to hear her story.

There was this boy I liked. Pwyll.

He was macho, but not too much. Bright, but not too much. But the thing I really liked was that he'd been in the Otherworld. For a year and a day he'd swapped places with a chief over there. That's something. Those kinds of men are different, when they've been touched in that way. And he hadn't gone entirely into himself, like some do, he remained a leader.

So one day I trotted past him on my horse, as he lounged about on a hill with his cronies. So blue the sky. But he didn't look at the sky after he saw me.

I would make him beg to fall under the hooves of my horse.

Plead to have my weight on him. And I wanted his weight on me, his big brutish mass. Yum.

Not recognising me, a rider was sent to try and talk. But no matter the strain and skill of the beast, it could never quite catch me. I made sure I always seemed to glide, never breaking to a gallop. Just a frittering of my fith-fath, pollen of my little magics.

I don't like it when kings send their servants.

The rider returned to the tump and the teasing men. The next was just like the first, till finally our man Pwyll himself elected to come. 'This is clearly between God and me. Bring me my horse and my spurs.'

Even Pwyll, with his skill and his horse's nimble leaps, could not compete. He rasped a request to me:

'Maiden, in the name of the man you love the most, please wait for me.'

That got my attention. That had some swing to it.

'Of course, happily. You may have made things easier for your horse if you'd asked some time back!'

I waited for the exhausted chief, drew back my headdress and fixed my true gaze on him. Strong gaze. Remember me, remember me, I am thinking. Remember me like a cum-cry and the Christmas feast and the best birthday you ever had.

Remember me like the heron lifting her wings over silver, Celtic rivers.

'Lady. Lady – where have you come from, where are you going?'

'Well, going about my business. And I am happy to see you.'

'My welcome to you,' spoke Pwyll. He seemed to mean it too.

Pwyll of the scars, Pwyll of the hunt, Pwyll of the shape-leap, Pwyll of the grey ford, big Pwyll looked quite undone. Giddy.

My heart was beating a thump.

'What's the business, may I ask?'

'My main purpose was for us to meet.'

'That's the best business I ever heard of,' he said. 'Would you tell me your name?'

'Rhiannon. I am Rhiannon, daughter of Hyfaidd Hen. Given to be wedded to a man against my will. Because of my love for you, I do not want him. So I come to find out your answer on the matter.'

I liked what he said in reply:

'These words can be tested by God:
if all women and maidens were made
available to me, it is
you that I would choose.'

My lad. God, he means it. He means it.

'Good. *Good*. Well, before I am given to another,
arrange a meeting with me.
Claim me. As I am claiming you.
A year from tonight there will be a feast
prepared in the court of my father.
Lord, do not forget your promise.'

And with that, I turned and left. But I knew from the flush of his cheek that my warmth remained. I was told from that moment on, Pwyll would not be drawn on the subject of me, not even to his closest. Some things are just too sweet to share. But he thought

[28]

of me in his bed, and I of him. He said I was Queen of the Wild Horses and that was it. I will take that title.

The year was up, a year during which I crafted my imaginings diligently. My man arrived, resplendent, at the court of Hyfaidd, with no fewer than ninety men in his retinue. Something immense was about to occur. The arrangement of the hall was this: Hyfaidd Hen at the centre, Pwyll on one side, me on the other, and then each according to rank and honour. A just hierarchy, from a time when such things existed, and will again.

This is when it goes off. Kicks off. Wild rumpus.

Some time into the feast, a young lad entered the hall. I knew him. Despite his youth he had weight, presence even. Tall, auburn-haired, silk across his shoulders, a pout. He sauntered his way to the high end of the hall, and addressed Pwyll. I could just tell what a clever little prick he was. Needed a slap.

'Lord. My business here is with you. I have a favour to ask.'

Generosity, the key to a real leader.
And a key to their derailment.

The words came almost in slow motion, I wanted to cram them back into my beloved's mouth.

'Whatever you request, as long as I have it, it is yours.'

I gasped, and a mare galloped a lonely valley.

'Why, why did you respond so?' I hissed.

'Well, he has,' piped the boy, 'and the gentry have heard it. My request, oh big-hearted Pwyll, is for the woman you wish to marry, and her provisions too.' Wide smirk, the hint of a bow.

The man Pwyll sunk into horror. As deep as Cheddar Gorge, as bleak as winter on Cadair Idris. He was without speech. I, not so.

'This is the boy they wished me to marry. Gwawl, son of Clud, a powerful man, of heft and ambition, drunk with followers. Godlike. And now you must give me to his son, or risk disgrace.'

Pwyll stirred from his bleak shore.

'I can't do this. I can't. I can't.'

I drew him close. 'He asks for my provision: this feast. That is not in your power to provide. I will give it to him, every chop, pudding, fruit and wine. He and his entourage will be sick with luxury. Little heroes, they will think themselves. Titans. Pats on the back. I will then arrange a meeting, in a year's time, to sleep with him. At that time you will hide out in the orchard with ninety-nine men, and I will give you a bag to bring. In the feasting, as he gazes over at the acres he thinks he is soon to plough, stagger in as a beggar. Call him on his own game. Generosity. And ask for nothing but this little bag to be filled with food. Such a small act. But if all the meat of Dyfed were to be placed in it, it would not be filled.

He will be sure to enquire on its appetite, and tell him that only an extremely powerful, nay, virile, nobleman could tread the food down in the bag, so it would cease its chomping. I will see to it that he parades such vanity as to clamber in. When he comes, turn the bag over so he is head over heels, tie up the neck, call your men of the orchard with your horn, and let them descend, descend with their fierce faces.'

Gwawl called the high table again, flushed now with his success.

'I need a reply.'

'As much as it is in my power to supply, so you shall have.'

A roar from the gleeful warriors.

Outfoxed the big man.

But not me.

A year later the meeting took place. The secret troupe stood steady under the apple bough, and Pwyll made good show as a beggar. Stinking, bloodied rags, a mess. A request for a bag of food, nothing less. Ah, but the bag was hungry. Starving even. A hundred years without so much as a crumb.

Gwawl bellowed: 'What is wrong with the bag? Our provisions are being gulped!'

Pwyll crooned, respectfully, 'It requires a firm and noble man to step into the bag, push the food down further and say, *Enough has been put in here*.'

At this, for a second, I gently touched the arm of the boy. 'My man. My bull. Get up quickly.'

A rush of blood. He leapt blissful into the bag. Bag was tipped, tied, and horn blown. From the place of the apples the men came. As each entered, each man struck a firm blow to the bag. Ninety-nine resolute, breathless blows.

'What's in the bag?'

'A badger. A badger in the bag.'

At this, a voice croaked up from the swill. 'Lord, this game of badger in the bag will soon kill me. I beg you. Slaughtering me like this is not how I should die.'

And this was how the pup saved his own life. He scampered from the hall and if you put your ear to the ground you will hear him scampering still.

From then on, we were grand to our people, Rhiannon and Pwyll. At the court in Arberth we presided over a huge range of guests, none of whom left without ring, brooch or wealthy stone. All felt confirmed, raised up in our presence, witnessed. That was the true gift we tried to give.

But after three years, visitors started to steal little glances at my belly. Still trim, no jut of a male heir. A dangerous situation. A group of noblemen had enough political heft to summon Pwyll, to Preseli in Dyfed. And there did they press him to take another wife, for the sake of the kingdom. They were clear that the honeymoon was over. He'd spill secondhand the news to me.

But Pwyll fought for our love, and gained another year till the council would meet again and only then would he accede to the wider good. And in that year I did indeed begin a lovely turn of shape. Goodness, magic, and the witch-mother were what my baby suckled on, there in the warm byre of my womb.

> But strange   strange   strange

On the night of the birth – a boy –
six women stayed up
watching over me and the babe

Six women fell asleep before the cock crowed

Six women greasy with fear
when they saw that my baby
had been
spirited away.

They knew it was their own deaths they were facing. And not swift.

Some awful thought shook the women – like a possession – and they daubed my sleeping face with the blood of pups, and when I woke, they screamed and moaned that I had destroyed my own son, wrestling him from them.

Sisterhood, eh?

Many times I offered them pardon for truth-telling, but so queasy were they that they gripped to the shrillness of their fiction. Rat-a-tat-tat. For the rest of their days they would have an ear for the battering on the door, the arrival of the king's men. Their sleep would be thin.

Stories like that have traction, are hard to conceal. The nobles brought the full weight of the law down on the back of heartbroken Pwyll, but still he refused to divorce me. But what was the truth of it all?

His grief made him blurry. He lost discernment in his wretched anxiety. Lost connection with the Otherworld. With me, his wife. With himself. After counsel with learned people, I decided to accept punishment, rather than the drawn-out scrap with six treacherous bitches.

The punishment? To sit by the mounting block outside the gate to Arberth, and tell my story to anyone I thought may not know it. And to carry guests to court if they so desired it. Few did. But there I sat, through sleet and snow, holding in my mouth a story that never was.

Holding in my mouth a story that never was.

Seven years was the decree. At the end of the day I would trudge back to court. At night I would stand by my window.

I cast my humours into the dark.

With my arms outstretched,
equine energies worked tirelessly for me.

[33]

❖

In Gwent
Teyrnon Twrf Liant
was lord, and in
his house lived
a mystery.

He had a mare that every May Eve would give birth, an elegant animal,
unrivalled. But the foal would always immediately disappear. Finally,
roused through conversation with his wife, he brought the horse
indoors and armed himself as the foal was born. There it shuddered,
a spring wonder, a budding leaf, a green wave in the bay. Even as he
walked over to test its weight, a vast claw shot through the window and
grabbed the babe by its mane. Teyrnon was ready and gave one cutting
blow down on the arm. Part of the arm, and the foal, slid down the wall
of his house, the tiny horse safe. Outside, the darkness was shudder-
shake with the scream of the beast and the lord staggered through the
door to finish it, but could not make out a form in the black.

When he returned to the doorway
he found a bundle,
a Moses, a Taliesin,
there in the candlelight

A swaddling of brocaded silk,
a summering field of golden curls,
strong arms, chubby and waving,
a cub reaching hard for life's pap

Though they could not help but love this spring arrival, as word
passed from travellers of my situation, suspicion grew in the couple
as to the boy's parentage. And he carried my own character: by four
years old he was negotiating with stable boys to water the horses. He
couldn't stay away from them. In the end, they gave the lad the very
horse that had been born the night he had been found.

They tell me he and his wife turned it endlessly round in their
conversations and concluded:

'If we send the boy home we will receive three things: the gratitude
of Rhiannon for being released from her fiction and punishment;
thanks from Pwyll for raising the boy; and finally, if he has
conscience, he will be our foster son and provide for us.'

They agreed to take him to us, blew the candle on the decision,
went to bed.

When they arrived at the gate of Arberth, I offered to carry them
to the court. Such was my muscle by then I could have done it. But
of course, no one wished it. Soon the tables were being gold-plated
with food and drink, the embers stirred and great logs lain on their
coals. I was back from my daily sojourn at the gate, and Pwyll just
returned from a circuit of Dyfed. When we saw the three visitors,
we batted other business aside to get to the travellers' story.

There was no shred, no follicle, no thin strand of doubt that this
was our son. It was truth. A kind of truth that breaks the fear-spell,
ruptures that imposter spleen to throat. Teyrnon raised himself and
gave good story of the whole affair – the magic of May Eve, the foal,
the black arm, the babe wrapped in silk.

And each word of the story worked on the skin and the flesh and
the bone of me, and scoured all possible confusion from Pwyll's
heart. It did. Stories can do that you know.

We would weave those broken years back together. Sing the old grief
song onto poetry's hazels. It would be a kingdom renewed.

I gave the name of Pryderi to our son. My boy of the horse-blood
and the May Eve.

Pryderi
who ruled the seven districts
of Dyfed, who conquered the
three cantrefs of Ystrad Tywi,
and the four cantrefs of Ceredigion –
the seven cantrefs of Seisyllwch.

Seven years holding a story in my mouth that wasn't true.

And I ask you, where is Merlin's sister?

This is supposed to be her age.

I am realising that badger in the bag is a station of the cross, a temple of disorientation, a shamanic spanking. Never saw that. Took her words to make it clear.

This is likely not the moment to be telling Rhiannon that Merlin's sister was probably 'made up' by an overworked Geoffrey of Monmouth, author of the *Vita Merlini*, or cut and pasted from any number of oral tales of the age, hardly a constant figure in the Arthurian tradition. No, this is not the moment. Not in this day of protracted hallucination. And who's to say this sister wasn't known round the campfires of Albion before she was sequestered into this story to appease whatever benefactor Geoffrey was cosying up to at the time? She seems awfully real to these people. As if they had no psychic life before they were written down.

Fakeskull

A few miles from here is curly-mopped, nose-smashed Robert Graves, hunched late by the lamp and the desk, quilling the living fuck out of day and night. He's in the little village of Galmpton, outside Brixham. He and his family have had to temporarily flee Majorca because of the Second World War. He's meant to be bashing out other projects, earning his keep, but dear Robert is possessed.

Possessed by a book that has to be born. Within twelve weeks or so he has a draft – *The Roebuck in the Thicket*. He'd fiddle with it for another fifteen years, revision after revision, but it would finally shudder its way into the world with another name, *The White Goddess*.

This book, this tangled tower, this thistly labyrinth, sucks in endless thousands of readers pulverised by the Second World War. It sells and it sells and it sells. Its mad ambition: to track through folklore, magic and speculation the relationship between the poet (mostly male) and his muse (female, cruel, beautiful). I can only ponder the kind of crucifixion awaiting Graves if he tried to publish it now.

The big, dangling dick of a problem is not just Graves's dividing-out of gender characteristics, vocation, etc. (it's hardly surprising in the era), it's that some of his sources have been proved to be bogus. They just made stuff up. Especially one Iolo Morgannwg (or, er, Edward Williams) who constructed the exciting *The Barddas*, whose work Graves merrily dug into as legit.

Passing off imagination as historic scholarship is foolish; a deceit, smoke and mirrors. And yet, when a Gravesian or Morgannwg transgression takes place is generally when people get excited. Something happens in the imagination when we give it the reins for a while.
Boom.

So, fuck the cynics. I mean it. Fuck them. You should be so lucky to carry one measly footnote from the deepest reaches of that book in your lunchbox next to the sandwiches Mummy made you. I am calling you a child and a snob.

That loping, nutty, inspired book gave colour, wicked excitement and appropriate ritual confusion to people looking to connect to the ancient world after a time of great suffering. Even in its tangles, knots and general lack of oxygen it's more properly bardic than we should ever have a right to hope for.

Maybe Robert and Iolo, and James Macpherson with his Ossian poems, are gazing across the scrying bowl of the river themselves, over the divining, glassy mirror, and reporting back as much as they are able to see.

Ah, I make a decision.

I am going to craft a magic in the middle of this book. I am going to create a road, a track, no doubt some would say a leyline, between the cottage of Robert Graves on the coast and the cottage of Ted Hughes way over on the eastern side of Dartmoor in North Tawton. These two bookends, supporting each other in some fashion.

They had enough thrown at them, let's back them up for once. So I close my eyes and it is

night outside Brixham and I'm scattering a trail of barley under the moaning, groaning streetlights. Agatha Christie is dribbling a drop of scrumpy as libation for her old friend before merrily disappearing into the darkness. I have a big bag of flour:

A trail of white under the moon
I am looking for hoofprints in it
There's crumpled first drafts
Of stuffed pretensions and gabbling vowel
Cretan gold and bent brown tickets
Into the British Museum
I am past South Devon College
Past Sainsbury's where I shopped
With the belly-swelled mother

Of my child a million years ago
Nipped up the shortcut
Past Berry Pomeroy ruins
A place so spooked Graves even
Wrote a poem about that very spook
Past the Brutus Stone on Totnes high street
Holding my breath for the rank whiff of incense
From the hippie shops – a wretched waft even in the dark
And I am up and tuck right again across the
Dartington estate
Where Alice Oswald is night-gardening with
A heavy cold stone tucked into her belly
I have hopped over Hexworthy bridge
Seen lights on in St Raphael's chapel
Is it you John Wesley?
Back at last your horse munching the flowers
Somewhere out there in the blooming dark
Is Pondsworthy and my aunt Met's
Honeysuckle Cottage where my folks
Honeymoon forever
Then I turn right right right
And fuck it I am flying I am flying my feet hurt
Not high just a little off the ground but with pace
By baling twine and bog
Bull skull and bracken
Through the depression of abandoned hamlets
So thick it hits you like a gasping
Terrible deathless thing the despair
Till I am at Court Green

Ted and Carol's place
Ted and Assia's place
Ted and Sylvia's place

I can't remember what time signature I am in
I swoop around like the Red Baron

The reaves the land divisions the time divisions
Are a-muck in me the stumpy little bread-bannocked
Walls collapsed my eviscerated slashed and burned
Sewaged and poisoned
Dog-eared dog-chewed dog-shat heart

I see a lamp on in the writing hut in the garden
But I don't know which time which time which time
I am in

If a *Crow* is being born or a *Birthday Letters*

I don't smear my flour on the door
That's just rude

Strength to both of them
Strength to their beloveds

I turn and I can see torches all the way back to the seashore

❖

Har holtes feond, ond hlaford min

And I chew the earth without anger

Seeing him alive and me dead

Ic eom wunderlicu wiht

I am a creature to conjure with

And he must not see me until the end

❖

But I do see him. I do see the rider on the hill. I started peeking a few minutes back and the bastard is keeping track with his gurgle-deep voice.

I can't understand mate. And I'm busy.

Let me talk about Ted and Robert again, turn the volume down on this, this egregore, this watcher. I mean, I've heard about this kind of thing. That if you do enough magical work, you attract the attention of a spiritual companion, a spooky being you half glimpse that sort of pads along beside you. Sometimes a parasite, sometimes a saviour. The whole thing is complex – they may become your lord or your servant but I, right now, am changing the subject.

The White Goddess was Ted's poetry prize as a schoolboy. He felt gladness and dismay all at once, that someone had already gazed into the rattle bag he thought was all his. But god almighty did he do something with it. There, even the thought of that is calming me.

There is another woman sitting up against a rock chatting with Rhiannon. She is small, trim and contained, black skin with a blue cloak. Trust me, she is there. You can see her too.

She speaks

—I am not part of a story, I am one who tells the story.

Sometimes they live in my jaw, on my tongue, in my saliva and imagination, other times they walk abroad, like Rhiannon here, sharing pork and bread by this river. People bellyache on about the bards being men, but this is you peering back through time.

You weren't there. You don't need to fetishise them. There are other traditions. The bardic schools and the information inside them weren't just sequestered breathlessly away. Women: grannies, sisters, aunts, mothers, we told stories too, sang songs by the fire.

We weren't scolded for it, we delighted the settlement when the embers glowed.

We may not have had a swan-feather cloak like the preening boys of the high hall, but we carried the nutrition of these stories just as much as they ever did.

Our cooking pots simmered, spat and made magically delirious the stories of our grandmothers, our hands pulled tales from the earth as wonderful as the sweet potato or the onion. Imagine that! We had our groves, our rituals, our mapping of the year. And don't you dare say we didn't. We have held fairy tales in our breast milk for thousands of years and fed them to our kids.

But we made the world, baby, we seized the sky, and the earth, fire and water. No nailed-up horseshoe could bar our way, no scuttled male-magic, we emitted loose chirrup and the ramshackle truth of fawn and cockle, our very mouth juice was a swagger den of the deep dreaming bell of things.

Open your mouth and catch my spit Wealas
There's stories in every drop, take it down
You lucky you know

We heretics, who praised the land not the landowner. Who were never committed to tenure, but carried the bundle of story through our births, betrayals, raptures and deaths. And, as I was just saying to Rhiannon here, don't be so sure that our age isn't coming, that Merlin's sister is not amok.

So, I have a story. A mad kind of love story. And I make a flour trail with it too, back to Rhiannon outside the court, with her husband not believing her and having to curate a lie on her own tongue. I send this to you, love, as a layer of hope and sustenance when you had to kick against the pricks.

And the little lady stood, stood in her vastness, in the late afternoon light, and started to tell a story, started to lay her trail of white flour under the sun.

She is the blue house of sound
That Taliesin never spoke of.

When Celyddon and Goleuddydd made love,
All of Wales bent their head for a child.

And the Holy Maker of Things was roused by such prayers,
And a spark of light flew into the depths of Goleuddydd's womb.

Her pregnancy was a true exfoliation: an unshackling, a fierce tuning to the green fuse of all things. Such sensory flooding gave her an animal distrust of the civilised, the neutered, the four-square. The sight of a doorknob would bring her out in sobs.

So she took herself from villages and out into the wilds. Alone but serene. Copse her bed, byre her home; curls rising like snakes from her head and twining with rowan buds and the pale shoots of saplings, nipples dark as cormorant, gorged with the secret milk of berries. For the nine months of pregnancy she was immense, utterly earthed.

When contractions began, all expansion abruptly ceased, and swiftly her shape reverted – like a hawk suddenly called back to the wrist – into the human, the finite, the housed.

It was in this disposition she blearily gazed around and beheld she was nestled with swine in a sty of pigs. In her shock she gave birth to a boy they would call Culhwch – meaning Pig Run.

As was custom, Culhwch was shipped out to be fostered by others. Over time, his mother fell into a sickness from which she was not to recover. At her deathbed she gripped her husband's arm, requesting that he not marry until he beheld a two-headed briar emerging from the mound of her grave. Then she called her old teacher and whispered that he was to keep the grave trimmed so nothing would grow on it.

Off he would scuttle with his clippers in the pre-dawn light. But a scuttle became a shuffle. Old teachers are old. After seven years he forgot.

One day when the king was hunting the green wood, he parted from his men, and rode quietly to his wife's grave. As he knelt, deep in reflection, he gazed down and beheld a two-headed briar peeking from the grasses. Ah. Bidden or unbidden, his time of mourning was at an end. The earth had murmured to him.

After taking counsel from sages and dignitaries, it was recommended that an ideal wife for him would be the wife of King Doged. No problem raised, and with a lightness in their hearts, they proceeded to slaughter Doged, seize his wife and take his land.

For her part, his wife was pragmatic and amenable to her new circumstance. What actually needled her most was her new husband's lack of virility. That she couldn't stand. His lack of a child. Seedless. It ate away at her.

One day, when strolling the town, she came upon an old seer, a woman who peered up at her through the rain and issued occult information: told her that her husband did indeed have a son, and to grieve no longer. He was perfectly fertile. Thank you for the coin ma'am.

With this brought into the open, Culhwch was soon installed at court. Beautiful to behold, a plan formed in the wife's mind.

One day, his stepmother took him aside and suggested that he marry her own daughter. There was no blood issue, after all.

When the boy protested that he was too young to marry she swore a strange destiny upon him: that his side would never brush the side of a woman until he married Olwen, daughter of Ysbaddaden, King of the Giants.

Under this weird incant, the boy commenced to rapid and furious blushing, like a strawberry, like a scarlet wound, like spring dusking, every time he thought of this woman (whom he had not met, nor even thought about). It was an excruciating and urgent development.

When his father located his scald-cheeked son, he soon heard all about Olwen and her towering father. The king considered his son's predicament.

'This is achievable, my son. All of it. Arthur himself is your cousin. Go to him to have your hair trimmed at his court and ask him to gift you the finding of this Olwen.'

Let me tell you of the boy's accoutrements as he left for Arthur's court.

Culhwch rode a grey steed, four winters old,
hooves like seashells, bridle-bit of gold,
a saddle of gold beneath him, two spears
of deadly sharpness in his hand.

His other fist gripped a battle axe,
the length of a man's forearm from
ridge to deadly edge, so sharp
it would make the wind bleed.

On his thigh a gold-hilted sword,
blade of gold, gold-encrusted shield,
the colour of heaven's lightning,
and the rim circled with ivory.

Running by his horse were two
spotted, white-breasted greyhounds,
both with collars of red gold,
wide from shoulder to ear.

The one on the left would
run to the right, the one
on the right would
run to the left.

The horse's hooves kicked
up four clods of earth,
like four swallows of the air,
two in front of him, two behind.

A purple, four-cornered cloak
hung from his shoulders,
with ruby balls at each corner
a hundred cows could scarcely buy.

Three hundred cows could scarcely buy
the gold on his clothes and stirrups
and his ride so light, not a lock of hair,
not a curl was disturbed.

At the entrance to Arthur's court the boy called up into the rain
and wind, 'Is there a gatekeeper here?' He kept his composure after
many miles. The torches flickered in the gusts, foxfire in the dark.

An enraged voice poked out into the bluster.

'May your head leave your shoulders for asking. It is custom that I am the gatekeeper for Arthur on the first day of January, and deputies the rest of the time: read them and weep young man – Huandaw and Gogigwr and Llaesgymyn, not forgetting Penpingion who bounces around on his head to save his feet, like a hurled stone on the floor of court.'

'Well let me in,' he countered.

'No.'

'Why not?'

A groan from the dark.

'Knife has gone into meat and drink into horn, and a steaming throng have already entered the hall of Arthur. Unless you are the son of a king, or a highly skilled craftsman, none are allowed in. Down the road a ways is a hostel which will give peppered chops for your belly and wine for your cup, food for your hounds, and a woman to sleep with you and a singer to sing for you. The circumstances are good, *down the road in the hostel*. Come back tomorrow.'

Shouted the boy:

'I will not. Open for me now or I will bring hot shame on the name of your king and raise three shouts right here that will be heard at the top of Pen Pengwaedd in Cornwall, and at the very bottom of Dinsol in the North, and even in Esgair Oerfel in Ireland.

When my shout is heard all pregnant women in court will miscarry on the spot, and the rest of them will find it impossible to conceive all their sorrowful, childless days.'

This halted the gatekeeper a little.

'You may rail against the laws of court, but nothing will transpire until I check with Arthur himself.'

The gatekeeper made his way to Arthur, who looking up from feasting asked, 'What news from the gate?'

'There is news,' said the gatekeeper, uncurling his tongue.

'Two thirds of my life I've lived,
As have you your own.

I was once in Caer Se and Asse,
In Sach and Salach,
In Lotor and Ffotor.

I have been in India the Great
And India the lesser.
I was in the battle of the two Ynyrs
When the twelve hostages were taken from Norway.

I have travelled: I was once in Africa, Corsica,
Caer Brythwch and Brythach and Nerthach.
I bore witness when you slew the warband of Gleis son of Merin,
And you butchered Mil Du son of Dugum.
I bore witness when you conquered Greece.
I was in Caer Oeth and Anoeth,
Caer Nefenhyr Nawdent:

Arthur, did we not see kings there?

But never in my life did I see a man so resplendent as the one
I leave at the gate in the cold and the rain at this moment.'

Arthur groaned.

'Good god. If you came in strolling, then leave us running. I give an injunction upon he who beholds the light then closes his eye to it. It is low indeed for us to leave such a man in weather.'

Ah Culhwch. He was primed for entrance.

When he arrived he rode his horse into the very centre of court, several rules of etiquette falling in one swoop.

'Hail Arthur, chief of the kings of our island. May the lower end of your house be as fine as your upper. May this greeting apply to all at court, favoured or not. May all receive its bounty, just as the whole kingdom may receive yours.

I come not for feasting or lavishment but to ask a gift. If I get my gift I will have deserved it. If I do not receive it I will bend my tongue to dishonouring you throughout the land.'

Arthur spoke: 'You shall receive it, as far as the wind can dry, the rain can soak, the sun reach, as far as the blue curls of the sea extends, the earth extends – except for my dear ship, Caledfwlch my sword, Rhongomyniad my spear, Wynebgwrthucher my shield, Carnwennan my dagger, and Gwenhwyfar my wife.

Go on, name what you want.'

'Not hard. I wish to have my hair trimmed by you.'

Arthur smiled. 'You shall have that.'

Arthur combed and carefully cut his hair with comb and scissors of gold. As he did so, unbidden, he felt a warmth in his heart before the boy. He spoke, 'I feel an affection for you. You must be of my blood. Tell me your name.'

'I am Culhwch, son of Cilydd, son of Celyddon Wledig by
Goleuddydd daughter of Anlawdd Wledig, my mother.'

Arthur replied, 'You are my cousin then. Give voice to what you
desire and you shall have it.'

'God's truth on that, and the truth of your kingdom?'

Arthur nodded and leaned forward. 'Yes. Speak.'

'Then I ask you to find for me Olwen daughter of Ysbaddaden
          Bencawr.
And I invoke her in the name of your warriors. I rise and give praise:

to Morfan, son of Tegid,
          so robust in his ugliness,
                    no weapon dared strike him

not even in the battle of Camlan,
          as all thought he was servant to a demon.

A river of hair roamed his face;
                    moon-yellow teeth;
                              a cornered bull.

He fought at Camlan,
          alongside Sandde Angel-Face,
so handsome a man
          no spear came his way
                    as all thought he was servant to an angel.

I send a voice in this ice-dark:

to Henwas the Winged, son of Erim,
Henbeddestr son of Erim,
Scilti the Lightfooted, son of Erim.

All three were wind and blur,

       never taking a track when they

          could gallop over a crest of trees,

leap the grey mountain,

      skim the green stream.

Their whole lives,

      not one rush was bent under their foot.

My heart flushes too

     with the name of Teithi the Old,

        son of Gwynham,

whose coast-bold castle

      was shouldered into sand

        by the teeth of the sea.

Who came to Arthur,

      was gathered in, welcomed to table,

but whose arm was swift to anger

      a man not fit for peace and rest,

and for that reason

     grew sick with a gloom,

        that took him down.

Ah, and Drem, son of Dremidydd,

      the Big Seer,

his roaming vision loped from Celli Wig in Cornwall,

    to the black north of Penn Blathaon

            in Scotland.

He could spy one green bud

      under the hoar-frost

        a hundred miles away.

He was firm with usefulness.

Osla of the Big Knife
        the one who placed his vast sheathed blade
                across any river that blocked Arthur's path.

A sterling bridge
                for the army of the three kingdoms of Britain.

I raise language to
        Gilla Stag-Leg
                        that one who leapt
three hundred acres in
                one swift bound.

Lord, we remember
        the vast-bellied Erwm and Hir Atrwm,

and how you would have to raid
        three hundred townships just to feed them.

They would feast steady till noon,
                and blaze up again at dusk,
                        shaking their goblets.

When they staggered to bed, they yanked off the heads
        of any wandering vermin,
                        as if no chop had ever glazed their lips.

They took the fat, they took the lean,
they took the hot, they took the cold,
they took the sour, they took the sweet,
they took the fresh, they took the salted.

If I quiet now, I think I can hear them chomping still.

Sol, Gwaddn Osol, and Gwaddn of the Bonfire,
> *that riotous bunch,*
>> *I raise the glass and remember –*

Gwallgoig too.
> *Many a village is sleep-sore from his revels.*

Sugn, son of Sugnedudd,
> *so plagued by heartburn*
>> *that he would suck up the ocean*

with three hundred proud ships afloat,
> *and gulp it down,*
>> *till there was nothing but a dry stand.*

Beloved Cachamwri,
> *Arthur's own servant.*

With his terrible iron flail.
> *Who could take a barn –*
>> *robust with thirty ploughs,*

and grind the crossbeams and the posts,
> *and the rafters,*
>> *to nothing but oat-size crumbs on the floor,*
no friend of farmers.

Gwefl, son of Gwastad,
> *our true Grief Man;*

when in his blue dream,
> *he would let his bottom lip fall to his belly,*

and the top he would fit over his head
>> *as a cap.*

A sorrowed mouth, big enough for the world's tears.

Uchdryd of the Cross-Beard,
              who would wrap his bristly red beard
                          clear over the fifty rafters of Arthur's Hall,
insulation for a sheep-white winter.

Clust, son of Clustfeinad:
              even when you buried him,
                          seven leagues under dark soil,

he could hear an ant wander
        fifty miles away, leaving its lair.

Ah, Medr, son of Medredydd,
              Gwiawn Cat's Eye,
                          Cynyr of the Beautiful Beard –

Medr who can shoot a wren
              right through its two legs,

Gwiawn who can cut the lid
        from the eye of a gnat without hurting it.

Cynyr, of whom it is rumoured
              great Kai is his son.

And what of Kai?
              Kai of the strange gifting.

Nine nights and nine days he can lie
              under the breathless waters,
                          a moon-track on the sea bed.

Nine nights and nine days he can live
              without sleep.

No doctor can cure a sword-cut
                            delivered by Kai;

he is a man of high skill,
                 as tall as the wood's highest tree when he chooses.

When caught by storm,
               such is his body's heat,
                         that a whole circle around him would remain dry.

When frozen in the iron-numb
                   gullies of Snowdon,
                          men would gather close
                     round Kai to dry their kindling.

Let wild fawn
                 always be at your bow.
Let your white-bronze rings and brooches
                 glow by the yellow candle.
Let the women
               with the dark river hair
                     be your companions.'

Arthur listened quietly, and with some admiration at the eloquence. Still, it was time for practical matters.

'Well, young chief, I must report I have never heard of the maiden of who you speak, or her father. But I will send messengers to search for her. I'll need a little time.'

'Gladly, you have a year from tonight.'

Really. Who would dictate such terms to the King of the Britons?

After a year there was no news. Culhwch threatened to bring satire down on Arthur's head until Kai stood up and growled like the black bear when starved.

'Careful, chief. You insult our man too much. Breathe. This is what I say. Travel with us. Until you confess that the woman doesn't exist, or we have found her, we will stay right by your side.'

A cadre of bright warriors were selected to travel with them.

And they set out into the dreaming

They came to a vast plain and a fort,
the largest in the world
but the more they walked,
the further they were from it.

In the evening they would be no closer
than morning, and the glorious fort
would beckon.

By sheer bloody persistence
they bent back the rules of play
and finally drew close
and as they drew close they saw sheep
without boundary, amok on the plain
and a huge shepherd on a mound
and a tattered jacket of skins on him
and a shaggy mastiff, as vast
as a nine-year stallion.

It was his custom
to bring pain
to any bold warrior

that passed.
And to scorch up
the land
tree or bush
with his breath.

They piped up, 'Greetings shepherd! And blessing on your prosperity! Are you well?'

He growled down, 'No wound vexes me. Apart from my wife.'

They ventured more, 'Whose sheep are you tending, and whose is that fort?'

He bellowed this time, 'Ignorant little torc-shakers! Throughout the world this is known by all as the fort of Ysbaddaden, King of the Giants!

I am Custennin, his brother, and because of my wife he has ruined me. And you?'

'We are messengers of Arthur, seeking Olwen, daughter of Ysbaddaden.'

'Then you are dead in your boots. Pulp. No one has survived that request, and many have made it.'

The vast shepherd got up to leave, grumbling. And as he did, Culhwch gave him a gold ring. Though he tried it, it didn't fit him, so on return to his home, he gave it to his wife. He eased wearily down onto his chair by the fire and tried to rest. But the questions came.

'Where did you get this ring, husband? Treasure it is.'

'A corpse on the tide washed it in.'

'Show me the corpse!'

'You will see him in the real soon enough. Culhwch himself has come to ask for Olwen.'

This was a game changer. She herself was aunt of Culhwch (she the sister of his mother), so she ran joyfully to meet the warriors as they strode towards their home.

So supernatural was her intensity of welcome, so focused her message of accommodation, Kai quickly snatched a log as she embraced him, sap pouring like whey and shape utterly twisted. This is what you call killing with kindness.

The bright warriors entered the hut
and the woman made her way
to a box by the hearth and opened it.

Out climbed a lad with curly yellow hair:

'This is the last of my twenty-three sons.
Ysbaddaden has killed the others.'

'Let him travel by me,' said Kai,
'and neither of us will be slaughtered
until we both are.'

Learning of their quest, the boy's mother
told them that Olwen came to her every Saturday,
to wash her hair in a bowl, and then leaves her rings.
Precious rings she never asks to be returned.

And, learning that they meant Olwen no harm,
she sent for her.

Olwen's robe was flame-red,

red gold torc about her neck,
like flowers of the broom
the yellow of her hair.

Waves' foam was
the whiteness of her skin,
whiter than cotton grass
her palms and fingers,
but whiter than the swan itself
her breasts.

Not the eye of a mewed hawk,
not the eye of a thrice-mewed falcon
was deeper or more beautiful than hers.

As the pinkest of foxgloves
her cheek,
whoever glimpsed her
loved her, utterly.

Four white clovers
sprang from where
she walked.

Olwen – whose very
name means
Track of the Moon.

She came into the house and sat beside Culhwch and the high chair.
As soon as he saw her he recognised her as the one he had loved in
his heart since the very mention of her name.

'Maiden, it is you I love. Will you braid your life to mine—?'

She cut him short.

'You are in grievous danger. Go to my father, and whatever he asks of you, tell him you can achieve it. If you do this you may win me. But if he doubts your readiness you will be lucky to leave with your life. He knows it is his death if I marry, it is prophecy.'

Culhwch and the men proceeded to the hall. Stealthily. As it is when you enter the hall of a giant. On the way they killed the nine gatekeepers of the nine gates and their nine mastiffs, all without a shout.

They stood in front of the giant en masse. He was barely awake.

'Greetings Ysbaddaden, King of all Giants! We have come to seek your daughter Olwen for Culhwch, son of Cilydd.'

'Where are my gatekeepers? Raise the forks under my eyes so I may see my new son-in-law.'

This was achieved by his fussing servants.

'Come back tomorrow. You will have your answer then.'

And, as they turned to leave, he suddenly hurled with full power one of three poisoned spears at their backs.

Good Bedwyr, he caught it and launched the spear back, rupturing the giant through the kneecap. Phwack and grind.

He bellowed:

You wild beast of a son-in-law,
savage, uncouth.
Like the gadfly's sting
this poisoned missile
has wrangled me.

A curse on the smith
that forged it.
A curse on the anvil
on which it was forged,
such is my agony.

Second day they arrived and did not ask this time but demanded: Olwen in exchange for her dowry and maiden-fee. And death for him if not.

He balefully growled:

'I have not consulted her four great-grandmothers and four great-grandfathers. I must speak to them. Come back tomorrow.'

As they got up to leave, he hurled again the second poisoned spear. This time good Menw caught it, and hurled it back, and it landed in the chest of the giant and jutted out his back.

Wicked son-in-law,
vindictive and sly.
Like the bite of a horse-leech
that hard iron has twisted me.

A curse on the furnace
that heated it,
and a curse on the smith
that forged it.

When I take to the hills
my chest will ache, my belly churn
and I will vomit into the grasses.

And they happily went to the lodgings to break their fast.

Third day.

'Ysbaddaden. Don't do this. Don't hurl the third spear. It's your own death you are bringing down.'

'Raise my eyelid, it's drooped. So I may see my glittering prize of a son-in-law.'

His servants busied themselves. The moment they did he hurled the last of the spears, with everything he had and a little bit more.

Culhwch grabbed it and flung it back. It roared into the eyeball of the giant and out through the nape of the neck. Grind and gristle.

Sadist of a son-in-law,
you have made me smoke-eyed,
when I stroll my eye will weep.
I will be beset by migraines and giddiness
at each new moon.

Like the bite of a mad dog,
a slathering dog,
a lunatic dog,
so you have pierced me.

And the men of Arthur went to their chops and wine.

Fourth day they came and implored again.

'Don't be a martyr. Give it up. You look terrible.'

He called Culhwch forward.

For hours the giant dazzled the assembly with requests more outlandish, more extraordinary than the last, but Culhwch gave a stock reply, 'Though this may appear hard, I will achieve it easily.'

And so the volleying match was raised to such a pitch the giant gave his most ornate command:

'*There is no comb or shears in the world which is capable of dressing my beard, because my beard is stiff, stiff like an irritable brush with angry spokes of iron, except, that is, the comb and razor and shears that hang between the ears of the terrible boar Twrch Trwyth – and he will not give them willingly and you cannot force him.*'

'Though this may appear hard, I will achieve it easily.'

'*For the hunt you will require Drudwyn the whelp of Graid, and the only leash in the world that can contain him, the leash of Cors Cant Win, and the only collar that can hold the leash belonging to Canhastyr Can Llaw, and of course the greatest of huntsmen, Mabon son of Modron, who was stolen from his mother when he was three days old.*'

For an age it continued. Nations rose and fell. Above, below, left, right, front and back, the stipulations of the hunt continued in dizzying fashion, but the young man held his nerve. Erect and unblinking:

'Though this may appear hard, I will achieve it easily.'

'*Oh yes, uproot those bushes near my hall and give the ground a good burn and I want it ploughed and sown so it's ripe by the time of the leaving of the dew and can be made into food and drink at your wedding, and I expect it done in a day, and only Amaethon will plough it for you and he won't agree and you'd need the two oxen of Gwlwlydd and he won't agree and I want honey that is nine times sweeter than the honey of the first swarm, without drones or bees (who won't agree), I want the cup of Llwyr which holds the strongest drink in the world but he won't agree and you cannot force him and the hamper of Gwyddnau and the horn of Gwlgawd and the birds of Rhiannon that bring the dead to life and lull the living to slumber and the cauldron of the King of Ireland and the blood of the*

*Very Black Witch, daughter of the Very White Witch from Pennant
Gofid to straighten my beard out as I prepare to be shaved. None of
whom will agree and you cannot force them.'*

Don't all fathers do something similar when their daughter is at stake?

'Though this may appear hard, I will achieve it easily.'

'And the big one, the tusked finger of a dark god, Twrch Trwyth,
will never be hunted unless you have

*Bwlch and Cyfwlch and Syfwlch
with their three gleaming shields,
their stabbing, stroking spears,
the carvers of keenness their swords,
Glas, Glesig, Gleisiad their hounds,
Call, Cuall, Cafall their steeds,
and respective wives, witches,
daughters and maidservants.*

Not one of whom will agree and you cannot force them.'

'Though this may appear hard, I will achieve it easily.'

At some point, in the small hours of the night, the list was complete.

Just locating Mabon was an epic itself within this creel of tasks.

Gwrhyr, a man of Arthur's who understood the succulent language
of birds and animals, walked into a deep forest and asked a blackbird
for whereabouts of Mabon.

*The blackbird told him to seek the ancient stag of the forest who told him
to seek the archaic owl who told him to seek the noble eagle who told him*

[65]

to seek the wise salmon of Llyn Lliw, who bore them on his shoulders to
a prison of stone, in which they could hear the wailing of Mabon.

Arthur summoned the men of Britain and gave full attack, and Kai
burst through the stone wall and gathered Mabon on his back, and
then fought his way out, giving no ground, a blur of skill.

Yet patient Arthur continued to stand by his word of help. That's
how you earn such a name.

He scooped up every warrior in the Three Islands of Britain and three
accompanying islands, then to Brittany and Normandy too. Arthur
pursued Twrch Trwyth across Ireland, fighting him ferociously for
nine nights and days, surrounding him with slathering hounds, but
only killing one of his seven piglets. The boar responded by laying
waste to one fifth of Erin. In private counsel with his astonished and
exhausted warriors, Arthur revealed that the terrible boar used to be a
king but the gods made him like this because of his wickedness.

Bloodshed and mayhem bang-crashed-and-bellowed their pursuit of
almost the entire stretch of Britain. It was the talk of every hamlet,
travellers' camp, every crossroads, every tavern.

Arthur and the hunt finally chased Twrch Trwyth down into the
blue acres of Cornwall. Mabon and Cyledyr (through astonishing
demonstrations of pluck and perseverance) had grabbed the razors
and shears, but still the bristled one maintained his comb.

Only down there, at the very south-westerly tip of the country, did
they finally take the comb – and you should know they paid hard
to get it, all the trouble thus far was mere play in comparison to this
final, terrible push.

And into the curly waves
Twrch Trwyth
and his piglets

charged charged charged
not looking left or right but slam-bang into the surf
surly and snarling.

And where he went then,
or what he did after
is not known.

Arthur, exhausted by the losses of the great chase, went to seek restoration in Celli Wig in Cornwall, to bathe long and deeply, and to throw off his bone-deep weariness.

Young men set the world on fire.

Culhwch gathered those who wished malice towards Ysbaddaden and made his way to the great fort, across the plain where it grows no nearer until it does.

The giant was waiting, preparing to die. Ready in his fashion. In his regalia of office, in his hall, with his people around him.
That's all there is.

And there, in that place, Caw of Prydyn shaved off Ysbaddaden's beard, then his skin, then his flesh to the bone itself, and both ears entirely.

'Have you been shaved, man?' said Culhwch.

'Oh yes.'

'Is your daughter now mine?'

'She is. But reflect that the debt you really owe is to Arthur. Without him you would have none of this. And now the time has come for you to take my life,' said the giant, bending his head to expose his neck.

Gorau, son of Custennin – the blond boy from the box, the giant's own nephew – stepped forward, roughly grabbed his hair and dragged him to the mound, severing his great head from his shoulders. He skewered it down on the bailey post and took dominion of both the fort and territories from the killer of his brothers.

And in the immensity of it all stand two kids.
Love's young dream.
Never spoken for more than a moment.

That night
Olwen and Culhwch
became lovers.

For as long as he lived,
she was his only wife.

❖

And Rhiannon is crying and I am agape. She whispers to me:

—*You heard that. That is Bard-Come-A-Fire.*
That is the greatest of our storytellers.
Not a boy in a hut with a stone on his belly
But a mother in a village under a tree.

And I am alone again, and the rain is tingling the surface of the waters.

✤

Is þes middangeard missenlicum

Wonder is this world, without compare

But he is stiffening his beard with sea salt

He is lighting red candles in the old kirk

He is making himself crooked

✤

I am not listening. I hex you rider, I wish your horse to be strayed.

I ride *will*, not fear, and I am going to talk history.

So: I am telling you about this kingdom of Dumnonia. Maybe I did already. Long before Devon or Cornwall, Dumnonia.

As the last Roman blew out the candle and ushered in the Dark Ages, this is the name-shape the far west became.

So says Solinus, and if he doesn't know, then tell me, who does?

I'm only kidding, I barely know the guy.

Gildas the monk called it *Damnonia*, to shame its chief, Constantine. Which is also confusing for the Damnonii, up in Strathclyde, or the other tribes around under that name.

Our scribbler Geoffrey of Monmouth insists that Constantine was in the line of Arthur, egging, then over-egging, then creating a whole bloody omelette of speculation that Arthur then belonged to the House of Dumnonia. Even a romantic like myself is not going to build his kirk on that.

But we gotta love Geoff. He wrote in a time of intense pressure: Normans officiously, ruthlessly and relentlessly taking what the Saxons never quite totally pulled off: the far west. The pressure, both literary and political, was coming from two fronts. By now, the twelfth century, Irish literary achievement was known and deeply respected, it helped plump up the infrastructure of church and saintly life, their Gaelic stories wove these lone, monastic types together into a powerful franchise. They gave them an organising shape.

Geoffrey beats back the Irish dominion for a second, stares down the Normans, and weaves an imaginal Arthurian tapestry right into the far west, thrums up the land's slumbering pressure points, cattle-prods the acupuncture of Dumnonia into electrifying, vivacious life. Bless the word-bruiser, the scrapper, the euphoric little god-torch.

Dartmoor:

you ocean floor, you houser of hyena, you endorser of highwaymen. Three hundred and sixty-five square miles of pungent weird. Sat in the barber's chair of infinite progress with your furious bonce shorn of trees, moon-belly pregnant with longhouses, burial cairns, clapper bridges, tannery routes, you beast, you utter beastie, still smeared vivid with naming; blaggard, indecent, scrumptious naming, roaring with story still visible on the rump of every tor, valley, pool and treacherous, swampy turf.

May you drain the petrol, the resolve, the very puff out of every lime-green hire car or finned and taxed caravan that touristy pootles along your ridged, granite, exhausted back. May you house hidden animals that no one ever sees.

May Dartmoor children crawl like glittering, lairy beetles up the coast, past Dawlish, Starcross, even Tiverton, and give a little of your magical stink to those that long for it, so they can stay there, and not come here. Let those good people sink emphatically and suddenly and maybe even blessedly into their place and just want to utterly stay there, beauteous and arrested by the buses of Balham, the cabs of Clapham.

I call for a sudden, sweeping, snooty disinterest in Devon from the rest of the world. Cock a snook, I beg you. Nothing to see here, move along. Don't worry yourself, let us come to you.

We always had allure, you see. From way back. Visitors Phoenician, Grecian and Gallic too, hungry for our tin, up and down the rivers they snaked:

ISCA
DURIUS
TAMARUS
CENIUS

I will stand up ablaze and lift the moor like a wriggling, green tapestry dangling in front of my thunderous face, all its rivers galloping down into my lusty, suckling jaw. All the giants will fall in, the farms will fall in, the tractors and the pixies will fall in, the taverns and the ice-cream vans and the secretive foxes and the cairns filled with hero gold. I'm so thirsty, you see. And so very, very hungry. Durius is moving fast round the bend towards Buckfastleigh and Totnes and Dartmouth, an icing of sunlight on the ragged ripple as it twists out of sight.

Dumnonia continues, here today, as you blink at my scratches.

It is quieter now, later in the day, cooler but no rain. Getting near dusk. I'm wheeling off the river shingle to head left up the long track that leads to the old-growth oaks.

I'm delighted to see the laughing boy of the lanes again, Dafydd just wandering about in the half-light looking at things. He smiles up at me and starts to talk.

—This bard thing you are thinking about. You should take heart. The bardic schools were fine in their way, but they decayed as things do. Life is seasonal. It's not to worry. But the essential stuff, the heart of the matter, the implicit roughage of what they sought is still available. It's to do with beholding things. Paying attention.

Me, I sang of the *chanson de geste*
Song of great deeds

That's what powerfully took me, the audacious,
grandiloquent leap into the most secret heart.

But I always made sure I came off worst.

I would puff up the heart, but play the loon not the bragger. I could
tell of centripetal structure, and caudate sonnet, imitative fallacy
and periergia, but you'd soon clout me.

I know you'd like leonine rhyme but I suspect you're already up to it.

I am cavalier, horseman, stylist of the heart, who bangs and clangs
the sword of the words into the melt of their feelings and all swoon
to my lion-rough mischief. I am the chant royal, and I ride with
Tristan over chalk-white cliffs to Tintagel which is lit with torches,
and bards yodelling my songs though I wasn't born yet.

It has warmed me so to see our hero.

Goodbye Dafydd,
Goodbye storyteller woman,
Goodbye Rhiannon,
Goodbye Finegas,
Goodbye Ted and Robert,
Goodbye Merlin.

I am going to the navel of the world now.

I am going to the centre of the woods.

✣

And I am watching him going into the woods.

I, Twrch Trwyth.

'And where I went then,
or what I did after is not known.'

It's known now.

And I bring ancient snow down upon this man.

✣

❧

Forst sceal freosan, fyr wudu meltan

Frost will freeze, fire melt wood

And the tusk god is runing the snow

I will meet Wealas and we will see what is

❧

How can the sky turn that odd grey-yellow in August? That piss-freeze yellow? And how is it that all heat has drained from the ground beneath me? Like a switch being flicked. And underneath flakes just about to fall, all I can see is red roses.

I wonder if this is one of Dafydd's tricks, the old troubadour. They are hanging off every branch, wrapped round trunks and even starting to weave up my jeans. I skip out of the circling parade of thorns.

Red roses.

I fell in love in these woods once.

So long ago it could be another life. A long time, another century. And so hard, so absolute, so all-or-nothing, the damage is writ large in me. And this leafy canopy has the sickness-memory of it, remembers the infection, watched the weight, the gladness, the wit, the sense, the un-sense, the rare peace of my character be ruined under the hooves of that long, terrible disease.

Yes, Dafydd, as you would likely say

It was a special love.

Loveskull

I defy you, you chloroform of the gods, you spreader of mayhem and elongated longing, I defy you, you grievous, inconstant, horrible bastard.

But love can't be defied. Never saw a single soul ever that could. The awful sweetness of the sickness.

Never saw any of us not become an instant utter twat the moment it slinked in.

But I am different now. Rebuilt.

Loveskull did not give me the language of a poet, but a killer. That's what happened by the time it had finished with me. One who culls.

Maybe that was my time in the swamp, swimming with a knife between my teeth.

Maybe that was my time carrying other people on my back, telling a lie from my mouth.

Oh yes, that feels about right.

But I see you in the woods looking at me, big pig, and I raise you.

Bring your snow, your flakes, I trust them more than I do these roses.

Flog me with the white stuff, take all this red, pumping blood stuff away, all this ardent, verdant, baby-mush, adolescent feeling-shite away.

What if I can't *trust* my feelings? What if none of us can anymore? Obi-Wan Kenobi got it absolutely wrong, the fucking hippie.

So wither, roses, wither

Wither
Wither
Wither

I don't have a story for Loveskull, you could creep between the lines of my words and guess guess guess. Loveskull withered Tristan on the vine, pulverised Isolde, caused Yeats to write words that touch all moon-struck teenagers everywhere.

The best poems are not written by the woman that got that last kiss, they are written by the woman that didn't. In myth there is a third place between desire and abstinence, between sex-show red and linen-clad white, between howling imbiber and vestal chanter. You may not want to go there.

Between the white flower of the hermit and the red flower of the lover there is a third flower that is not mentioned.

It is the black flower.

This is the gift of the roses that I am just too fucking angry to talk about.

Griefskull

There is a layer of skin on my face now, but my skull has been Griefskull. I only have to touch the jaw under my beard to know this. Not special, elite grief, but the grief that is daubed on the lintel above all of our doors. It's there when we glance into the mirror at 3 a.m. as we take a piss. Who is this weeping tramp in my bathroom and how did he get there?

So you will have to take my anger for the energy it is. As the only thing that got my body out the Somme and dragged its barbed-wired heart all the way back to Albion when damn those torpedoes fell.

Let me tell you something. When my great-grandfather was fourteen, he was lowered down the side of an English ship on a rope and with a stick he pushed the German mines away. He was lowered hundreds of times. Fourteen years old.

This is how you earn a name like BOOM.

So here I am. Between skulls. Trying to earn a name.
Things growing on Griefskull like moss on bone. Facial tics,
ludicrous opinions, long silences, some terrible absence when I try
and love again.

These last few years my body tries to kill itself while I sleep. I stop
breathing utterly and find myself in the dark, crawling and vomiting
and wheezing around the room trying to kickstart the whole life-
affirming process called breathing. Breathe, you fat bastard, breathe.

But it's not diet or booze that caused my body to start doing itself in,
just common or garden-variety sorrow. Maybe when I am a new skull
I will start to take my hands from my own throat. This is a spiritual
condition, not a lifestyle issue, and it needs healing. I need healing.

White flakes fall on the sharp, black fur of Twrch Trwyth, and he
keeps his small, furious eyes on the middle-aged man ranting about
roses. He grunts with satisfaction to see that the track behind him,
out of the woods, is swiftly being covered with snow. He's so self-
absorbed he doesn't notice there are other eyes watching him now.
There is a bull, with one blazing eye, an eye that rolls round and
round. Its belly scrapes the ground, and is hot as a pair of bellows.
Next to that, as it gets darker, yet more eyes flicker open.

Men and the wound.

It is the archaic, righteous mandate of the boar to gouge the thigh of
men. Dermot of the Love Spot got killed this way, it took the puff
right out of Tristan and in a fashion it happened to the Grail King
too. And this groin wound is what stands behind all the digging,
fracking and mining we get up to every chance we get. What do you
mean, oh preacher? I mean this. Just to keep old man Grail King
alive, they dug up:

carbuncle and moonstone
onyx and chalcedony
coral and bestion
pearl and optallius
ceraunius and hieracitis
pantherus and androdgma
dionysias and agate
sapphire and emerald
turquoise and lipara
diamond and topaz

And they thought it not nearly enough. It's contagious – angry white guys digging stuff up.

Oil-soaked seabird, you know what I mean.

The very shape of the wood is changing. It is contorting, expanding, bringing its night shape, not its day shape, and still the snow falls.

All the other woods, the little ones, the copses behind council estates, chip shops and golf courses all over this darkening country are quietly pulsing, pulsing like a heartbeat.

And above them, the remote stars circle, and pulse back.

They have every right to be looking at me. The animals. Whacking the diesel into my car, poisoning the air with endless flights, all those sparkling waters nestled in the back of the fridge. Night-blind to the consequence. Ho ho ho, you 'lover of the earth'.

So yes, let this delegation have at me.

I am making my way to a hill fort, an Iron Age hill fort. A ridged, moated, rough circle, that people lived, died, fucked and conjured in. It's prone to mood swings.

I've slept there many times, the place sometimes thick, terrifyingly thick with magic, and then other times sour-aired and flat. It will not display itself for whatever wish I may bring to it. And that means I trust it.

It has never tried to paralyse or enchant me, as some places have, I've never needed professional help to wiggle back out of its humours. Some places you do. They clamp shut on you, tendril you into incapacity, mineralise you, mossify you. And despite the tantalisation of our animistic selves, most of us don't want that, not really, nor anything like that. We want the T-shirt, not the encounter. But Ted is down the hill, on the river, fishing in the half-dark, shouting up through the snowfall

—CONTACT, LAD, CONTACT!

When spirits come in the forest something happens first. It gets quiet. You get about ten minutes of acute, padded stillness. It's not like any other kind of stillness, any other kind of quiet, any other kind of atmosphere. This is your moment to run, if you still have the legs underneath you.

Otherwise, the assumption is, you're *in*.

I am crunching through great drifts of snow now. Everything is crusted but I am so rousingly hot. The top layer of stacked flakes is already becoming ice.

Little Red Riding Hood skips down the path to meet the wolf.

We follow the crumbs to the witch's hut.

The Handless Maiden enters the wood at the darkest part where there is no path.

I will get to my fort and I will take my rest
Though the woods are dark and deep
And I have promises to keep
I will take my rest

I know something is about to happen. I feel I may be about to disappear.

I am six and I am standing by a red postbox on the high moor, because I know, whatever happens, someone would come in the end to collect the letters and I would be rescued. There is a white fog everywhere but in the centre is a boy in shorts by a bright red letterbox, his left hand cupping the freezing iron of its casing, his face jutting out.

I am walking through the woods to Cockington primary school where they feed me little pints of milk with a crusted crown of cream lolling about on it. These are the woods behind the estate I live on. The woods my mum walks me through to Cubs, where after we will have chips for fifteen pence. The woods where I make my dens, the woods where my dad will first kiss my mum under the arch, the woods where I first heard the wind through beech trees and knew it was the sound of the dead.

The woods that are my holy hills of South Dakota, my Mount Kailash, my Glastonbury Tor, my Cadair Idris, my Uluru. Every time I climb the beech I am scaling the World Tree, valiantly clenching the broad trunk between my un-strong kiddie thighs, shifting up onto a branch so I can gaze up at Odin, the All Father, and his great ravens Huginn and Muninn, *Thought* and *Memory*. They swoop round the high branches, telling me things that are to come, and making me cry. Below is Tumnus, with a lantern, telling me to hurry hurry hurry the White Queen is coming. So I climb down and go to school. At lunch I will sit and not want the liver, or the kidney, and especially not the rice pudding with the synthetic jam plopped in the middle. God no. At the lunch table I close my eyes and think of Sherwood Forest, and what Much the Miller's son would be eating, and dear Marion, and Friar Tuck, valiant

Will Scarlett, Alan-a-Dale, and Little John and Robin himself. I know I know I know, as I keep my eyes clamped shut at table, and hug myself, that Robin is the twin brother of Arthur, his green ally, the leafy-sovereign and shared custodian of this island. Does anyone else know this? And I know it's not fucking rice pudding they are eating out there in the dusky forest.

I am a teenager now, and I am at a convention in Wales for young Christians. I haven't quite become one, but people would like me to be. There is the oddest moment, where a kind of wind comes into the room and people are speaking in lots of odd voices, and any empty chair seems to rattle. This is not *Songs of Praise*. It is frightening, and heavy, heavy in me, like raw fear is heavy, but also good, because some uncorralled and obliterating spiritual power is showing itself. It knows things about absolutely everybody. I want to run away as fast as I possibly can, before it articulates my wretchedness.

And I am in Canterbury, leaving the side of my young wife in the middle of the night to go to my work as a cleaner of the art college. I walk along the ancient city walls, soon to mop mop mop the empty building. January night crowds in, sharp, blue and magnificent, and I wonder if this is all there is for me, not hearing the tick tick tick to detonation hidden under the pillows of my wedding bed.

Soon, in a lonely gully in Snowdonia I will encounter the thing I have always sensed and played with through my imagination. But it will be nothing like my imagination. It will be utterly outside myself, but will force itself into myself, in the way it's always been done, out in the lonely places. And that will be that. All of this is in my bundle, the bundle of my life, my snow-wet bundle I carry in this blackening, ashy, snow-Saxon, snow-Celt darkness.

My ancestors are not just people, they are rivers, hills, caves and hawks. They are rain-bears, thumping their sleepy belly for sex and meat in the middle of a Siberian winter; they are the green ink in Lorca's pen; they are twelve young stags in an autumn glade.

My people are with me now as I climb up to this thing that I am scared of. This becoming.

Let it be known to all that I was here, that I sparked the earth properly wild with my words, that I took kindness, money and love, that I scarified wickedness, that I failed and was human, that I became less for others' good, that I bent open my prison bars and was free.

I clamber up the ridge of the ancient compound. It is now almost completely dark.

Something else is there.

In the centre of the fort is a large, dead horse.

It's on its side, and its upper flank is ridged with snowflakes. It already seems to be freezing.

Underneath, from the jut of jaw to its cunt it has been sliced open. Gutted.

A pile of belly and intestinal pipes are heaped up like a ruddy mush in the melted white.

And from inside the horse comes a voice.

Neb is min niþerweard

My tooth is long

And I may bite you

Wealas

You have to come with me. Walk towards me.

[84]

No I don't want to fucking do that. No part of my body wants to do that. If I wasn't so catatonically frozen already I would turn tail and run into the bank of watching eyes. My thigh is wet again, and not with snow.

I crunch towards the terrible, gutted beast. The beast with no insides that is talking to me whilst it snows like never before in the middle of August.

I am absolutely terrified, but I kneel down and stare into the gaping, massive, pitch-black belly slit of the butchered horse.

And I am looking into the eyes of a man

A man squeezed inside a horse

Covered, butcher-thick with horse blood, horse vein and horse sinew

He is a terrible huge baby cutting itself out of a womb from the inside:

Look, I made this for you.

I am the Hunter.

You say you want to meet Bardskull?

This fort is the top of Bardskull.

It is underneath, that skull. Underneath this snow, soil, root. It was right underneath you the nights you and your laggard friends loafed up here. Its tongue is the river.

Now, my Numbskull, Childe the Hunter is going to crawl out and you are going to crawl in.

This horse-womb is the fontanelle of the Hill Skull. Get in amongst
these stinking ribs and fall into the marvellous.

Nothing has ever felt less marvellous.

Childe finally, after so many hundreds of years, rolls out of the horse
onto fresh falling snow. His cloak has disintegrated at the back and I
glimpse greenish tattoos, almost like a map down his spine.

He is standing now, in a way. His feet aren't there, just a kind of smoke.

I can hear the sound of Twrch Trwyth, snorting with disquiet. The
sound of helicopter blades all mixed up with his juddering anger.
All electrics swoon and sway down the southern belly of the moor:
Ivybridge, South Brent, Bucky, Ashy B. In the Exeter Inn, the lights go
out completely at the back snug and the fridge is doomed to defrost.

BANG BANG BANG

Go the Salvation Army drums, stashed away in the village hall cupboard.

And Twrch Trwyth and his shrieking dark piglets once again will
cleanse this island of all falsehood.

The great boar king will drive far, far out into the green Torquay
spray the unjust, wicked enchanters with politic gob.

BANG BANG BANG

Go the car bonnets in every wayward garage from here to Plymouth.

And I tell you this

The slaughterhouse of language did not begin here. It did not begin in
the cider bar of Newton Abbot where we fill our jaws with smoky, flat,
stultifying vats of the stuff.

And here I am at the end of this story trying to crawl back into
its beginning, trying to stuff all these words back into my mouth,
all sentiment, all barter, all seance I indulged in, I take them back.
Cram them in so hard my teeth are pink with blood and regret oh
lights of my hut I see you

But it's too late

It is too late

I don't know

I don't know about this at all

And I am in the horse

part two

pixillation

RíXí LLATION

And it trails behind me. Woven into the tail of my name is wolf.

Shaw = Sithech = Wolf

The wolf I'm after is not zoo wolf, or Latin wolf, measurable wolf, endangered wolf.

This is ghost wolf. Long-gone wolf. Kaput wolf. Bang bang wolf. There are no wolves in merry olde England anymore.

You won't learn a single fact about them in what happens next.

This is seance, what happens now.

♣

Because the old stories say this is not a horse time but a wolf time.

Because for the sore awfulness of this century we need more fur, not less.

That's the root of the trouble: a hairless mind. Hairless mind has us far distant from cormorant and eaglet, from birch bark and anaconda.

Understand me, there's a great deal about people I like. There's a vigorous gleam of the unique in a few. Danger lurks in the observation, but it's undeniable. But humanness seems truest and most vivid when smeared into the petri dish of the mad-bad-and-beautiful expressions of a wider earth.

To have a bald mind is to have black-magicked yourself away from those wider nerve endings.

A pox on the house that brewed that up.

I'm starting to wonder if things actually *were better in the old days.*

Let me set adrift my confession to you.

One hundred and one days the spirit of wolf can take you.

The human that becomes a wolf when the moon fattens. Lupercal.
If you can survive the 101 days you may have the fur lifted clean
from your bones and think pleasant thoughts again. Avoid all
wildlife, stay indoors, wear white, utterly domesticate yourself. No
lovemaking. I heard this once in a Widdicombe pub, and it's stayed
with me. This last little glimpse of oral folklore.

But this ceremony is all wrong now. This doesn't fit the dark
buzzing of our times.

To be more deeply human we could do with more wolf. More
animal. Less animal and we make terribly deranged decisions, and
everyone pays.

What will this look like? Every day I will walk into a wood and
sit under a hazel bush. I will carve out 101 days where I have my
head turned in the direction that the feelingness of this ceremony
dictates. On the outer layer of the encounter it's not complex; on
the interior, God only knows.

A wolf has more information in five seconds about a forest, more
acuity of focus than anything I will locate within this protracted
encounter. I know that going in. Aping that is not what this is, though
I admire it. This leans on what they call a poetic state of mind.

And if you sneer at that, then forget it, read no further.

So the remit is simple – not praying away wolfness, but inviting it
in. A reversal.

I will sit under the hazel and sing my calling songs and see what comes. I am not gambling for crescendo, climax, coda. I'm just going to keep turning up.

Such an idea gives me the jitters. So I have to do it. The deepest part of it will not likely fit into words.

To have a wolf move through my mind.

Be prowled.

Be stalked by my own name. To find out something of my own name. To possibly earn it. To be howled by an extinction. A beautiful ghoul. This is the compulsion, the way my head has turned. First time in a long time I'd have the mind to do something like this. To invite in a kind of discomfort.

Forget the undead, zombies, Nosferatu, that's not what's tickling this into being.

And I have to turn from another animal first. You see I have suffered these last years. Ordinary and terrible heartbreaks, and in that suffering I crawled into the belly of a horse. She offered the refuge, and I was glad to take it. If my way of thought is scrambled and mad to you, or rattlingly unknown, I say again you should stop reading. I can't dally. I can't stretch wine-scored words on the rack of sobriety. I have to carve my way out.

I have to break from a mare. From Macha. From a horse goddess.

ALL OUR LIVES WE ARE CRAWLING IN AND OUT OF ANIMALS

Some are stuffed with dust, some have their balls cut, some are petrified of electric fences and loud bangs. Some piss on the carpet when their owner comes home, some square up to grizzlies. But all my storytelling, all my years of wordy ramble saved me when I most needed it, and the horse goddess found me. Stalked me. I had paid an anticipatory penance that she was prepared to recognise. So one night I just climbed into her.

I am here, talking to you, me the slumped scoundrel in the ribs of Macha, this gleaming rotunda of horse, I gnash my way out of the massive. *Clack clack clack* my smacking sticks bang me out of her bone cathedral.

Goddess of horses I am astonished to leave. I am in my astonishment to be out of you, such were our centuries together. To the rinky-dink world, it was five years, but it was centuries to any gradient worth the count.

I was there and I loyally pilgrimed your clip-clop beatitudes. I climbed into you when the pain was set to eviscerate me, and you, angel-nag, you took me in. We rode with the Tuareg across cold night-timey desert. When you turned yourself into a blooming deep-sea whale and swam the Liffey I was there, and it was there in the stout-black perfume of it all I suddenly knew someday I was to be wrenched out. Like a smirking drunk hurled bleakly from God's own tavern. And I would mourn and belabour such expulsion, wicked plead with the innkeeper. Out of Eden. My obscenity would dictate it.

So yes, holiday's up. The passport has enough stamps. I have enough exotic infections. I am home. I know I am home when I sink into the *vargr*.

That means *Restless*.

I have become restless. Means I am healed a little. I address all this to the creaking forest I now stand in front of, horse gut to my heavy belly, equine red ribs to my hips.

I know what is coming is going to be messy for a while. Won't make sense. Crashing about in the bush talking to spirits when I'm meant to be gluing my hands to the lions in Trafalgar Square. It'll be static and distortions for the most part, but something may come through. This rather odd process is the deepest thing I can offer in this moment of climate emergency.

I do this because I simply don't know what else is left to do but to sing your calling songs. I honestly don't.

Yip Yip! Announcements:

I am the piteous cripple you old-time spirits have spooked before. It is time to change temples. One hundred and one days I will be in this prowled state, this hidden kerfuffle of clamp and leap. The woods will be my lupine monastery.

Strange that a horse would birth a wolf.

I will cut a rough slit in the slurry of a Devon hill and make a chilly nest. I will make a den for the pagan dark. Devon, Defanscir, Dumnonia – *the people of the deep valley.*

That's what it means to be Devonian. More than cream teas and furtive witchcraft and more Tory flags squatting in more bullish farmers' fields than black hairs that flood the shoulders of Tony Cleave, the greatest butcher for fifty miles. This is the only place I trust enough to take on this foolishness. To embed this incant. This place can have me if it wants me. Almost half a century of the bashing sea and yellow-gorse moors in my love-spun ears and heart-sick eyes.

Some particulars you should know. My nest is limited to roughly a thirty-foot circle, perimeter articulated by flour and whisky. Very little to alert the eye. No dreamcatchers, no showy wafts of Tibetan scents. No Green Man figurines. There's just a middle-aged guy visiting a place, over and over. Shuffling in and out.

The nest is a configuration of flushed oak, low clouds of spiky ivy, florid vine and bracken with a pronounced case of erectile disfunction. The whole thing is a little on the slant. Very little light. But that's good. Deer tracks from north to south, a dog fox that noses occasionally, a sparrowhawk I see maybe twice a week. At its centre is the little hazel bush, where I will sit and call. Towards the end of this ceremony I will move to the woods' very heart, an old Celtic hill fort.

So the darkness on the outside
And the darkness on the inside
Will make a covenant

Vargr vargr vargr

I will ride the restless.

This is October. The forest is hiding its strength. It's faking weakness. Every branch crunches, cracks, bemoans its lot underfoot. I limp over a leafy quiff of foliage. This first day is piss-sodden, beautifully wrecked by rain-sluice. And gulp gulp gulp goes the happy copse. Bracken is a very distinct, very bleached tan, lopped off to one side like a parting of hair.

I'm actually going to have to begin this.

I clack and church the air with my old horse belts, the kind that used to hang on the necks of the heavy horses – the Percheron, the gypsy cob. Big fellas. I swing them and fuck the place knows the sound. Grinds that sound in its crunchy forest-teeth like morning has broken and peace has broken out. *Knows it.*

clack clack clack

It's a sound that disrupts consciousness.

For the ones to come, I do this
For the ones to come, I do this

Women climb under my pelt
When they want their shape to leap,
I slip an owl feather between their thighs
For a baby to grow

You can live hundreds of years
If you place my tooth on your chest

I'll tell you this about this time we are in. If you don't start to
understand a wolf then you will never know the etiquette of the day.
If you can't howl, my friend you are already dead.

shake it off

song one

clack clack clack

I was a third brother, and the son of a king. Grew up near power,
witnessing power, but a little back in the mix. Such an arrangement
would suit many of us. It did me for a long time. Stupefying luxury and
low expectations. But I was a dull bird compared to my shiny brothers.

And it was a bird that was stealing my father's apples, and he fierce
hoarded his apples. Why wouldn't he, they were solid gold. He
almost lost his mind over the theft, turned ugly. Face raw red like a
thousand nights on potato vodka.

My eldest brother strode into the night to catch the thief. Stood up
like Hercules from the south, alone in the orchard. Of course he
fell immediately asleep, and my second brother fell asleep the next

night. Both bullshitted our father, said that they stayed up all night, but the lost apples spanked reality into the circumstance.

It was a strange thing, but father said nothing to their fabrications. It is something, the first time you look your father in the eye and tell him a lie.

It was my turn, the runt. But I had my silly lad wisdom. I sat up in a tree that would not give me rest. A thorn throne, immune to seduction. Never get comfy.

I saw it was a bird of fire that took the apples. Like a visioning I saw it. I could not catch it, but grabbed a tail feather to show Dad. The feather cheered him up. Made him skip for a moment. Never seen him skip before. If the feathers alone could do that, then what about the whole damn thing? We three brothers trafficked in the sheer possibility.

My eldest brother Dimitri was off on his big horse in a shot to locate the bird, riding his pride. Acres of time pass, decades, centuries it seems, and he did not return. My second brother Vasili went and also disappeared. My father was weakened without his sons – his Suns – and it was a fierce and persuasive conversation I had to have with him to let me go too.

I left on a white horse with a white bridle and saddle, and rarely had I been happier. The whole world was with me that day. I was a giddy boy.

Days later I came to an immense forest, and before the forest there was a stone tablet which read:

If you go left you will die and your horse will live

If you go right your horse will die and you will live

I did not have the imagination to just proceed ahead.

Well, bless you nag but I went right. Deeper into the greening and over the hours I even forgot about the stony mandate. Whistled to myself and thought about women and feasts. Jolly boy on his jollies.

A wolf came from nowhere and ate my horse. Boom.

Ate it up, all of it. And me screaming and crying and helpless like a little baby.

Then the fucking thing speaks, wolf-croak:

—*This is not a time for horse, this is a time for wolf*
Get on my back / I know where the bird of fire is

It is a thing to get on the back of wolf. It took me a moment to do it. I had to leave something inside myself, just put it down. Something civil.

Wolf fur is thick and deep, they move in a way ungodly to the settled life, there is little fat on bone as they dip, dart and break from the rough – and me clinging alive alive oh, glancing quickly back at the bloodied ribcage of my crunched and gobbled horse.

But he didn't lie, the wolf. I noticed that.

Oh he took me to a cage with the bird in it. There it was, in an open meadow. I freed the bird but some longing came over me for the cage itself. Just surged into me. A fanciness, a raising of rank, surely my father would be doubly proud if I returned with the cage? That extra swagger.

—*But I told the boy. Do not cage the wild. I told him*

It's true, wolf told me, but there I was, cock-of-the-north, tugging on the great weight of the splendiferous abomination. That's the cage, in case you are wondering. The wretched thing had a hundred invisible threads attached to it, the tug on which brought warriors, blades, all with deadly intention.

I was brought to a king who recognised the value of having a nobleman in his debt, and a thief at that. Of course, there is always something that a king wants. So I asked and he replied, and I got to live a little longer. Kings always have a weak spot. And in this case it was the Horse with the Golden Mane. If I stole that from another king, then the bird I would get.

So off me and the exasperated wolf travelled to the next kingdom.

I sneaked into the stable at night to take the horse, but oh in the moonlight I was enamoured by the ornate bridle hanging on the wall. What would the king think of me if I brought that with the horse?

A desire swept into me, possessed me, a darkening.

—But I told the boy. Do not bridle the wild. I told him

It's true, wolf told me, but there I was, the laughing boy, tugging on the heavy weight of the bridle. The damned and enspelled thing had a thousand invisible strands of declaration on it, that brought soldiers, daggers, malice.

I was brought to a king who saw that having a prince in his pocket was no disadvantage, and one not afraid of a little burglary. So I asked him what he longed for. And he smacked his thin lips and revealed what he most desired: not a bird, not a horse, but a woman. Fair Elana, a woman who lives far over the hill, at the edge of the furthest ocean; who is almost a holy rumour. The soul itself, some softly murmur into their wine. Bring me her and you'll get the horse, he said, merry and deadly as all kings are.

And I think by now I was the wolf, there's no pretending, or maybe it was the wiser part of me.

—And yes, I was him now, even as he travelled on my back north, past lakes and rivers and encounters that clean the dirt of civilisation from a man. North to a green place where Elana would be with her women and her mother. We hunched in the treeline under dripping leaves and admired them.

Do not be foolish and think this a mortal woman. And there was no way I was letting the boy's idiocy or simple greed blow the encounter a third time. I waited till she was near us and I pushed into view.

A woman may take a wolf over a man these days. They say I snatched her, but I didn't. She ran. She ran to my back. She had her own nose for the wild rumpus.

I don't kidnap: I kill or I invite.

And they are on my back and they are falling in love, aren't they? And he-that-is-me is weeping and wailing that now this is the real thing and never to be repeated surely I could weave some magic so that they can stay together. He's all teary.

So I make a big gesture. I leap into her shape and present myself to the king and he gives Ivan the Horse with the Golden Mane.

Whilst Elana and Ivan picnic, I endure and sneak from the lovers' chamber several days later. The prince was meant to say my name three times and forgot, such is love's woeful amnesia.

Everything he says is true. It is a shame I'll carry, this forgetting to call the wolf. But we brought the horse to the second king who – cutting a longer story shorter – gave us the bird and suddenly Elana and the wolf and I are back at the edge of the big black forest next to the tablet of stone.

And the wolf the wolf the wolf would not take another step to the domestic.

For he would have been riding my back, wolf on man, if he'd taken another step. Is that not a degraded and backward move? His fur would have dropped away, his yellow fangs crumble, claws grow blunted if he caught the spicy whiff of court. He would smell wrong to the forest forever after.

It is the most awful thing to smell wrong to the forest.

So wolf turns, and something in me turns, and he is back in the immeasurable vast. Out of reach. And I can't see him, and something complacent settles in the absence of his restlessness. I can't quite reach him. So, I decided we should get cosy.

Never get cosy.

We sat and we feasted, me and the woman from the edge of things, wine uncorked, sweetness on lips. And we relaxed didn't we? The grand unstretching, the massage of safety. We fell asleep. And when we sleep come my brothers.

You remember them?

My two false brothers. Dimitri and Vasili. The liars. Who eyed the Firebird, who eyed Elana, who eyed me in my relaxation, my terrible vulnerability. And they with:

Empty hands
Empty hands
Empty hands

They decided to become men of action. Having pissed the money away, itchy with clap, they would become men of action.

And they took their swords to me, their malice, their wickedness. I was mangled, turned over, mashed and trampled. The bird of fire was taken and a blade to Elana's throat, grim murder promised if she breathed but a word to our father that it was not them as the grand heroes of all things. The redemption would be theirs.

And I remained as the great bloodied lump, gleefully piled up, legs where there should be arms, ears where there should be fingers. And there I would have stayed if not for wolf.

—And I fleet-foot it through the rough and I come to my friend but upside down and all dangly, destroyed in the muck and gunk of himself. I think we all come to our friends like this one day. Two minutes left to his own devices and now this. But I saw something unimaginably old, I saw raven – raven who is from the beginning – I saw raven about to take an eye from this mash-tangle. Through respectful force I convinced her to fly to a faraway place and bring back the waters of death and the waters of life for my wrong-footed friend. And she flew – over everything and underneath everything and through the door of every ghostly century till she brought back the waters. The death water reassembled the lad in the correct order at least, dusted him down, reconstellated, reconstituted him. But waxy he still was in his way. So a lick of the life water onto his blue-ridged lips. He gazed up, and smiled like dreamily receiving good news, 'How long was I asleep?'

He's an idiot, but he's my idiot.

Takes a lot for a wild thing to survive past the forest edge, to not be pixellated by the stink of the civil. But runt is on my bony shoulders and he rides back to culture not on the back of

man-brain
horse-thought but
wolf-mind

This is me, Ivan. Don't skip over my upside-downness. Quickness to you it may seem, but not to me. If I walk back to people without a wolf, they are going to carve me to ribbons. I had it coming. My brothers who are as much me as wolf is me were just following their sleazy little mandate.

They are the terrible guards at every village gate, passport control, city wall.

I roared into the palace on the back of the wolf, there was my father, there was Elana and she broke rank with all enchantments, all threat, all conditions, all spells – she stood:

'THAT MAN THERE IS MY TRUE HUSBAND

The one that is letting his mind be run through by a wolf.'

And the king gathered his kingness into him and felt the texture of truth in her heart-shouts.

What happened to my brothers I cannot say.

My wife the queen rides a wolf now
Me the king rides a wolf now
We will make wolf cubs

And I tell you, reader, right now

This is not
A horse time
This is a wolf time

pharmakon

And then I was poisoned. Me, Martin.

Within hours of telling this story to the forest. In fact I poisoned myself.

In my ramshackle dwelling I have made myself sick with half-cooked meat. I suspected the coming trouble even as I inanely gobbled the lamb down. I ate from the hunter's trap because I was not paying attention. I am convulsing and sick, and still the story circulates my mind as I sweat and curse my stupidity.

—do not cage the wild
—do not bridle the wild

—work with the wild
—listen to the wild

And we have to wrestle the authority figures who've set up shop inside us.

I am curled in a crescent moon hump, shuddering under a blanket, looking out the window. Get up you little quitter. I'm yellow, but I'm heading up into the bush.

The rain is cold and constant. I am going back up the ridged tractor marks then onto deer tracks till I am back in the wolf-womb.

In my feeble funk, I am thinking about Elana, her at the edge of the world. She's not your girlfriend, not my mother or sister, she's Elana. I wonder if I can drag myself to the woods I may glimpse her. Sometimes she's called Vasilisa, or even more ancient, the Woman of the Golden Roof.

Today I walk into the wood a new route. That's important, as I know these trees. Need to surprise myself. I need to go in a wolf way, not a horse way. A chest-high flank of brambles and thorns that I flail at with my feeble staff. I am suddenly thinking of Sleeping Beauty.

I realise this sickly reverie about Elana is something to do with how to talk with my own soul. Surely that is part of this vigil?

That at this time in my life, it is likely only the wolf in me the soul trusts enough to talk to. The rest is too florid, too public. Wait, that is a big thought, I have to think it again:

It's only the wolf in me my soul trusts enough to talk to.

Fuck.

Rather wolf's truthful danger than the sleepy breeze of another false suitor. I don't pretend to know what Elana quite is, but then we're not meant to know. She can't be franchised.

I realise I am trying to get at least a momentary glimpse of this soulfulness. A shy audience. And the intelligence it brings. A shimmer not a sharpness. But the rain is beating me back today, the coming night is beating me back, thorny ridge is beating me back.

So my wolf wants to talk to my soul and my soul is currently a sleeping girl, just so you know.

I had to be poisoned to meet my soul.

And I am in every arrow

I erupt and diverge
I erupt and diverge
I erupt and diverge
Into the incredible

song two

clack clack clack

I am a young girl the other side of blue thorns,
Whose family forgot to invite the witch to my party,
Whose people got jitters at the thought of the witch.
What else can happen without her but
That I prick my finger and fall asleep?
Witch in exile, when that energy is abandoned, we all fall asleep:
The servants, the hounds, the ale-tasters, the singers in the gallery.

I was fifteen years old when I found the secret room in the
          ancient tower.
All fifteen-year-old girls find the secret room in the ancient tower.
They find that witch part of themselves.

Within it was taboo.
Within it was a spindle.
The last one left which hadn't been destroyed.
The thirteenth wise woman placed it there.

And I wasn't really asleep. She replaced me with a changeling.
Me, I had a hundred good years' education with the woman of the
          winds
Before I slipped back into bed, a moment before the prince arrived.
Some mischief, you see.

It was a magical act, to get everyone to look the other way.
While they gaze at the thorny castle, I get my days on the high street.
I, Briar Rose, *am* the witch now, and I will ride the wolf right into
          Trafalgar.

I learnt to walk on my hands and sleep hanging from a tree like a bat.
And this time it is not the prince slips through thorn, it is wolf.

Trouble your soul to wakefulness all who read this.
Become wolf, slip through the thorn-wall, and come find me.

Kiss my lips, and it is *you* that will wake up.

❖

OK, that's all I've got. My shirt is drenched and I have to wobble back home.

I can hear the wolf blowing his conch shell from the woods tonight. I returned exhausted and gut-sick with the bad meat, but he is playing on the wind and the rustle-rain. He is on his hind legs. I am terrified because I can see my cottage through his eyes from the treeline. I can see myself at the desk, scribbling and sighing.

And now it is morning, blue heavens, scud-happy clouds. I appear to have survived the night. And I am going to get my old man stick again and beat a path.

There is a woodyard nearby, spouting Mordor-like crashes and bangs, and the occasional wrench as some old-growth personality from the forest is thumped to the sod. Every nut on every tree seems to be lobbing itself in my direction, and the thorn flank is still resiliently giving me grief at every stagger. I wonder if the insistent pricks are pissy little ritual cuts. I gasp up great bellyfuls of pungent forest air and look at the vines wrapped on the nearby trees, as pronounced as a smackhead's veins; ridged, mossy, obstinate. This is already tedious.

So fucking *say* something.
I'm coming every day.
What can I do for you?

I hear a thump coming from a shed next to the treeline. Bang bang bang. I walk over to the shed and in it, thumping to be liberated, is the full pelt of a Polish black bear. Lolling skull, the whole thing.

It's wedged between deckchairs, sleeping mats, paraffin lamps and dry wood. It's keen to be on the move. It fucking growls at me.

Now, you should know I put it there. I'm the dungeon keeper. You should know I slept under the beast in a tent, many years ago. A long time I slept underneath it. And the forest is telling me to show a little respect. As I write this, my hand is perfumed with the oils I have rubbed into its fur, my shirt reeking with the smoke I have wafted under her nose, my throat hoarse with the prayers and apologies I have sung in her ear. Her recent residence is demonstrative of a time of such woeful heartbreak in my own life I had let go of certain essential manners. And I have shame for that.

And I remember when I married a bear when I was a young girl.

song three

clack clack clack

In three tents on the taiga lived my family: mother, father and my sister and me. My sister was married, but I was unwed. My beauty was odd, and made my parents anxious, so they kept me hidden away, lest hungry eyes spotted me. I became rare. I shared a tent with an old woman who would feed me, but my parents rarely visited. When I couldn't face the loneliness, I would slip into my parents' tent, and get down under the furs to be hugged close by them.

One day, as usual, I was sitting in my tent. It was a day I was alone, and a day where I suddenly saw the flap of my tent being pulled up. But it wasn't a human hand, it was a bear's muzzle doing the pushing. I was agog with terror, couldn't even scream. The bear dragged and snuffled his way into my home, up to his black furry belly, and put his great paw over my mouth. Soon me and the bear were gone, out into the darkening taiga. Stolen away.

It was autumn and the time of snow was coming.

On arrival at his den, the bear packed up the entrance and encouraged me to lie close to him in the warm darkness. Soon we were both asleep. Whenever I awoke, hungry, I would wake him and make gestures that I needed food. I somehow knew he wouldn't slay me.

He would let out a low growl and place his big paw to my lips. Sucking at the thickest part a delicious fat would drip from it. This was satisfying, and soon my eyes would flutter and I would fall asleep.

As the days gradually lengthened I woke in the dark with the bear shifting his heavy weight onto me. Unable to resist, this was how I became his wife.

When it started to get warm, the bear unpacked the entrance and went looking for food. With his great forest mind, he had no difficulty hunting, and would bring back hare, or reindeer or ptarmigan.

But these endless bloodied chunks of meat proved too much, and I begged for a fire to be made. He made another growl and disappeared off into the larch. Soon he dramatically reappeared with a flaming torch in his jaw and even a knife in his paw. It was impressive. Spits were whittled, even more meat brought in and I got my roast. This was what I survived on.

Soon the snow was leaving and colourful flashes of berries started to flirt from under the white, melting crust. I knew the bear loved berries as much as I did, so I started to roam abroad, bringing them back for the feasts we would share.

One day when out picking, I heard the hiss of a human voice. A male voice. It was my sister's husband, a one-who-is-alight, a shaman. He had been looking for me all winter long, over land and water. And finally, success.

I sauntered over, but carefully, as if I were still hunting berries. He spoke again:

'Where on earth have you been? Who has taken you?'

I quietly muttered back, 'A bear came to my tent, carried me off, made me his wife. He likes me close to the den, not wandering off.'

The shaman nodded. 'Even now he'll be unhappy. When he thrashes his heavy paws around say, "Grandfather, why do you attack me? The berries are getting fewer and fewer, and I miss my parents and family, I'm restless."' The shaman followed his advice with, 'But you must get back to this very spot.'

Well the bear was concerned, and started plucking great clods of soil out of the earth and bellowing, but I told him all the shaman had advised me to, and he calmed, listened and grew still.

The next day I pretended to saunter off after those succulent berries, but instead hot-footed it to the shaman. He emerged from the foliage and told me to run on. To get home. He then dropped to all fours and became a bear, a large bear with a bell on his left ear. He spoke:

'Run faster than you ever have. But as you run, try to listen like never you have before. Listen to what erupts behind you. When the earth crash-bangs with thunder then us two bears have met. If my bell grows loud and bright then I am winning, but if it fades, then he's ripped me apart.'

I ran, over stream and pale tump of larch I ran, up steep gully and down the other side, through dark grasses, faster than I'd ever run for anything. Sure enough, soon I heard the clash-crang of the ground a-pounded and I knew the bears were in combat. After a while the bell dimmed and almost stopped and I feared for my life. Then, bit by bit, it started to ring, it picked up its brightness, its tempo was strident and clear, and I realised the shaman must have won.

When I finally crashed into the tiny settlement of tents I did not enter my parents' or my own, but crawled into my sister's and fell faint. Soon the shaman, now in the form of a man, pushed back the flap and, awakening my sister and my parents, tended to me. Now in deep fever, I surged in and out of the world but eventually, on the third day, my fever broke.

In a little while, my belly swelled attractively, and all realised I was pregnant. Some months after that again, I gave birth to a boy, replete in most everything, but with two things added.

He had the ears of a bear.

Over time, Bear-Ears (that was the name I gave him) became a powerful hunter.

I have combed the hair of the black bear now, I have again scented it, oiled it, brought fragrant smoke and food to its snout, and now I will sleep under it, just like I did back a ways.

The door and the windows are open to the full moon and the river nearby, fit to burst with rain.

To make a road is to make a leash, isn't it?
Ceremony makes us a good, obedient child
To make a road is to trample it down, over and over
To flick off the days on the paper stuck on the fridge
My black pen is my black wand is my black arrow

And now my black coffee. Before a damn thing, the coffee.

you have to bring me something

is what I learnt today. Scurrying late into the woods, chill, sky
looking slapped-arse pink, raven and crow having it out to my right,
some melodious but unnameable trilling from my left. A typewriter
tap from the birch trees. Glorious stink of moss is raised up in crisp
air to some almost heavenly bouquet. Scent is so vital. I suspect
I'll keep banging on about it. I think weight and brightness of air
is as important as any astronomic constellation for circumstance
of ceremony. Dampness brought havoc to Coleridge, dissuading
poetics and bringing on gout. The electrical and the magnetic
interested the romantics, the poet Peter Redgrove claiming that the
reason Sunday feels so tangibly different to us as a day is because
so many electrical sources are turned off – factories, shops, etc. –
though sadly I'm not sure how much of that is the case anymore.

Squatting down on some mulch masquerading as a fallen branch, I
find myself zonking out, just blanking out. Now the boy's not well, I
grant you, so my concentration is not what it could be. My eyelashes
are hot. Now it's flu or some lesser cousin.

I wonder why the werewolf is so much more terrifying than Yeti
or Sasquatch, why those two seem more innocent. We can sketch
them with a few lines, but werewolf is always in such vivid, ludicrous
detail.

Hunkered down on wet Devon mud, squelched amongst ferns and
bracken and endless small holly bushes, breath visible, I get – for
about two seconds – a sense of a-long-time-ago. The telepathy of
the forest sometimes engages in this blankness I'm experiencing; it's
like I'm getting quietly scrubbed. It's not an emotional enterprise,
I simply don't have to feel much of anything at all. There's no
crescendo, no judder, no grief, I'm simply in the place. Head lolls on
my chest.

I don't know how long I am there but suddenly it is almost dark. I heft onto my stick and drag myself up. A surprise. The top of the staff is missing. A significant carving of an owl, an owl of gold. It's just vanished, with no huff, puff or associated drama. I remember it when I sat down and now it has gone.

YOU HAVE TO BRING ME SOMETHING

I have been remiss today, and forgotten to bring something, so the ceremony has taken something. That tends to be how it goes. Forget at your peril. There is now some loss for me to leave in the den. I loved my totem, my fetish, my golden owl fith-fath. I leave the staff too, but I know I've still been shamed.

I track back through the bush, crashing about, and notice a trail is emerging from my daily libations – I'm not taking any form of usual track or road. As it is near dark I slouch out of a sheer wall of dark trees and bring a dog walker almost to his knees in fright.

And it is another day now. I've been wobbling in and out of the woods, often into this weird blankness. No one knows I am doing this, absolutely no one. I'm surprised to see dragonflies in October, and, as I follow the trail of one, I am suddenly overlooking the river Durius. From underneath me on the high bank the waters are snaking towards Buckfast and on to the sea. I blink hot, sickly eyes.

On the waters
Past my cottage
Go regal Boats of Fire
The boats Walter Raleigh sent
To tackle the Spaniards

We are never happier than
When we are sending
The Flaming Boats out
To tackle something, anything

They will process to Dartmouth
And disappear into
Surly Albion waters
So forbiddingly thrilling

I watch entranced with my battle-hot eyes.

—He needed to pay more attention to his cock

says a voice to my left. It appears I have company.
The voice is coming from an old man. I mean indescribably old.

—More sex, there would have been less torment for everyone that
the mad old bastard had to 'discover'. And they call him a magician?
I am a magician, and I give you a story.

I know this has happened fast, but this is how it is for me. This
is how I experience things. I am watching Raleigh's Boats of Fire
accompanied by a Finnish magician. A minute before, it was just me
and a river. OK. A little pushback from the spirit world. This guy is
famous, I think. There's a big book about him.

He leans on his staff and words glide out from under his cloak and
surround us.

This is some mad shit he's going to say, hold on.

My songs made pretty much everything. That's my gig. I make
through what I spake. I am Vainamoinen. I skim through the marshes
on my blue elk and feel good about things. Wind in my beard, sun on
my shoulders, like a successful older rock star. Great teeth.

But I can't find the warmth of a woman, I help create the fucking
world and I'm scouring the lonely hearts columns.

I'm always fighting with a younger guy, Joukahainen – sometimes he wins, sometimes I win.

What I'm going to tell you lives in every blues record you ever heard. Machado is telling you this, Polly Harvey. Even the Stones say

WHAT A DRAG IT IS GETTING OLD

One day I got into a pissing contest, challenged the younger guy on his spiritual knowledge – which was ZERO. He had a toddler's knowledge. Now I had him. I addressed the little shit:

I dug out the ocean, pushed up the high mountain.
I was there amongst the seven immense heroes who erected the
        sky's pillars.
It was us that set the moon and sun on their paths,
It was us who loosed the stars into the ink-black heaven.

That turned his piss to vinegar.

The lad wanted to scrap and I grew angry.
I upheld my chant
And the earth shook. *My* earth.
Sometimes a younger man deserves a slap.

I turned his sword into a lightning bolt,
I made his crossbow a streak of rainbow over the lake.
His arrows erupted into a rabble of hawks overhead,
His sleigh became a log on the grey water,
His horse a boulder, his whip a reed by the lake.

I gave his whole ancestral line the jitters.

Don't pick a fight, you little prick, just don't do it.

He offered silver I did not want, and fields I did not need.

But then he found the sweet spot, he found my longing-song.

'Reverse your magic and I will tell you of the deepest woman. My
sister. She's a May blossom, as a fruit you will find none riper. She has
a kind of honey that will turn you into a mad bee, drunk on the wing.
Many men throng around her, but none has received her betrothal.'

That caught my attention. I'll do an awful lot for a May blossom.
Make any kind of oath for a girl of the orchard. Stupid bastard that
I can be.

Anyway, it was bullshit and I never got with her. Let's move on.

I used to take my longing on fishing trips. I must have caught
thousands of fish but that one most evasive – my heart's desire.

Many more came to me, in their hundreds, beautiful, but not quite her.

I got really miserable. Someone should have stopped these nutty
trips, but I kept going out.

Once a fish said she

Was to be the wife of my life
The chick by my hip
A baker of honey bread
A warm bed, an eager pillow

But that I was just too fucking stupid to catch her.
That I would never know how to keep her.

Then that sly little bastard Joukahainen got me. He shot my blue
elk and I crashed into the sea. I was swept off as he assisted my
inelegant departure with all sorts of undoing spells: that I bob for
six years, drift for seven summers, splash for eight, then spend six
years as a fir tree. The usual horrible shit. Revenge time.

For a few days I was out there in the bleak, I tell you. An eagle came, thank all available gods – a Lapland eagle, a magic eagle, not too big, not too small. It remembered I'd done it a favour – left a perch for it whilst felling for the Oslo district – and so carried me, gripping its wings, till it dropped me by the deep sea.

I was a mess, an unrighteous mess. I mean, let me tell you. You have nothing on this.

You are King of the Tatars in comparison.

My back had a hundred wind-lashes across the shoulders, one hundred wounds to my belly, chest and thighs; my hair a vast, erectile tangle of salt braid, my beard stiff with brine. I took a right kicking.

A maiden of the sun came walking in the dark woods, saw me, brought others. Louhi, great mistress of the North, told me to forge a new road, cut a new track, to speak out the grief, not let it languish mad in my chest.

Don't let grief languish mad in your chest. *Tell your people that.* If you tell them nothing else from your ceremony, tell them that.

Do that, a bride would arrive. Coin wouldn't cut it. Had to be a sophisticated, spiritual activity. Make something called a *sampa*, a magical object.

Well, I was old enough to know I couldn't do that, but I knew a man that could.

Ilmarinen the craftsman.

It takes some years to baldly state that reality. It was a thing few noticed, but you should.

It's as epic to name another man's gifts as it is to make the world.

We can't do everything. Icarus catches the scent of smoking feathers.

So here's your teaching moment:

Old men are lonesome and even when they may glimpse their long-lost love they likely lack the skill to keep her.

And with that he's gone. Cheery old sage. Fuck.

I know something was just delivered to me.

I know something about Joukahainen and I know something about Vainamoinen.

I am the young man of huff and puff and the old man embarrassing himself for love.

I am being digested by a swamp whilst walking through the consequences of my ancient spells. The 101 days are a hinge between youth and age.

Something is ending in me, something is being born.

Do I need wolf eyes as I grow older? Their accuracy of assessment. I think Georgia O'Keeffe had those eyes, Ronnie Drew from the Dubliners, Muddy Waters. No wool drawn over those steady lids.

I have made my creations – I have – have laboured at the forge, dug oceans, spat forth giddy strands of star and wonder, and sat impotent and ridiculed for my sheer lack of years. I have been eviscerated for occupying that most tiresome of shapes, that of a young man. Young men are rarely elegant wolves, more humping dogs.

As I leave I walk into a bank of clear, gold Wagnerian light.

Every time I'm in the wood it's as if the trees are in positions from a yoga class, very slowly changing their postures over many years. What they do contribute is their nut fall. They've gone nuts. As we all eventually go. Nuts everywhere. But the memo seems to be incremental not frantic. The trees appropriately frustrate human time signatures.

Talking of time signatures, that distant bloody woodyard's clangs and bangs sound like a slow-motion drum solo, or some wheezy backing from a lost Tom Waits song. Down there is some wizard steering his canoe of sound all the way back to Africa. What is the drummer calling? The secret drummer in all the mechanical whizz-bang? The machines in all their chomping are calling, calling, calling. Calling stories is like a calling of medicines, or familiars. I have a few:

Epic medicine.
Folk medicine.
Fairy medicine.
Even a little bit of
Legend medicine.

These have been very precarious to gather, and have poisoned me on more than one occasion. They won't get me well till they've seen me weakened.

It takes a while for a story to reveal its particular power, and as a storyteller you can never locate it on the page, only in the telling. There will be outward signals. You get sensitised to the outward signals. Wait till you see it writ large in front of you.

Some stories are smooth and self-sufficient, others needy, requiring endless rounds of reassuring; others built for the roar of the tavern, some little scrappy puffs of magic that don't stay for long and refuse to learn your name. Some stories you couldn't hang your coat on, others you could your soul. Stories to be lived by, stories as caution, stories as seance, stories as witchcraft, stories as mass-inflicted healing, stories as full-on gambling with the fates, stories as seizures of truth-telling, stories as hypnosis, stories to outrun history, others to confirm it.

Every time I drag myself to the forest this is what I'm calling forth, and also what I'm supplying.

I will be a year older tomorrow, and it's first frost today.

Our allotted years. Our black little sticks of time.

It's natural to devour the stuff, to tear at time, to sink our jaw into the ever-disappearing, ever-shrinking flank of time. Mystics say some of us don't want to be born at all, and hover for decades at the curly fringe between our mother's legs, staring sorrowfully out. Many of us only get born near the end of our lives.

Me, I wanted to get born.

Today the boiler in the cottage has neglected its perennial wheeze, and fallen into a sulky silence. I gather up armfuls of dry oak from the shed and sprint the twenty yards to the front door, the cats nonplussed under the lintel.

Now the woods again.

I am slipping under again out here. Into nothing or suchlike. First thought, best thought said Ginsberg. No trying. Don't try. In all this water I feel drier than ever, my mind getting progressively dried out.

Today these are the only kind of thoughts the wood is giving me:

When you walk on your hind legs you are a villager
When you walk on all four you are a forester
Life means shuffling between the two

Woeful a warrior as he scatters
Death-beads into a grave
Joyful a mother as she cleaves her plait
On the safe return of her son
He will not speak much
But she'll accept it
Just to have his shape by the fire
And I keep remembering

There is a golden owl hidden in the holly

Weeks have passed like this now. The weather is releasing a kind of death sentence on many living things. The great roughing of late autumn is here, the rousing, the creak, the crash. The river is some berserk cascade, great arcs of fish flipped up from the foam like wriggling silver wheels as they bang-boom their way to the ocean. There is no song stronger than the seasonal – NONE, it cannot be neutered or reasoned with, it is its own uncanny reason, the witchy canter into sleep and age. It's getting dark again.

king of the tatars

I have been struggling at night: sleep apnoea, acid reflux, nightmares.

It is old Vainamoinen climbing into my body.

He's been a constant since paying the price of entry with his mad story. As I struggle out into the dark for that second piss, he is pleased with his occupation of the property. It's fat old guy stuff.

But I'm leaning into it.

A few days ago I met a young rock musician, a lifetime younger than me. I deliberately dressed dull, made myself small, so I could locate more oldness in me. I called it in, the diminishment. I blandified myself. That's not how I see old age exactly, I just wanted to try taking up less room. It was a little terrible and made me quiet later. I stood naked in front of the mirror like a scald-crow bloated on battle-meat.

But all the lightning in all the forest is in me. I was told this *by* the forest.

That is an odd compliment I was given here in this chill, sodden lump of trees. This out-of-condition crazy man, wheezing and staring at the river smattering by, the waters caring not a jot for my conditional, half-vanquished heart.

I walk back to the cottage and old man Vainamoinen walks through my mind with me. Takes the lonely road with me, and whispers more private words to me in the black. I eat it like bread.

Ah.

And suddenly the key is in my door.

Vainamoinen is not banging about in my soul, he wants to enter my culture, my cottage, my people.
Oh story man, you can cross under the lintel.

Wildness has entered inside now.

When wildness has entered a cottage
The cattle of old sounds emit their warmth
There is woozy lowing, and milking,
And a sparrowhawk in the rafters

When wildness has entered a cottage
There are oysters in the pan,
Gillyflower wine
And French doors open to rain

When wildness has entered a cottage
Your hands have weight but
A reluctance to swing
And Limit is a goddess
You are grateful to lie with

With the old man in residence I have been sitting up at night to aid digestion. Thousand pillows. Well, we ask for a shape-change and there we have it. In the morning my neck is cricked and there is a kind of nausea when I twist my head. Dreams are perpetual and knackering; since the ceremony began, they simply never stop.

This sitting up is my uncomfortable tree that Ivan recommends.

And I remember having a blue elk shot from under me. I remember that it is a good and true thing to name someone who can perform a task that you cannot.

An assault from the outside world begins, just to make sure I realise I'm low under the bar of goodness.

Days drift by with jabby messages from disappointed people, any occasion when subterfuge has been detected or suspected or just plain made up, Christ I can't remember. I have bags under my bags under my tired and suspicious eyes. I must warn every single human being about my fundamental lack of availability, I must make a sign, like Coleridge's swinging albatross. I must create a deterrent to expectation. I'm sick of it.

I've been reading about Coleridge's bad teeth today, and how he would tear through a Dorset cornfield, massacring the stems in pursuit of a flighty little poem catching wing. Damn the torpedoes, in he goes, infuriating farmers. The job of poets. I'll hang his mashed-up teeth from the gate. That'll dampen ardour.

It is Halloween. That weird time is about to happen. I have made my daily crawl to the forest, scored another visit off my note on the fridge; the ritual has been observed. I have slathered the forest in the supplicatory oil of language, so the hinge between old and new year – the Celtic way – will not make much of a shriek as the door opens and the whole heathen horde flood out and into my garden.

I believe in Halloween. Just have a look round when you take your stroll out to the woodshed, or take a piss in the garden. Something is a-swirl, rampantly amok, cranked up.

All over England tonight hippies are scrawling notes and hurling them into fires with crimson string. Waggling their dreamcatchers about. One interpretive dance after another. No one can seem to pummel this doggerel out of us.

I can hear Vainamoinen shouting through the dark.
Then I realise it's me doing the shouting:

I'm an old man
Gonna get on blue elk
With my blue heart
And head to the North Farm
Find the woman of milk and light, cream and grace
I'm the young man fixing to thump
My black magic arrows in the old man's arse

It's important to betray the man who helped make the world

I am falling in the green horror of cold water

Mermaids and ghouls attach like barnacles
Taunted by my never-bride the fish girl
As a toddler binds me with his ranting spell

Good god. It's hard to hold the cottage together with all this going on.

clack clack clack

A little peace please. Gentle hands undo the rope from the gallows. Walk amongst charred tipi poles and scoop up the children. Let the fawn find her mother under dark oaks. The bell from a far-distant village is clear tonight.

I am saturated with this Ouija rain and Ted Hughes is fishing, always fishing by the dark river.

—Contact, boy! CONTACT!

Holy October weather, please protect all that is small, and good, and trying to grow.

I give thanks for my years, and more so for my beloveds.

Lorca is smoking on the porch, linen suit, peering hopefully into Devon rain.

Lorca you handsome goblin, don't get mud on your espadrilles.

The spirits will come to you, don't sweat it. You are spooky enough for them to hit you up.

clack clack clack

In the last minutes of the old year
I clap twenty times in the thick dark
From my perch
Many owls hoot back
Calling-song-to-calling-song

And for hours after I chew dirt-black air, my pagan meditation.
I burn letters and wealthy things just like the hippies do, that
crumble then spill out across the garden like tiny flaming teardrops.
It is dark, so purplish dark, and the vast interior in me has been
roused still further by looking in at my lit cottage windows, the
whiff of an oak-wood fire some distance, this charcoal night
smoking away around me. I've never seen a lit cottage at night
and not longed to be inside it, but to be outside is grand also.
And tonight, on the first night of the year, I am again watching
myself at my table.

And I watch the inside from the outside, sickly at the treeline,
weakened and neck still nauseous-tight I watch. I am in touch with
Grendel. My hand reaches for the door and the singing, then slinks
back into the holy dank. I will sleep in a cave.

This ceremony is making me be in all sorts of places at the same
time. I'm disintegrating.

It is a day later now and Jesus-in-the-manger-with-all-the-animals
did a storm come. In my dream I was somewhere out at sea and
then I woke in this kind of time and everything was flung open:
open windows, open doors and an oak coming down on the car.
Bang down it came. Thor thump. In comes the gateway to winter,
and is there not a naturalness to some frail old tree coming down? I
manage to get the car started and pull it in snug to the cottage then
drag heavy shards of soaking tree back into the long grass.

And old Vainamoinen made it through the night. Even in the rain
I see him processing to his wedding. At this point I have absolutely
no idea who he's marrying, but he seems thrilled.

I think he's leaving me now. He had some kind of point to make,
something to address, and now he's off for what is rightfully his.
Magnificent.

Some see him on a stallion of black, others a raven of power, a mighty griffin, but he is, in fact, riding a wolf. He is distinct as chokecherry amongst elms: six golden orioles sing on his shaft-bow, six blue cuckoos announce him. He has made it through the night. So many times he hasn't.

I am standing in bare feet and covered in mulch and oak leaves with car keys in my hand. I've stopped waking up where I went to sleep. He and his people, two hundred strong, are processing like a tapestry through the rain and the forest. To the wedding. He walks with a tall bear forged in the womb of the sun.

I watch them for a long time. I can't hear the woodyard anymore.

And it goes on, the walking in and out of the woods. I could have just gobbled some psychoactive plant, but I can't trust a ceremony without a great swathe of grinding boredom in it. That showing-up-ness. I can't just ride disorientation and thrill.

It continues to be cold and nutty, nights just mad crammed with dreaming.

I told you some friendships were going up in smoke, I know I did. Almost from the moment I started the ceremony. Kidneys are pricked thick with porcupine quills.

Doing this thing is like Ivan tugging on the Firebird's cage, it tugs on hundreds of invisible threads in my wider, more visible life. Everything's on high alert without quite knowing why.

The wood has strayed me today. Got me lost. Suddenly I find a new track, not my usual through the thorns' boogie. I've been muttering for a new track, even without knowing.

Yet again I feel sickly and I see the forest in a strange way – the sodden lime-and-orange leafing, the sluiced ground, the brewer's droop of the bracken. Again, I see in a strayed way. I see as if something much older than me is seeing everything, but through my eyes. I am weakened and drop my stick.

Have I walked this land before? Before I was myself currently? Do I discreetly appear, every six hundred years or so? An old one that sees everything through my latest, temporary eyes.

I spend more time stacking wet wood in a dry shed after the heinous weather and wait by the fire, just watching it get dark. I feel open to attack. The hay's unbound and the storm's coming.

So there will be a little magic: a herb heated to full crackle on a pan, a blowing of smoke, a name mentioned. A warding-off. I am vulnerable, I know this, but I will be wicked terrible to anyone who comes to take advantage of the fact. You will rue the fucking day.

Cold has bottomed the whole conversation out, Fenris cold, there is a blue god of water and freeze, snake-charming its way across the west country of England.

And god of mercy, the dreaming.

This night-time pummelling. I know the texture of such eruptions from shorter – much shorter – vigils in the wilderness. But this is relentless. I don't know what to do with this. I don't think there *is* anything to do with most of it. I just waddle in and out of the forest, frequently fall into this odd blankness and then writhe through the night. It's the kind of dreaming you experience when there's not much air in the room and the radiators are on. Breathless and hallucinatory. Feverish. It swallows all my imagination for the next day, as I doze at my desk or propped up on wet roots.

That's interesting. It imagines me, rather than me imagining it. I can't. I'm too knackered. It's put my own thinking into deep freeze.

Goodbye dear autumn, winter comes gliding.

It's important to get out the gates for a while, every few days. Away from the wood and cottage. And after the geriatric-in-residence that is Vainamoinen, I've been looking for the company of the older. By and large people don't seem so old, not anymore.

Seventy seems grand, not old, not really. No one is sucking sweets under a blanket by the fire. The old I meet are not thinking they are at the end of their lives; they are still vital. But is to be dying to mean not being vital? I have to check that habitual thinking. I am presuming this vigour is a good thing. I find myself cheered by it. But what happens when it is the end of their lives, how do they click into that particular gear? I've seen more morbidity in a twenty-year-old goth. These elders, they tell me to live as if I expect to be three hundred.

Some of these old folks walk me to the beach, to a brown pebbled beach, where a snarl-up underfoot has you wheezing and a-totter before you even make the sea line. I gaze out for a little minute looking for those fiery ships but something else happens. There's a lone trumpet. The consequence of such ships. I look and there's more old folks assembled. Memorial Sunday, and they stand up in their dozens, maybe a hundred.

And almost immediately I am weeping, such is the effectiveness of the ritual. The earned sorrow of it. No talking circle or curated catharsis could do this. It doesn't matter what you think of war, or armies, or soldiers, this is grief sifting through families and through memory.

I loiter from the freezing winds in a promenade shelter and practise being old. As I watch the waves I think of my constant companion Dylan Thomas. We are swimming out, me and him, fat as piglets on the grayling waters, laughing boys in the swirl. I can see the White

Lion Hotel on the shore and gesture we should go scoff black beer and whisky. And then I am back in myself in the promenade shelter, watching a smoke of crows on the hotel's roof. I must drink as much of this sea weather as I can before the forest takes me back again. Glug glug glug.

Later I make my way into the woods, and there's a big mist coming down from Buckland Ridge, Alaskan-looking mist if you know what I mean. Great flank of austere grey, like a stairway down the oaks.

The woods have told me they want me dry for a while, no drink, but I can at least slip some of this glorious watery air into me. Water makes all the delicious smells of the forest unfurl themselves. More glug for the slug.

I am wearing a dead man's coat today, a glorious knee-length jacket of Donegal tweed, flecks of burgundy and teal, right-hand pocket lining disintegrated. It's always the pockets, isn't it? Forty quid but absolutely worth it. That mist, that steel grey mist opens its mouth and talks to me. I stop absolutely still and listen.

This is what the mist says:

—You should know that Inuit children do not come from a woman's belly. They have to be dug out of the earth. You can find girl babies fairly near the surface, but boy babies are trickier, further down. You need to dig.

Your kids come from the earth. From out of the earth. And you frack.

Fish are actually flakes of wood created by an old man whittling by a river. Every flake of wood from his knife falls into the water and becomes char, lumpsucker, halibut, salmon.

The first woman was one woman – Putu. Not Eve. So many men wanted her that they all pulled at her in different directions and she

[131]

came apart. The men would scamper off with their body parts and carve the missing limbs from walrus ivory and the thigh bones of a boy. She would reanimate and become another, then another, then another.

Putu means hole.

All stillborn children are the Northern Lights, that's what you see up there. That wonder is all the stillborn babies dancing with their afterbirths. These never-children, forever dancing.

A little story.

One baby is one baby too much for a mother and she leaves it in the snow. Fuck that, baby says. It travels around in the skull of a dog as a kayak, uses an old man's thigh bone as a paddle. He tips over his brothers' kayaks and they all drown. When she awakes, the mother finds the abandoned baby sucking on her tit in the dark looking up at her.

The mouth of the mist closes and I keep walking on through the rain.

i see now i see

And in these pages where I rant about dream, a Big One came. The gears finally shifted.

With Vainamoinen gone, there was even more space in me for a dream. To soak me in the thing. A dream to get through the pores of my skin, to rattle the wolf awake a little. X-ray me now, and it may not be a human skeleton you see wandering round.

And this dream, this big dream, this great, lumbering fuck of a dream was going to take all purchase in my wider reality.

And I dreamt, oh forest, oh listener, I dreamt. The ceremony dreamt me.

I finally saw the wolf.

Out at sea I saw it. A sea wolf.

It was like a drawing from the front of a children's book, one of those hand-drawn maps that gets you all giddy about the journey you and the author are about to take.

It looked like Britain, Ireland, mainland Europe, but where there was usually the waters of the North Sea there was a vast wolf, absolutely massive. Big enough for a culture to walk across.

Its paws clipped sharp the Norfolk coast, the enormous bone and fur of its massive head an island, then the long swing of its body a trackway people walked, and slept and made camp on, back and forth, till its hind legs gripped the bank of Holland. Out there is wolf. There are ridges of little black hills, forests, caves in its shape. It is a fertile place, the flank of the wolf.

Some people would call this Doggerland, but that is its day shape.

At night its shape is Wolferland.

Wolferland is its dreaming shape.

The thing that keeps Wolferland going is the stories that people tell as they walk the wolf.

Stories – folktales, mythologies, little gossipy tidbits – are passing from the island of Britain back to the mainland, and these stories seem the miracle, the dark equilibrium, that keeps this animal hump, this flesh bridge, compact between these hunks of land. And not separate from them, really, but fused.

Many times I tell a story I am walking in Wolferland. I am bartering with the far-off lands: India, Persia, Lapland, the Caucasus. I am muttering into the night across the slow-breathing body of the beast.

Some may wish England to just float off from Europe as Elgar plays, but Wolferland is a way it can't.

We, in our thousands, need to camp out in Wolferland. Make a covenant with it, draw our dreams into it, let our hawk-selves circle it, our salmon-selves swim it.

Trade stories, sing songs, massage its bones, walk the secret miles of this archaic passageway.

I am energised but confused by the dream. My head is fuzzy.

Doggerland I know scraps about. I knew nothing about its night twin.

Dogwood made a decent Mesolithic fish trap, the bendy stem at least. You could make a dagger or spear from its heart-wood.

Dogger, like the Danish, *Dag*, dagger.

A land bridge, plenty of birch, hazel, later pine, hordes of wild horses, bison, grazing aurochs. A precarious but also abundant existence.

Oh of course. *Of course.* This is why this is happening. Got it.
I start a ceremony to make contact with something more than my own hairless intelligence, prompted by a churning world. And where does the dreaming take me – it takes me to a time of rising tides. Where everything you loved disappeared.

Doggerland went down.

Your offerings didn't work, your sympathetic magics, your fith-fath, your fucking nothing. Shamans gabbled and shook, swine were slaughtered and tied upside down to pines and fuck all helped, waters rose and Big Mama Earth, lovely old Gaia, took everything you ever loved away and buried it under the waters. Sometimes in minutes.

'Fuck you, British motherfuckers,' smiled cosy, vegan Mother Earth as she watched kindly over all of us. 'Namaste, you ignorant, pebble-worshipping pig shits. Drown.'

part three

wolferland

things to know

One. **Wolf gives Swiftness**

The wolf lives in rye. They know this all over old Europe. Children would be warned of the wolf in the rye, no ordinary wolf. When wind passes through the field, the old woman says that the rye wolf is running. The rye wolf hides in the last bale to be cut, then leaps into the loaves itself. Like a communion. You are taking of the wolf when you eat rye bread. A child with swiftness has the rye wolf in her.

Two. **Wolf gives Direction**

The Wulvers of the Shetlands are something that stands behind humans and wolves. There is a shy goodness to them. Covered in brown hair with a wolf's face, they are known to fish and leave the bounty at the houses of poor families. They keep vigil by the window when a spirit prepares to leave a body. If you were lost on a lonely track a Wulver wouldn't take advantage, but show you the way to the lights and warmth of your home.

Three. **Wolf gives Culture**

They said about the Irish that every few hundred years all the people, en masse, would become a pack of wolves. And it was poetry that they would bring back in the fangs. Nutritional, wayward, proper poetry. Did you check Kavanagh's fangs? Did you have a good grope with Yeats's molars, or did he have too much of the slathered Fenris about him? It must invigorate a culture to take the shape of a wolf once in a while. A whole people take the wolf-shape. An island. A Wolferland.

the track out of town

And on the 23rd of November a ghost came to me.

He seems slender, and his clothes are from a hundred years ago. But even from a distance I can see who it is. I can see who this man is.

This is Hamer Broadbent.

This is my great-great uncle.

In all my feeble bleating, I have called him.

In all this calling, I have called an ancestor.

In this wolf-womb a ghost has woken up.

You should know I never expected this, never hung this encounter as the skeleton of this ceremony, nothing. I don't know what is going to happen now. There has been no literary plan to this. To do that would cheat me more than it would you.

There's a banal level of commitment required to all this. It doesn't feel creative or whimsical. You just have to keep staggering up.

Hamer was born in Manchester, 15th June 1861. He died 28th June 1945, age eighty-four. He loved his sleep, Hamer. Could crash anywhere. Nothing fazed him – no bench too hard. He told his friends that the key was to relax every contour of the body, then rest was inevitable. One clenched toe and the deal was off. The little Christian yogi was into stress relief. Ahead of his time.

Hamer came from a group of Christians that were done with artifice, pomp, any form of smoke and mirrors. They wanted to get warm by the words of Jesus and that was all the sustenance they needed, thank you very much. As everyone knew, you couldn't buy

Hamer. Loved Turkish coffee and wore a Panama hat, but that was as far as the affectation went.

Hamer had a heavy but divine yoke on his shoulders. He had to tell people about his faith. He had one of those travelling ministries. He left his Suffolk farm and took himself through Turkestan, the Caucasus, Armenia, Poland, Russia, Finland, the Arctic Circle. And when that wasn't nearly enough, Hamer Broadbent, my great-great uncle, took himself into the deep wilds of Siberia. He slept by campfires, travelled on the backs of wagons down endless, rutted tracks, suffered and was raised up by his God.

So, as we can surmise, a capacity for easy sleep was essential.

With just a little black bread in his belly for nourishment, Hamer would find himself preaching in overpacked rooms – sometimes a hundred in a garret made for twenty, with not the merest crack of window, due to the terrifying cold of a Transylvanian winter, the heady reek of an oil lamp pleading for oxygen.

At one meeting, a man more bear than human confessed to the joyful slaughter of more than two hundred, just for the sheer exhilaration of taking life. And over time he bent his head for forgiveness. Even the dreaded Cossacks sometimes attended the gatherings, with hair-curling stories of rape and terror-bringing.

And this mild, gently humorous man stood in the blood-soaked slipstream of confession and held his nerve.

They say wherever he passed, people sweetened their own manners afterwards. And that wherever he lay his head, he became native. He slept when they slept, rose when they rose, got involved with ways of farming, herded cattle, would play with the kids. And then, at night, would talk scripture at the kitchen table. In simple, spacious, invitational language. Nothing like some village priests who often liked to make things obscure and difficult for the villagers. In fact, a fair amount of Hamer's time was spent defending people – often Jews – against Church corruption. A great enemy was what he called 'priestcraft' – when a priest or church interposed themselves between the worshipper and the divine. And this enemy he encountered many times over.

At this moment Hamer arrives, and for the first time I see his face. The easy grin, the blue eyes, the neatly trimmed beard. He speaks:

—And here's what you didn't know.

I got the bite. I got the loup-garou.

One day in deep winter I was walking the long road out of town. Far from anywhere. It was snowing and properly, deadly cold. I was trudging along, no escort, when two huge wolf-dogs set upon me, set upon my right leg. When they'd made a deep incision, they immediately turned and loped into the white. Like they were never there, but for the blood on snow and the terrible bite.

Three hours' bloodied stagger to the nearest cottage ensued. I dressed the wound myself, with an Indian balm I always carried – Christian yogi, remember – and within weeks the wound healed without any trace.

I have my fur on the inside now.

And my blood is in your blood. Think about that.

I am a man of the bite.

If your calling songs hadn't been strong enough, I would have had nothing to walk upon. Your songs are making this wolf.

As a man of the bite I will walk across Wolferland, through the reeds and swamp, over rump of hill and by salty reek of ocean. In my peregrinations I will bring stories to be told, stories given by the people of the lands I travel, in exchange for the news that I bring.

I mean, where does it stipulate that a missionary has to be living to do their work? My bite is my passport.

(Wow, that's the spirit, Hamer, the *ghost* missionary.)

Anything other than God that brings division amongst people, I oppose. So in this time of separation and mistrust, I will help you with your weave of stories between England and the mainland. I will not traffic in anything I regard as corrupted or especially profane. But I think I understand the exercise, and I will help for a little while.

And you, my great-great nephew. You will chew on a Bible every now and then, turn those fiery words around in your heart. That's the deal. Forget about church, forget about priests, absorb just the stories and the teaching.

I will agree to this. If a Christian ancestor bitten by wolf-dogs in the middle of a 101-day ceremony has arrived, then I will take this as the next step in the ceremony. I think the ante has just been upped.

The very next day he is out of a dream and in the forest. It is a Sunday, with another heavy mist, and my uncle's here. Silver beard and handlebar moustache, neat three-piece. Amiable, not bothered by the fog. Well, he's dead, I suppose.

—I walked back across Wolferland for you, and into the mainland. Y'know how they found the land under the North Sea? Doggerland?

I shake my head.

—A fisherman found a harpoon shaped from deer antler. Down there in the depths, came up in a trawling net. Even before that they'd been bringing up mammoth bones, and any number of more recent animal remains. Something was down there.

It came out from under the last Ice Age, gradually assembled its curvature and took on a fair number of human settlers. There would have been laughter, and babies born, and sulks and forgiveness out there under the black wave. Land. It was the waters that took it soon enough. Climate change, you see, hardly new. Study of it through time they call

PAST DISASTER SCIENCE.

But what you asked me to walk is not quite that either. It's substantial, equally hidden, but different.

Wolferland is distended imagination, not a place you can jab at on a map. It's made up of every roused thread of magic-thought that's ever roved between England and the big lands beyond. It's as much a binding agent as Doggerland.

Wolferland is the dream twin of Doggerland.

It's older than any temporary upswing of tide.

Wolferland is a bone bridge of timelessness and time bound, and identifiable in almost all British folktales and mythologies worth their salt. Coleridge crossed it, Blake, Shakespeare practically had a bus pass so frequent his trips. It is a footbridge for the roaming soul, robust enough to walk on. Merlin knew it, Taliesin too. That bridge built the Arthurian romances, brought us chivalry, all sorts of hidden secrets returning from the Crusades. They still glitter in the branches of the trees out there, those secrets. They brighten up the bushes like candles of flame.

And walk it I did, and asked around. Talked to the great-grandkids of those I knew back then. Prodded them as they slept. Turns out many I prayed with ended up in the Gulag or concentration camps. Some of them think I should have stayed nice and cosy in Suffolk. But tell me this: where else was I meant to take my faith? Any other response but my endless walking would have been dereliction of duty. Some words are so disturbing and so true, all you can do is walk with them.

But the people talked, they did, as I stretched myself into twenty places at once. And I have these stories here, this high currency, to make stronger this Wolferland you have fallen into.

I walked through clouds of greylag geese and flanks of vast horned aurochs to get you these. I saw some ancient-looking man on a blue elk zipping back and forth.

I, your wolf-bitten uncle Hamer, bring these back to you. From Siberia.

song four

clack clack clack

This happened back a ways. I was hunting, autumn, first snows. Out on the taiga me and my companion go, to feed the Ket people. Our people.

We hunted small things at first – took down squirrel, padded after sable, laid entrapments for ermine. Nothing to boast about.

But night caught us. Suddenly we could taste life ending in the back of our mouths. Quick as that.

We gathered wood for a night out, but then we found an empty bear den. Much better.

We made a little fire by the entrance, brewed up a kettle of tea, and looked up at the yellow moon:

Moon of the Old Buck
Cold Udder Moon
Genuine Udder Moon
Moon of the Waters
Making Leaves Moon
Moon of Warmth
Velvet Antlers Moon
Moon of Love Among the Wild Deer
Moon of the First Winter
Muscles of the Back Moon
Shrinking Days Moon

Then clouds came and blizzard hit us. The cave had grasses inside, and we filled up the entrance by bundling my big fur coat, and slept under my brother's. It was very dark, warm, and soon we were asleep.

Suddenly we were awake. The howl of the snow-wolf had stopped, and we could see light round the lump of furs blocking the entrance. We crawled out. We didn't understand – the world was working backwards.

The snow had melted and the sun was high and happy in the sky. This bent our heads. We couldn't follow it. We shuffled off back to our home.

Our children stopped still and stared when they saw us. And they didn't look right either. They were stretched. Bigger. They ran away. But our wives laughed and cried and tugged at us.

We had not been away for one night.
We had been away all winter long.
When you sleep in a bear's place, you do what bears do.

And from then on, whatever the predicament, Ket never spent the night in a bear's den.

Hamer lets out a long breath.

—And that's what I did. Me, Hamer. Everywhere I travelled in my life, I did like the locals did. Ate what they ate, slept when they slept, fell in with their breathing. And I tell you, if I had ended up in a bear's den, I may have hibernated too.

Is this what you are trying? Are you claiming modern life requires a kind of enforced hibernation? To lie with your flank against a big brown god? Have you lain back in the wolf fur to be as they are? Some will want to kill you too if you do that.

These Ket became what the Japanese call *Yamabushi* – One Who Sleeps in the Mountain. Those Ket men slept in the den of their god, got rubbed and scented in the dream, got contorted and preserved in the storm, carried the infection of the animal powers back to their people. It may be that it scared them, but it never stopped them telling the story now, did it? Wouldn't you lose a few months to be connected to the Bear God?

Whole cultures should lie back in the fur of the bear, the fur of the wolf. It is only a wolf howl that can articulate the deprivation of our times, it was only a wolf howl that could articulate Gethsemane.

Under BRIGHT YELLOW MOON

Let us imbibe Bear's wintering fat
That would be a communion
Jesus would understand

I didn't quite expect this from uncle Hamer. He has the sacred wind in him.

—That is today's story for *your* hibernation, my young nephew.

And that is more than enough.

I go back to the cottage and he goes back to wherever on earth he is abiding.

absolutely skulled

Seeing a feeling through to the end of the sentence.

Sentence. A word in a dictionary, a stretch in prison. A judgement.

I feel just shattered, eight weeks into this. Heavy. I feel spoiled today, wretched, as if I have done something despicable but I can't quite remember what it was. I would assess that the sensation is awareness of personal sin. Of unripeness. It's not specific, but it falls like a cloak, and me exhausted underneath all of it.

I'm not sure I want to see the little saint again. That's what people called him, how they experienced him. A knyght is rarely a hero to his squire, but it appears Hamer pulled that off. That rarest of moves. A move that only occurs when you've got God blowing on your wingspan. The wolf man is a Christian. Christ as wolf. Wolves don't generally get an easy ride in the Bible, but St Francis was a fan.

But I trudge out to the forest anyway and wait for him. As I've wittered already, I am realising that so much of this experience is about fidelity, and so little about imagination. It's about turning up. Expectancy is a blight, but there it ticks ticks ticks. For something to happen. Well, today, just like the last dozen or so, everything seems just the bloody same. Why in the name of everything decent didn't I elect to do this in summer? I will keep saying this.

Forest is nuded now, flattened, big grey-gold sky. This place is now so little about language, so much about silence. My silence anyway. The river is still in full-boar-roar, and night falls in minutes. The moment it lands is an end to day-thinking and day-seeing. Witch twigs, night crow screech, creepy medieval shapes. I shuffle from foot to foot in my now customary semi-trance state. Head lolling.

Things come out at night, they just do. Not all unease is paranoia.

Seeing a feeling through to the end of the sentence.

Or a ceremony.

A hundred and one days is long enough to get properly lost. I'm lost now – labyrinth lost. Twisted ankle and out of signal on the moors lost. I'm never really out of this. The thing trudges back to the cottage with me. Everything is event.

When everything is event, you can build a universe of meaning. You just have to get good at maintaining edges, boundaries, ditches, moats filled with explosives. You have to delineate, absolutely, you have to, or you are scampering off to crazy town.

Be careful with your curation of significance, your buffalo hide scratched with your watering holes and sacred mountains. Know where your kingdom's walls are erected. I'm having to do something like that here, because I'm under such a flood of stimulus. But if you wave the billhook of discrimination too early then you hack at the world tree at its roots. Best let it have its way for now.

I'm scowling at a freezing December treeline. I keep my gaze brisk for the gentle stroll of Hamer, the crunch of Vainamoinen's sledge, a young witchy girl staring at me through a wall of thorns. I know when I walk back into that forcefield anything could happen, anything could reveal its hand. And, as I am experiencing, whatever does pulls on some copper wire to a part of my life out in the wider frame. Has an effect in some other area. This odd lumbering back and forth. What on earth did I expect, no bleed?

Oh shit. I can see him. I can see Hamer. He's patiently waiting by the hazel bush, hand lightly tracing the bark. He'll have a story. Why in the name of god did I begin this in autumn? I could have picnicked my way from one end to the other, rather than this protracted hallucinatory march through drizzle and blight. I have literally just said this I know but I'm knackered I'm repeating it. It's a BIG thought.

No small talk today. Hamer stands and begins, in a voice that is not his own.

song five

clack clack clack

How did I become a Singing Man? I will tell you.

It was a cramped cabin: me, mother and my two brothers. Smoky, dark. A bash of logs, squeezed up against endless tundra. My brothers were big and lively, always hunting, but I was a feeble thing. I'd curl round the stove whilst they brought home meat.

My name is Kunachi. Mother was my companion, leaving me to drag myself around in the snow collecting firewood. I think she loved me especially.

One day at dawn I heard my brothers shuffle and spit, and go off to hunt. I slept on, but a storm, a crazy storm, picked up and roused me. I saw the door was flapping open, and all the heat drained out of the hut. I called for mother but for the first time she wasn't there. I'd been sleeping on the stove, and fell off in my panic, injuring myself. Bruised my side, my hand. I crawled to the door. My legs didn't work.

They'd never worked.

It was a carnage outside. The winds had given a beating to the forest: trees were down or even ripped from their roots, the air swirled and gnashed with timber. To my left I saw mother, gripping deadly tight to the cabin. I thought I heard her call:

'Come to me my boy!'

But it could have been the storm, mocking me.

After that she was gone.

I fell into a weepy fever, and my brothers came back to an iron-froze cabin, a missing mother and sickly brother. We set out to look for her the next day. I was in a kind of papoose. We travelled a way.

It was a thrill to see the world. Mountains caught in sun-glow like bright humps of blood, a dazzle of flowers for miles in each direction, in the far north the blue-white sheen of snow.

What happens next, you may not believe. I can't tell you exactly that I knew I had these powers, but I can't tell you exactly that I didn't.

We camped by the ruin of a lake, now overrun with grasses. All this light came into my mind. I knew things. There was a sparrowhawk tearing up my blood. I told my brothers to pull up the grass. All of it. They were surprised by me finally having an opinion about anything at all, and such an odd request, but they did so. Hours passed and most of the grasses stayed high and impertinent. When my brothers rested, a mad strength came down upon me and I crafted a great snake of rope, three times wrapped around the dry lake bed.

This gave me a little leverage with the boys.

After they vainly attempted to dig up a tree I had requested, I pulled the thing straight out of the ground by the lower branches and chucked it into the sky.

The snaky rope was attached to the top of the tree, and the tree managed to root itself in the very air, an impossible thing. It braided itself to the invisible and I was agog.

I spoke:

'Our mother is not on this earth, she must be up there. She must be in the sky. Let's climb up the rope.'

There are lots of little surprises up there.

In the sky there are many silver roads that shoot off in many directions.

And me, the cripple, did I tell you I was a cripple? I think I told you. Found I could walk up there. Finally I could walk.

My brothers were impressed, but also terrified. The world was fast changing in their minds. There was no light in their minds, I could see that now. They elected to make a fire for three years by the rope whilst I wandered, looking for mother. Two stay, one leaves. Often the way.

Silver road I take
Strength to my legs it gives
Silver road I take
Strength to my legs it gives

So much horror, so much joy in me all at the same time.

On my silver road I walked, twice coming to a silver hut that would spin, flashing with light as it did so. So similar were the huts, I'd swear I'd ranged in a circle. But the maidens that lived in them were different.

The first had skin as white as a range of summer cloud, cheek shy and pink like the dawn. She invited me to stay with her. I ate a little. But wouldn't stay. I call her Dawn Cheek.

'Maybe your mother's up here, maybe not. Long road behind you, longer road ahead. Stay with me.'

I wouldn't settle so easy, so she sent me to visit her older sister. I had to take the road to the right for that.

A different kind of woman, the same kind of woman. It's hard to explain. She had cheeks darkening red like dusk not dawn, and eyes that glittered like stars. I call her Dusk Cheek.

She fed me and told me I was right to search. To not languish by the rope like my brothers. That my mother was carried off by Thunder itself, a spirit, who had her trapped. She gave me a sword, from her own wall, to kill him with. She told me to be a man who walked straight, to not deviate, not get turned around, to not stop even if it seemed I was walking into the Northern Lights.

She told me that a rider on a white horse would come. A snow horse, ivory horse, glowing horse. And that he would jump off and approach me, and that was the moment I could have at him with the blade.

So I left, and I tell you, I did almost walk into the Northern Lights. Wanted to. They almost came into me, tugged at my frame, to fringe me with blue to yellow to red to green. To contort, expand and shrink like them. In the shape of the lights I could make out mountains, pale larches, grey lakes, meadows gorged with flowers. They were the deepest enchantment.

I heard once of women in the south, women with the heads of ancient birds that sing songs that make sailors go mad, pine to death for the sound. The lights do something like that. I thought it was a heaven.

[153]

Suddenly the horse was there; the milky, snorting horse. The rider got off the beast, walked towards me and I struck him. Just as the maiden told me to do.

Everything erupted, lightning flash, thunder. I dropped the sword. I dropped all intention of harm and was a piss-wet boy crouched on the stove again. Crouched over an ember as the world raged around me, whirling and crackling.

I was on a snow-ridged plain, no elegant silver road, no working legs, just flailing about on the jagged ice coat that lipped the flakes. My hands were raw and salmon pink. A voice spoke:

'You made this for yourself. You did this. Strutting up with your sword, not telling me what you wanted. Those maidens had you for a fool. They lied to you. Let's see how much resolve you really have to find your mother.'

So a crawling wretch I was. Gradually the crawl became a limp and I could hobble. Not the stride of the silver road, but not the agony of the ice-crawl.

I remember crossing a lake, ready to drown if I must, but the water froze under my feet and then I saw that dream-rope of the heavens again, the Northern Lights. They would swell up before me like the tips of an immense forest, then sink back down into the driving current of a wide and lively river. Blues, greens, reds, so staggering, so humbling.

At the very edge of the Northern Lights I came to a huge house, a house of eight windows. A threshold constructed of ten elegant gold beams. I'd never seen wealth like this, I'm not sure anyone has: a gold-tiled floor, a bench that sang songs, a stove that told stories. I know how this sounds, I know. Crazy.

And then there was my mother.

'My boy! My boy has walked to me, on his own feet he has walked!'

Mother was as lithe and as radiant as a young larch, her voice like songbirds in its branches.

We sat on the singing bench, I told her things she did not know. Everything that had happened.

Then she told me things that I did not know.

'A long time ago I was wandering with my man and my two kids. Your brothers.

A bear came for us, killed my man and leapt for me. Thunder came, from out of nowhere, Thunder came. Lightning killed the bear and a rider on a white horse appeared. Thunder had saved us.

I lived with the rider, with your brothers, for one year. I got pregnant with you, Kunachi. My little magic baby.

Thunder is your father.

Three times he visited as you grew, and the third time I went with him.

It was the only way to make you walk like Thunder, Kunachi. To come find me.

That was me calling you that day, not the storm. And you came.'

So I came to know my father at last. He was often busy, distributing water, but I know what it is to have a father's affirming gaze on you now. I know that feeling and have brought it deep into myself.

He asked me if I wanted to stay, and I said no. To gift me he walked me to the three barns he had in his yard.

FIRST BARN: at first I thought it was filled with moonlight, such was the gleam, such was the brightness. It was silver and gold.

He offered me my fill, and I refused.

'Ah, you don't care to be rich.'

SECOND BARN: lightning streaked across the barn, mad-a-hum, winds wiggled bound up tight in leather sacks, rainbows stacked high and jubilant in one corner.

I refused. These were his work things. He'd need them.

'Ah, you don't care for power.

Then I will choose the gift. The gift is in the third barn.'

THIRD BARN: just a tiny little stick. A stick with three knots in it.

My father picked it up and gave it to me, saying:

'When grief stalks you, hollow out the knots and look into the hole.'

My mother and father were at peace, and so I hurried to my brothers.

As I ran – and run I could now on that good, straight silver road – I passed by the huts of Dusk Cheek and Dawn Cheek. Dusk Cheek made excuses about the sword – saying it was a bad wedding which is why she'd counselled death – but now wanted to travel back down to earth with me. Dawn Cheek wanted the same.

Imagine my brothers' flushed joy when the maidens appeared with me. With the three years almost at an end they were about to extinguish the fire. They didn't ask much, just stared at the maidens. One by one my brothers and the maidens slinked down the grass rope.

You know what happens, don't you. You can feel it, can't you?

When they got to the ground, my brothers my brothers my steadfast brothers set light to the rope.

The grasses, so dried these last three years, were a flume of spark, a sharp splutter of fire.

When the rope broke, I waved my father's stick and it stretched to the ground, like a totem, and I descended.

My brothers and the maidens were long gone. It didn't make sense. These men were not wicked. They had fed me as a child, me and mother, and now they betrayed me. One glimpse of the maidens.

I am not sure I had ever really submitted to sorrow until that moment. No sense, it made no sense.

As I wept, my father's stick started to twist and turn in my hand, as if to get my attention. It was like it was alive. I remembered what he said, so hollowed out the knots and peered through.

First of all I saw tundra.

Then I saw Nenet people, the ornate embroidery of their clothes, the cheery and plentiful display of their tents, their elaborate sleighs. I could hear singing, I could smell meat, the beating pattern of their tambourines.

I've seen a lot. I've seen houses with gold beams and maidens of dawn and dusk, but I was held fast and weeping by the sight of those people and their happiness.

Secondly I saw taiga.

Through the knot I saw blood-sun mountain peaks and the fur of trees. I saw the Khant and the Tungus, driving their deer across bright little streams and up steep valleys, singing and laughing as they worked, singing and laughing as they played. This was a heaven too.

Thirdly I saw Yenisey.

I saw the Yenisey River, the deep and ancient beast, merrily filled with rowboats and bigger ships. I saw the Russians coming: I saw sacks of exquisite cloth, high-quality flour, vats of wine come onto the bank. I saw deer, ermine and fox skin be loaded up, great mammoth tusks that took three men to carry. I saw little fires on the bank and the Russians making toasts, sharing wine with others, and dancing round the flames, as much bears as men.

And I saw some of these things before they had happened. Gazing through the knots on my father Thunder's stick I saw in a prophetic way.

And as I saw, I sang.

I sang of everything I had lived through, and everything to come.

I sang of my brothers, who were quickly abandoned by the maidens and now run around the tundra eternally; skeleton men, trying to get the maidens' attention up in the clouds. I followed them with my eyes, but there was nothing I could do.

I have sung for a hundred years now, moving like a nomad wind from place to place. I am still little cripple Kunachi, gathered around the heat of my songs.

As I see, I sing.

And I sing you this story.

This is how I became a Singing Man.

cranes at dusk

And the next day our man Hamer was there. Steady Eddy. Again
no facile civility, no gossip on the weather. Just him, erect as totem,
robust within his slim frame, speaking old-time words.

song six

clack clack clack

My sisters and I had watched the men for some time. Seen how they
cut and quartered their days. We watched them from a distance.

Yudjian was a hunter, the oldest. The younger, Hodjugur, he kept
a tight homestead. It was an effective arrangement. Yudjian gave
himself so totally to the hunt he was out before dawn, before our
Father the Sun even majestically peeked his head over the edge of
the hills. A little later we would watch Hodjugur apply himself to
organising the yard, milking the cows, feeding the horses. We all
cooed when Yudjian would give chase to an elk or wrestle down a
bear. He brought home many pelts. We notice things like that. But
me and my sisters, we liked the way Hodjugur went about things
too. We elected to visit him, when big brother was out there nosing
a wolf track.

We flew to him, we seven cranes flew to him.

We circled him – they say on the side of the sun our wings rustled
red and fiery, then passing through the shadows we became an
indigo blue. Around and around we circled, a kind of casting. And
we caught him in our net.

We came to rest. We gently let our white feathers fall to the ground and took our other shape as young maidens. If he was scared, soon he was happy, and if he was happy, soon he was ecstatic. We did affect his labours, I confess. He forgot the stove, the milking, the sweeping. It was a sweet time we had together, and too soon our Father the Sun grew weary and started to cast his net of shadows. We gathered our skins of white feathers and flew into the cold, dipping light.

It surprised Yudjian to come home to an unlit fire, testy horses and unmilked cows. He had to gather the wood himself, even collect the water. Hodjugur made some excuse about sleeping all day, and his brother took it in good grace. Not so the next time, and the time after that. We would come every day but swore young Hodjugur to silence about our visits.

But Yudjian, he was not stupid. Absolutely not stupid. He was scented with so many animal powers, so rubbed up against the forest his wolf nose knew magic was afoot. And he had a little of that himself. Learnt out on the ice floe under copper moon. He was a man of art and skill.

One day he squashed himself deep into himself and became a flea.

It takes a shaman to know a flea can be as useful as an eagle. He hid and patiently watched us for hours, saw his brother in the delirium-thick of us. He wasn't angry, more mesmerised, like a whole other dimension of possibility had arisen. Which of course it had. As dusk came and my sisters took off into the coming darkness, he grabbed my white feather skin, trapping me. I watched my sisters arc away from me. Streaks of snow in the dark.

Yudjian said this to me. The hunter said this to me:

'I have admired you this long day. I understand why the cows don't get milked, horses fed, fire stoked. They never could with one such as you. How could anyone concentrate?'

I replied, despite myself:

'Keep talking.'

'Now you look at me. Take me in as I've taken you in. If you don't want me, so be it. I will return your skin. But if you want me, stay here and make a life with me.'

No man has spoken to me like that. Nobody. His brother had never spluttered such a thing. Utterly clear. He shone when he said it. And I agreed. There and then in the dusk, just like that, I agreed. It felt ordained in some way, like there was a magical touch to it. I flattered myself it had taken lifetimes for us to meet, as lovers always do.

I did a thing you may find strange. I asked him to hide my white feather skin. To keep it out of sight. I didn't want it there to torment me, or risk anyone's grubby hands on it. He hid my skin in a heavy iron box with three locks, and hung the keys on a high peg.

I have to tell you it was happy times. It was. I'd be giddy to see him at the end of the day and he me. But it was not so sweet for Hodjugur, not at all. I suppose he remembered the days he had us all to himself. He slouched about, refused to help with the daily chores, lost all his charm. One day I caught him with my feather skin, holding it up to me with a stupid, teasing look on his face. I was weakened, and my voice was more like a crane call than a maiden's voice when I asked for it back.

I offered him my earrings and he refused. I offered him my belt inlaid with silver and he sneered. I offered him my knife, with intricate carved handle and inlaid sheath and his eyes bulged. That he wanted. I threw him the knife, he threw me my skin.

Oh my skin my skin my skin

Not under iron not under a man's dominion

Oh my skin my skin my skin

I wrapped it around my frame, still not quite intending to leave. I loved him madly, my husband. But as I stretched my arms, almost afraid to take wingspan, my sisters flew into the yard:

Six cranes circling in the dusk
No one can resist six cranes circling in the dusk
And I flew away; a heartbroken stroke I had, but away.

And I came home and my wife was gone.

My idiot brother was clutching one white crane feather. And for the first time I took my fists to him, my fury to him. I flogged the stupid little shit with a heavy, braided whip.

When he was pulped and quivering, I stopped and gently cradled the feather. I took my gaze from him and stepped out of our yard.

I rode a golden horse out into everything that was outside our settlement. I took all of life on. I would eat my way through tiger fur, crunch bison skull, swim a hundred miles under the ice, just to find her.

I rode for many days, till my head drooped in the saddle through lack of sleep. When occasionally I rested I pressed up against the flank of the animal for warmth and protection from the winds. I flashed through forest, meadow, swamp, till finally I was at the foot of a high mountain. Biggest I'd ever seen.

I left my horse grazing and I climbed the thing. Why I climbed I'm not sure. Took not hours but days. I was spent as I finally crawled to the top and beheld an ornate white yurt. Inside it huge skins flush with fur covered the walls, and there was a golden cradle in the centre, containing a baby. A bird, a Chichah bird, was rocking the child. It spoke to me:

'If you are Yudjian, if you are searching for your wife, you should walk over here and behold your son.'

The little one stretched his arms out to me as if he knew me, quite the cherub he was.

I changed myself into an ermine simply to entertain the lad, running around the cradle as he giggled, and hid when I suddenly heard a voice. It was my wife walking in. And my heart walked into the yurt too, it did. She was all my gladness. She slipped out of her crane skin to cuddle the boy.

Oh, terrible what happened next. What I did.

Something landed in me as I looked at her, suddenly returned like this. It was a madness that came over me. A clutching, terrible madness.

I grabbed her white feather skin and threw it onto the fire. I wanted her back forever, you see. An end to the flying life. You may not approve of what I did, but I think you may understand what I did. Mad that it was. I only thought it for a second.

'Why did you do that?'

She spoke those words and died in my arms.

Horror pushes you into new ways of being. I was doing these things before any shred of me knew what it was I was doing. I found myself outside the yurt and leaping onto a low cloud, a cloud that took me up and onto a great road of stars. Up there is another kind of world, Upper Earth.

It was not that different up there, there was enough for me to orientate.

I walked the starry road and came to a yurt. Inside was a woman, combing her red hair, hair four times the length of her body. It was spilling over the edges of the eight-legged copper dais she sat upon. She combed it with a comb of gold and carefully gathered up the hair around a silver staff.

I asked the Daughter of the Stars to be my wife and she agreed.

I requested she gather her dowry and I would meet her on the top of the mountain below. I continued along the great road of stars. I came to the yurt of the Master of the Moon. Inside was a woman with silver hair, hair six times the length of her body. Spilling over the edges of the eight-legged copper dais she sat upon, she combed her hair with a golden comb and gathered it around a silver staff.

I asked the Daughter of the Moon to be my wife and she agreed.

She wanted time to pack and I said I would meet her on the top of the mountain. I continued to walk, and I could hear this shaman of the moonlight happily calling her dowry of cattle.

I walked so far that I walked past the night. I walked into light.

I came to the yurt of the Master of the Sun and went inside.

Inside was a woman combing her golden hair with a golden comb, hair eight times as long as her body, wrapped around a silver staff. Oh such bright hair that poured over the edges of the eight-legged copper dais she sat upon.

I asked the Daughter of the Sun to be my wife and she agreed.

As she prepared I moved with the cloud and returned to the mountain with my child and wife. In the yurt the Chichah bird still rocked the baby, and my wife was still dead.

I dressed my dead wife in my own clothes, covered my hat over half her face and hid.

In time, and from three directions, from three roads of sky came the Daughter of the Stars, the Daughter of the Moon and the Daughter of the Sun.

They surrounded the body, assumed it was me. For beings like that, it was no great issue that they were marrying the same man. The issue was that I was dead.

The Star Daughter spoke:

'I can revive a dead man so he is only unconscious.'

The Moon Daughter spoke:

'I can revive a dead man so he is only in a deep sleep.'

The Sun Daughter spoke:

'I can revive a dead man so he comes back to life.'

Star Daughter leapt over the body and the breast shuddered, just
        a little.
Moon Daughter leapt over the body and a hint of rosiness returned
        to the cheek.
Sun Daughter leapt over the body and she came back into life.

With that resurrection my hat tumbled from her face and her hair cascaded down her back. The game was up.

At that very second my son cried in his cradle and my crane wife ran to him.

The three maidens looked at each other, and understood things very quickly, as they were prone to do.

Sun Daughter spoke again:

'There is a mortal wife and child here. This man is not for us, sisters. I leave my dowry with them.'

The Moon Daughter also left hers, and, face flushed and to avoid humiliation, the good and proud Daughter of the Stars left hers – though making it clear her father was not such a wealthy man.

❖

And so, I, White Crane Woman, was born again. I came back from deep spaciousness into this hectic world.

With my husband, child and great dowry we returned to the homestead. Swaying happily alongside us were three-times-ninety herds of cows.

When we saw Hodjugur running towards us he seemed different, older, broader, taller, more handsome. Certainly less of an idiot. It was good to see him. He would become a master of the herds.

So I am here, amongst you people of earth, with my skin of white crane feathers revived. There is no iron box, no keys, no foolishness.

When six cranes circle
In the dusk I fly

They sing my calling song
They sing my calling song
They sing my calling song

When six cranes circle
In the dusk I fly

❖

So few of us have the crane feather anymore, let alone a marriage to the sacred bird.

Iron-box thinking is what is killing us.

Burning the crane skin is what is killing us.

Our forgetting of heaven is what is killing us.

It is getting cold and dark for even a ghost now.

—Go inside and feed the cats. Listen to your records. No booze. Read the Bible. Cook a chicken, make a fuss of your kid. Love that kid, wrap her in as much affection and truth and beauty as you can, she's the best of you, and then some.

I've got one last story from the far-aways for you tomorrow. Then my part is over.

You have to keep heading to the Northern Lights, my lovely little cripple. Crawl on, nephew.

Oh this morning was beautiful, I have to tell you. Yes, the rain, the chill, but in tandem with this great burning swathe of orange through the mist. I think every leaf that is coming down has done so by now, the great and grand mulch swung low onto the sucking soil. The owls hooted and prowled till almost dawn and the heathen air swirled round my bedroom as I wrestled with cavernous and magical dilemmas. Soon it will be Christmas, just a week away. This, December 18th, and, I am presuming, my last day with Hamer. But I don't presume much anymore.

Even as I write these words it's clouded over, and the woodyard is rasping away in its Mount Doom kind of way. I am bringing whisky to replenish the woods, and maybe even Hamer will take a drop, you never know. The winds are up now, and there's that smell that could promise snow.

There he is. Always so light on his feet, so unruffled. Maybe a fox, or a tap dancer.

He smiles as I daub Talisker in the pits of tree roots and make prayers. It's a little early in the day for him to take tipple. He speaks:

—So this last story. I wanted to bring you tales from the furthest parts of my travels, from distant, majestic Siberia. This should release all sorts of questions into your bloodstream.

song seven

clack clack clack

It's something to look at your daughter and see a wild animal. But I think every mother has had the experience.

I am old Kytna.
From Kichiga.

One day my daughter Ralinavut went walking and did not return. We searched, we searched. She was full grown, not a kid, and we did not know what could have happened. Had she got lost, injured herself, frozen and been drifted over with snow?

These questions turned my guts to vinegar. I tortured myself for three years with the not-knowingness. My man too.

After three years I went to a shaman. He shook the world loose, gazed his blood-eye into the centre of his sorcery and returned with news.

'She is not bones under the snow. She is alive, you were right to come. She lives with a wolf pack, far up in the north. Place called Talkap.'

To hear those words, those strange words, after three years.

Alive.

Against my man's urgings, I packed for the north.

After one hundred steps I turned into a she-wolf. On step 101 I had not foot but paw, not hair but fur. I bounded now. I crunched and leapt now.

After moving a long distance I saw reindeer herders up ahead, so became an old woman again. They knew nothing of my daughter, though kindly offered me a reindeer to travel on. I refused and in the morning took my hundred steps and on 101 became wolf. Wolves are faster than reindeer.

And as I ran I saw a handsome he-wolf ahead. We played a little and I asked him if he knew of a pack in the far north. He bent into his memory and said he had seen such a group, and seen an unusual being amongst them, half-human half-wolf.

'That must be my girl Ralinavut.'

'It must be. Some magic between human and animal, stretched as tight as a drum.'

I stayed again with reindeer herders and set out early after tea and meat.

Oh, and I see my girl. I see her at last. Oh, my gods I see her. I am approaching.

As she-wolf I pace in a circle round the pack as they devour deer, and I begin my calling song:

clack clack clack

There is nothing on the snow but wolf
And with them is my Ralinavut

I tighten my circle as she looks round

These are serious wolves who never hesitate
And with them is my kid Ralinavut

My girl pads towards me

How could you find me, mother?
You should not have come, mother

I make my third circle

Your name is Ralinavut, a woman name
Your name is Ralinavut, not a wolf name

I am old Kytna
My daughter is Ralinavut
Sometimes we are woman
Sometimes we are wolf

That breaks her heart in a wonderful way.

It is a great thing to run through the snow with a daughter like this
We run past the Chukchi reindeer herders
We run through larch and leap the slim stream
My old husband sees us and somehow he knows
He is losing his mind with happiness
As we bound towards him
Moving between shape

He is losing his mind with happiness

[170]

I am old Kytna
My daughter is Ralinavut

Sometimes we are woman
Sometimes we are wolf

❖

To lose your mind with happiness. What a thing.
To know that sometimes you are a woman, sometimes a wolf.
And that all along, old Kytna had the wolf way in her blood.
But why torment yourself for three years?
My uncle is leaving me with a story of many loose ends.

He smiles his easy smile and stands.

—I will be leaving now. But I am glad to meet you for a time, my
descendent.

You will have to prowl Wolferland yourself, see what comes. What
is coming to both of us is Christmas. And I remind you gently again
to observe your part of the bargain. For every story I told you, read
one of the thin-skinned Jesus, who asks terrible things of anyone
wanting a life where not much happens. Jesus my burning wheel, the
terror of corrupt spiritual teachers. He's as radical as anything you
could possibly imagine. You just have to break the crust of church
from the energy of the message.

I'll see you again, little cripple.

And with that, dear Hamer slipped away. Down the hill a little.
Towards Spitchwick, taking the river walk, a lark ascending. I will
hear his singing always.

banging tunes

I am getting stronger now, less murk. I am banging Drake's drum
in the garbled greyness of this late December day. Did you know
Francis had a drum? Some speculate he was gifted it at Devil's
Point when he sold his soul to the devil in exchange for the storm
that scattered the Spanish Fleet. But it wasn't the devil. It was Dyer
from Wistman's Wood on Dartmoor, it was Bucca from just over
the Tamar. It was the raw, sometimes ambivalent magic energy
secreted in the far west. It is sworn the drum was heard beating from
Buckland Abbey when the German fleet surrendered in 1918.

But I don't beat the drum for war, I beat it for jubilance and
invitation. That's all I know. Don't overthink, just beat. Don't rob
a moment of its lurching joy. I beat it for the sheer magic of the
totem. I hope the Nanai hear it, and the Ket, and the Evenk, not as
a thump of dominion, but as a pulse of connection. Somehow, now,
with everything shouting to everything else, I change the pattern on
Drake's drum.

Because it's not the drum, it's what you play on the drum.
I don't repel in the pattern, I invite.
The drum thump is a paw beat.

And Wolferland is growing, the claw and fur moving out from
Liverpool and the mystic Wirral, back to when there was land between
England and Ireland, that far back, when we were all bound up.
14,000, 15,000 BC. When there were people there before we were here.

And in the end, if we are having an ancestral reckoning in all of
this, I must skip that way once or twice. It's my perennial and fierce
compulsion. It's my people, you see. The blood-daggers of my veins.
Mayo, Galway, the Connaught region has much of my source in it.
Oblivious till I spat in a glass and a whole world opened up. Twenty
years telling of Finn and the Fianna, never for a second knowing I
was speaking words directly from my ancient, ancestral haunt.

[172]

So stretch if it is your true shape, dear Wolferland, clamber round these isles and make one great wolf-shape, diverse and churning though the mass of it may be, and let me wrench my mad ceremonied skull in that direction and see what could come. I have absolutely no idea. There is no map, only unmapping, there is no map, only submission.

I am blessed
And could bless

That's what Yeats said, when he was a little older than me.

I am thinking about Yeats because I am thinking about Ireland. Thinking about when I taught in his tower, even slept in his bed. Thinking about when I read out loud his poems in his bedroom and a large bat appeared and swung in widening orbits around me as the words cut green the air. When I finished the bat was gone – a real, proper, non-metaphorical bat – and I glimpsed out of the window and saw the little lane leading up to the tower filled with cars, torches and people. It was a majestic and rather severe thing, Thoor Ballylee. Phallic and compact. Later I would drink potheen at midnight outside the small town of Gort.

There's more than a few connections between Devon and Yeats, more than a few. I'll tell you about one. His grandfather William Pollexfen was born in Brixham in 1811. The house he was raised in is just a few miles by motor down the Plymouth road. At a decrepit age twelve, William took himself to sea, eventually settling in Sligo. His daughter then marries into the Yeatses and everything happens.

Yeats, continually remaking himself, a commuter between islands, a man to not just receive a spiritual message but to pummel it from one side of the tower to the other until it gasped out every dimension of its disclosure.

Yeats – some back and forths:

LONDON—SLIGO
SCEPTICISM—BELIEF
MYTHOLOGY—CONFESSIONAL
ARROGANCE—SHYNESS
UNREQUITED LOVE—MARITAL FULFILMENT
MYSTICAL RECLUSE—PUBLIC FIGURE

Remember Blake – *Without contraries is no progression.*

It takes that kind of tension, and requisite toughness, to make the art that Yeats makes.

Yeats becalms the great waters with his poems, there's a structural permanence that evaded me for many years simply because I did not care for rhyming poems. I didn't quite understand what he was up to until I gazed up at the boxy jut of Thoor Ballylee. A gust of wind wasn't going to knock them over, these poems. A shaman is happy to become dust, a magician wants to be remembered.

They say he was a man always peering out of windows and sighing loudly.

Willie's not going to come sit with me in the wood, I think I can tell that. Not that he didn't languish this side of the Irish Sea enough times. But he is truly somewhere else now. I can feel it at the very edge of me, but I can't quite access it. Somewhere bright and high. Byzantium far.

Oh the slosh is upon me now. I wonder how many times I can crawl to the rapidly shrinking doorway of your gracious attentiveness and inform you that, yes, it's fucking raining again. The fields, the lanes, the trees, the hedges, everything is on the bloat. All distended with moisture. All kinds of Devonian magic tied up in the smashing grey sluices of rain winnowing their way past my pile of rock and roof. No wonder Hamer skipped off. It's 3 p.m. and almost dark. God it's utterly glorious. Sausages for the pan, fried up with butter and garlic, and soon, soon, a suck of wine. Even the forest gives a reprieve for a drop of red when you're mourning an absent uncle.

Who abides in the grizzled thatch of Irish Wolferland? Who's cutting turf from the bog with Patrick Kavanagh and Seamus H? Brendan Behan is sitting on the drystone wall watching and holding their porter. A slop, a plop, a drop in his jaw. Luke Kelly and Grainne are playing chess and the whole ground, the fur of the Wolferland's back, is teeming with hare and swooping merlins, speckled salmon in the diddiest stream and every secret nook you lay your hand in there's a warm duck egg. Gawain urges Gringolet on, looking for a bed in the Wicklow Mountains. If you look through the tavern window there are Moorish poets and Basque sailors.

And most of all, over there, for once, it's not raining. That I know.

So it seems the Gaelic world has come crashing into the shape Hamer left.

I will sleep on it and see what remains in the morning. There are saddlebags on the porch, there's grain in the cellar and Connemara peat in the fireplace. These arrivals are not convinced about the booze rule either.

These multitudinous kingdoms
Expanding and contracting,
Blowing wild across the fields
The whole chanting night.

It's morning now, 20th December. They must have shifted. The cottage is empty but there's a thin smoke coming from the treeline. Campfire. They are all here, and at the same time I am all alone. It's the oddest thing, this emptiness and fullness, crashing about.

Now it is evening. The death-cold has arrived, the kind that has moved through settlements for thousands of years, picking off the old. I can see the ancients quietly standing up as the others gaze into the flames, taking themselves off into the trees. They have that taste in the back of their mouths that tells them it's time.

I have been in the woods looking into the sky-night. It was the strangest thing.

One moment it was a deep indigo with a mind-jolting array of white and yellow stars lacing its foreground. I glance down for a second and when I look up it is an utterly different painting. The stars have gone. The indigo is now dulled coal. No iridescence. From ecstasy to depression in five seconds. From the keenness of the gull to the blindness of the mole, just like that. Informing me of something I can't quite grasp, but brutal in its execution.

I slept today, plenty. My two aged cats curled up at the end of my bed. As my eyes closed it was late afternoon, when I opened them, night. Or the late afternoon version of pitch-black night you get at this time of year. It's glorious. I will be alone for much of Christmas, which is not the emotional misstep that many would presume. It makes my continual forays into the woods easy to manage and it buys me a little time to take stock.

But my mind is under lock and key to this interminable ceremony, no intelligible progress report possible. My mind can't 'take stock' in any sense of the phrase, it hasn't been able to turn up for duty in that way since maybe back before Halloween.

Hunched in the dark I can hear the river roar; tipping and garnishing the sound is the forever-shriek of my tinnitus. My friends and loved ones are scattering tonight, to all corners of the country. Ho ho ho. To not be doing that has its delight too.

THERE'S A LOT OF SPIRITUAL ENERGY AVAILABLE
WHEN YOU SLIP OUT OF A CIVILISED EVENT

Who slipped out?

Bukka White became a wolf
Ronnie Drew became a wolf
Germaine Greer became a wolf
Maggi Hambling became a wolf
Marie-Louise von Franz became a wolf
Virginia Woolf was already a wolf
Beefheart channelled a Howlin' Wolf
Lorca made love with a wolf

And Joe Strummer loved them all
Danced to his boom-box
Dreader than Dread
And shouted like a Rasta:

MORE FIRE!

ONE COLD VIBE
WON'T STOP THIS HERE BOOGIE

Beefheart said it first, and Strummer took it into himself somewhere
quiet and then told it to me, an almost-stranger, one day years ago,
and I tell it to you on this cold night, with the death-chill.

Our time has the death-chill on it. So I give you a Hope Chant.

All the oldies have changed their mind about death on the tundra
and run back into the village, come back as ancestors not spooks
and are shouting and mischief-making:

ONE COLD VIBE
WON'T STOP THIS HERE BOOGIE

Spirits from the deep, who never sleep
Be kind to me
Spirits from the grave, without a soul to save
Be kind to me
Spirits of cold and ice, presiding over crime and vice
Be kind to me
Wolves, vampires, satyrs and ghosts!
Elective of all dark, wild hosts!
I pray to send hither
The great grey shape
That makes all men shiver!

This Slavic incantation, with all its enjoyable, ghoulish theatre, is not what I am in the grip of.

In 1484 it was literally a sin to believe in werewolves, but by the late sixteenth century they were seen as very real, in fact in league with Satan. Career Christians with large brushes sweep all pagan characters into the pit with Old Nick. Black and white. Nature is not to be trusted and bristles with vast, ghastly, positively wicked forces. You kiss the hand of the pope with a ring on it expensive enough to feed a village for a year and you think wickedness resides in the wild?

Christ.

Wolf rubs up against Roma against Black against Irish against Dog. Fucking white-land. Thank god we didn't succeed in that.

This is the opposite of all that, a scythe to that, a Heyoka to that, an upside-downness to all that.

It is the shortest day tomorrow, when darkness will take the house. It'll be the death of Tristan and Isolde, but also the gleam seed of their return, as a snorting royal horse carries Isolde who is a Hawk

[178]

of the Sun back from the night into the fullness of midsummer. Across the sky this will happen; in our shy, romantic, cautious hearts this will happen. Light will be restored, just as right now darkness is being restored.

I went out into the thin brief light and spilt whisky on the roots of the hazel bush. The glass of the bottle was so cold it stung my fingers. All colours look doctored, Photoshopped: loopy-loop lichen, a pale and brilliant green. Everything is about staying warm: most of the cottage is portioned off – I flit between the bedroom and kitchen, the cats omnipresent at the end of the blanketed bed, thirteen years into similar procedures with me.

End of decade. It was a mosh pit, a victory march, a grief hole and a smackdown. I tapped out a couple of times, and staggered to my feet just before the bell. Wobbled and flattened – older and wiser, I hear. I have no clear thought about how I would view myself at the end of it if I glimpsed myself at the beginning.

I can't conceive of any of it without the old stories. Without the terrific unrest they bear down, bare-knuckle hard on my jabbering consciousness. Never like this though, at the end of this decade they parade under the lintel of the cottage. They squat like shouty punks in my most delicate of dreams, hysterical, flash-mobbing my musings as I walk the river; they refuse to wash up, and steal books as they please.

There is this final push though, this final month before this is done. Only ceremony will be the guillotine on this meander, this pummelling of the unseen. There will be an ending. There just has to be.

I wonder if I will have more pups. I wonder if there is a wife out there in the dark. I wonder if I am a husband. These are not yearnings, just questions. There is not quite a sorrowedness to this, just that scrag-end-of-the-year wondering. People wonder such things staggering back from nightclubs, whilst filling out tax forms, even squashed up in retirement homes. We wonder. About love, companionship, gentle care. I wonder if I am too wolfish for that now, though those that know tell me they are all wolfish things.

If anyone ever reads this, they will know such howls themselves.

But if the bottle falls BANG on my skull tonight, and the serious dark floods my bright brain, then let it be known this was alright by me. This was all alright. This arrangement of life.

ALL OUR LIVES WE ARE CRAWLING IN AND OUT OF ANIMALS

There was an old seer that came to Ireland with the daughter of Noah. When the waters rose round the high mountain he was on he became a salmon. Salmon of wisdom, they say, the very salmon Finn tasted at the bank of the Boyne. Fintan his name. Fintan mac Bóchra. A repository of knowledge.

When facing a flood become a salmon.
Swim in the waters that come to drown you.

It is the shortest day today, a Sunday. Yesterday endless thousands of deeply committed pagans skipped off to celebrate, not bothering to actually check the date. Maybe it was just easier for them to fly their freak flag on a Saturday. I will go over to feed whisky to the tree roots in a little while. Today I've seen rainbows, a bauble of grey rain on every motionless object, and little birds cruising for worms.

But what I haven't seen yet is a story.

Born in the same hut as my father and my daughter I was. My father smokes his last cigar on that Octobering night. And swish swish swish goes the Devonian sea, and groan groan groan goes the forest behind our house, and me a baby all crammed in with the books and the records. No phone to break the deep reading, no car to unchallenge our feet, and why would you with all of old Torbay to explore?

Then I am being walked to school and deciding it was alright for the day, but I'm glad I don't have to go back tomorrow. What a miracle it was to reach up to a bookshelf and fall into a kingdom of story. Or to be enswooned to the storying of a landscape by walking it almost every day with my father.

What's that word, *finesse*. My dad finessed the landscape. He showed me the fissure points and the song lines, the minefields and holy wells. Did it all by speaking it out, storytelling, hour after hour. And then by five I was finding some of them myself, scrabbling in the copses above the estate I lived in.

I was finding my Wolferland even then, getting stretched and strained by a place, and a sensation of being set aside. Not in a grand or declaratory sense, but of being pulled to the side of life's playground. And suddenly I'm approaching half a century and it is Christmas. Christ light.

Did you prepare a table before me
In the presence of my enemies?
Did you anoint my head with oil?
Does my cup overflow?
Do I dwell in the House of the Lord?

There's many that would say I don't.

Today is Christmas Eve. Scuddish clouds, a smidge of blue, a storm passed through about 5 a.m. Mild again, and this odd, sweet tang to the air. Wind is up. I dreamt of an old mentor of mine, laughing in some imaginary corridor below my bed. A lung-smoked chuckle that meant spirits were having at him. Those moments he lives for. A cackle in a corridor. It was wearisome to hear, and broke me from sleep. It is not to have meaning extracted from it. I fed the cats and went back to rest.

Later I make a god-awful mess of my kitchen table, making little oil paintings on it.

I hang one on a nail and in horrible slow motion it slips behind the radiator and won't come out. The heady stink of wet oil paint smeared on radiator fills the world with fume. I have been thinking of the painters I loved twenty years ago. I used to paint a lot more. Basquiat with his genius rattle of urban hoodoo and scattergun language; the pale, frail-lined intensities of Agnes Martin; the outsider mythologies of Ken Kiff. Kiff made some wild paintings for a book of British folktales. I have it under the projector so it's tottered high enough to watch movies on the wall.

I have been getting my days mixed up, but I am sure it is Christmas Eve. Soon I will take to the woods again and rest myself against the hazel tree.

And I was in and out and it pissed pissed pissed down. Nasty hard. Fuck it. I cleaned the house and listened to Spanish medieval carols from the last century.

COMES A VISITOR

It is blustery and blue dark now, stars consistently on display. Far away I can see the lights of a home. I lay out a plate of lamb, delicately sliced, good cut, and a glass of rare Black Pot whisky. I have been smelling brine for hours and I think someone is coming.

He stands in my garden, me watching from the porch. He outstretches his sword with one hand. Lays large crumbs of salt across the blade. Shows me he is a sea-wolf.

song eight

clack clack clack

—I long for God's mercy
I, a lonely traveller
Exiled, I sail aimlessly
And without destination.

There's only one port:
Memory.
I've seen my people killed
Over and over.
My heart has shut shop,
Silence has dignity
And speech is no cure.
This taking to the sea
Hasn't worked.
I imagined land, loved ones
A lord to serve.
Fuck all.
It's just been breaking bread
With sorrow.
It used to be so different:
I sometimes pretend
My lord is still alive,
I bend my head and kneel,
Open my eyes to putrid gulls
And sea-billow heaving.
Alas, cup of brightness,
Alas, majestic prince.
Alone in this night
It's as if you never lived.
Driving snow pins the earth tight,
Winter is a deep horror.
Men and women are fleeting,
And this earth rolls into emptiness.

This earth rolls into emptiness.

I gesture to the lamb and whisky, but he
Stares ahead at me. He is pale as snowflakes,
Still holding his blade horizontal at his chest.

—I will tell you of a tall woman.
Fifty foot tall, chest seven feet across.
The only thing that had never grown were her paps.
They found her on the mainland.
They had tied her hands behind her back
And cut her massive head off.
Purple cloak on her back, that's it.

Bigger woman still lurched up on the Scottish coast.
A hundred-and-ninety-two feet long. I swear it.
Her nose was seven foot, hair sixteen, seventeen foot
Between her paps.
Every part of her was white as a gull.

Big women frighten some people.

❖

Well he's frightened me.

*Please sea-man, take the communion of food and drink on this
Particular night, a night for a spark of light in the dark.*

This night crammed full of carols and booze and television shows
also has Saxon sea-men wandering the forest, seaweed on their
boots, looking for their comrades. They wander the dark groves
of Wolferland.

They walk in and out of me all day long.

But for now he still stands, blade un-shaking, so cold in the dark it
would sting you if you touched it. So cold it's hot. I walk back to the

cottage and close the door. I will light a candle at the window for
his boat.

I am him looking at me.

And now it is a Christmas midnight and it is glorious.
Seafarer, did you find Bethlehem? Did you find your
Fellow rowers, transformed as three kings?
Chest thick and happy in the warm hay.

Head there. There are no simmering girls in this forest,
No trough of brandy, just a canticle of owls a-bliss with a baby.

Such a night. Peace sweeps the chase.
As Muhammed Ali said:
'It ain't bragging if it's true!'

skinny horse, rusty sword

COMES A SECOND VISITOR

Unexpectedly the night was a wrestle, and not the pleasing kind. It
appears I had to revisit a particular wound, its unstitched, unholy
self, its depth without end. A wretched gutting. For once the cats
are not mewing for food, so I lie in the dark and move in and out
of this weary, pulverised state. To be rid of it, oh to be rid of the
infection.

But the morning is sweet. The trees seem to be standing straighter,
the sky is robustly blue and there's even a ridge of frost on the
ground. And, I promise you, most of the lamb has gone. The whisky
glass is frozen to the table. I hope there aren't too many pissed
robins careering around.

I have slunk into my Levi's, sheepskin boots and Donegal coat. I leave the cottage and take the walk to the river, crunching the white as I do so. So slap-fresh. It's so vivid out, the shadows of the oaks are like huge charcoal snakes. Australian landscape in my mind, though I've never been. As I walk down towards the water there are tiny birds swooping about, lots of song, and gushing tributaries of rainwater spilling down onto the path. There's an orange crest of trees, but near the edge of the river is a blueish mist, making the air grainy.

The river spumes with a pearly green foam, but in a still spot I can see an angler. It's early, and it's Christmas Day, so it's a surprise. His bearded face is covered mostly by a bashed-up hat and I hear the wind-up radio he has next to him. It growls away as he casts then settles back on fur. Big guy.

'And the BBC celebrates Christmas Day with *Words of the One-Eyed*, reflections on life by the wandering god Odin. Also known as Ruler of the Gallows, Battle Wolf, Spear Master, Grim Mask, Rune Scatterer, Maker of Magic Song.'

I sit down the bank a bit, avoiding the melting frost, and listen in. I will not look again at the angler or his circling birds, two dark skald-sticks above him.

song nine

clack clack clack

A greedy man
Unless he reins it in
Will scoff to his downfall.
Sober men will frequently
Mock a fool
About the risen hump of his gut.

You are going to get damaged
With your constant talking
If you never winch your jaw shut.
A blabbing tongue
Unless it's been tempered
Earns its owner painful consequence.

A fir tree rots
Lonely by a farm,
Stripped of all needle and bark.
Unprotected.
People are the same.
If nobody loves you,
How much longer will you live?

Don't just give big things;
It's often the smaller that
Carry the most heft.
Friendships have been forged
From me just giving a chunk of bread
And a bowl of soup.

Get up early,
If you don't have a servant,
Get straight to your labour.
It's more than time you sacrifice
If you snore on;
For the early riser, you've already
Won half the wealth.

There is joy at evening
For the boatman
Anticipating supper,
With just a little way left to row.
But you can't trust these
Autumn nights.

Things can worsen
In just five days,
Let alone a month.
Cut wood when the wind is blowing,
Crest your boat on the waves,
Enchant your lover in darkness
(Daytime is full of peering eyes).
Respect a ship for its speed,
A shield that protects,
A sword for its keenness,
A woman for her kiss.

Gulp ale by the fire,
Skate on ice,
Buy a skinny horse

And a rusty sword,
Feed the horse
And let your dog sort itself.

A snapping bow,
A roaring fire,
A keening wolf,
A skalding crow,
A snorting pig,
A tree without roots,
A cresting wave,
A kettle boiling,

A hurled spear,
A smashing wave,
Ice but a night old,
A snake that is striped,
A bride's words in bed,
A snapped sword,
A bear that wants to play,

A king's child,

A sickening calf,
A bolshy servant,
A prophet with good news,
A dead man on the battlefield,

The killer of your brother
(Even in a public meeting),
A house half-torched,
A horse too fast
(One foot breaks, it is unusable),

May never your trust be such
That you completely trust these things.

No man
Should ridicule another
For falling in love.
Such sickness
Often claims a wise man
Quicker than an idiot.

It's only you that knows
What's alive in your heart
When you're alone;
And the greatest pain
For a person of wisdom
Is to have nothing to love.

This happened to me
When I waited amongst the reeds
For my lover that never came.
She was all my flesh, all my heart
That wise girl,
Though I could not claim her as mine.

There are words here I need to absorb. Words that speak directly to my night-time wound. I untangle myself from the crunchy, shining bank of grass and start to make my way back to the cottage, the angler's radio wheezing on.

Some say Odin was the first Santa. That the eight-reindeer sleigh is based on the eight-legged horse of the wisdom-soaked god, Sleipnir – *The Sliding One*. That he visited homesteads in the old Yule time of year.

Some say Odin is Woden, but you get hurt feelings all round if you cram the gods together like that. They are both complex, both dealers in battle, but I haven't yet heard Woden speak of waiting amongst the reeds for a girl that never came. Both Woden and Odin lead the Wild Hunt on occasion throughout the year, so must be acquainted with our Antlered Lord on Dartmoor, Dyer and his hounds of Yeth. Keep your head down if they ride by.

Soon I'm squatting on my little mossy seat under the hazel. I'm admiring the buds still in repose, enjoying the stretch of branches, like pale outstretched fingers. I've been thinking about that Odin counsel down by the river, so today my calling song is a set of Old English maxims. These lived on my fridge door once, typed out and taped on a postcard from a beautiful, dying man in New Mexico.

song ten

clack clack clack

Living well is to get on with what needs to be done.
If you have inspired advice, say it plainly, but when privacy is needed
Write the words down. If you have a song then let's hear it, when
You have to make a judgement, then do it. Today is always the day

For action to be taken.

Be wise about what you've got.
If you come across a fine horse, be good to it.
Where is the man who has everything he needs?
Show fidelity to your friends. Night will settle soon enough,
And you'll yearn for a companion on the dark road.

A shape moves amongst trees –

When the wolf finds you alone
It will not reflect on your fame in the village.

In this darkening world
Grey wolves are always ravenous
And have no thought for mercy.
You have to do the thing that needs doing.
Wrap tight a bleeding wound, when slander is frequently inflicted
Call forth revenge. Arrows wither without a bow,
And both are feeble without an arm of strength.

When you exchange treasure, the heft must weigh the same,
But keep in mind that God allows strange outcomes.
Guard your house, keep what you can, but know that when
A tree falls there will be no more growing for it.

Show the trueness of your heart in how you do business
Because God abandons the thief. God sees the whole affair,
There's a dark shape to it all. This is accurate for all of us,
Even if we have particular theories, particular cheery songs.

A man of degree acquires songs and plays them on his harp,
He feels less alone when he does so. Be vigilant to how isolation
Becomes terrible, how horror tracks you like a boar through the
Crunching wood!

When the boar comes you need a friend stoutly by your side,
Clutching a well-crafted spear. Don't let gossip ever separate you
From your kinsmen. Be true, and the chill of winter's cold will
Not bring grief as you play chess with your friend on a dark night.

We get weary, day after day of hard things. Like rowing against the
Wind, straining away, yet you must also know you are a man of the
Right spirit. Be steady, clear of heart, always ready!

There's no haven in this world. Ever since Cain killed Abel there's
Been nastiness soaked into the dirt of the earth. And this is where
You are going to have to live, amongst killers and thieves.

There's no other place to find. Every day such people whittle long
Knives.

So be alert with a hard shield and sharp spear, a bold character.

A weakling's heart is no reward,
But a man of courage deserves his bright helmet.

Ah, such catnip. All of life in those few lines.

The terrible stranger on Christmas Eve I saw once more. Same place,
me on the porch, him in the garden, just a little light from the French
doors. Christmas darkness around us. He spoke to me one last time,
words from a Celtic sea-god. He moves between Old English and
Gaelic. It wasn't quite a calling song, it was like a fleeting and very old
memory he was attempting to retain, almost under his breath.

Oft him anhaga are gebideð

Often the lonely one prays for mercy
Sea-bashed Bran

Beholds the grandeur of an ocean
Dashed about in his coracle
In my chariot I see him
Presiding over flowers

Bran grips timber
Sees a curly head of waves
I see a crest of red-headed flowers
Utterly perfect

My host is numerous
Though he sees only my chariot
Rivers pour forth honey
In this domain of mine
Under his tiny skiff

Is a fruit-heavy wood
His coracle has nipped the bluff
Of a forest without decay or imperfection

Dig in Bran, keep rowing
The Land of Women is ahead
Evna with her manifold bounty
You should reach before the sun is set

Before the sun sets. A land of women. There's been precious little of
that in all this gallivanting. It's absolutely pissing down, you will
be shocked to hear, and I am sheltering under bear fur in the green
wood, contemplating whether to break a little taboo of mine and
make a fire in the dry spot under the western oaks. I decide against
it, and will have to use words to keep me warm.

Words have kept me warm for getting on for fifty years, I hope they
won't stop now.

Parzival sleeping in armour as the snow drifts – he needs a story
The Handless Maiden wandering the forest – she needs a story
Raven bringing light to the world – even they could do with a story

Here's something far from any well-worn track.

song eleven

clack clack clack

It was Pentecost. Pentecost at the City of Legions. Pentecost at Caerleon-Upon-Usk.

Pentecost – so often when an adventure of King Arthur's was to unfold. The holy spirit descends and swarms the recesses of our deranged conscience. Pentecost is the sounding horn for clip-clop forays far out into the teeming forests that surround the settlement. Into the mystic.

There is gossip in the gallery that Arthur was in his cups when he did what he did.

When he publicly squeezed and hugged and laid hot kisses on his wife the queen. It was not unusual for Arthur to speak lovingly of his wife. But the etiquette of court required limits to such voluble displays of affection. Even Merlin looked away. The room stiffened, demanded a response. Pentecost was a ceremony of poise and deliberation.

'Why did you do that?'

'Do what?'

'Have your hands all over me at such a public moment. Such a religious moment.'

'Because there is just nothing I love as much as you. Amongst all this wealth, you are my deep delight.'

'So you are saying you love me so much, you know the workings of my heart?'

'I think I know you care for me, that your affection is known to me.'

'You are grasping, witless on this issue. You have got nowhere near either the nature or the heart of a woman.'

Bright Christ, the court heard that.

Silence, and the king gathered himself, though wretched and slaughtered beneath his cloak.

'I call the heavens to bear witness now, that if I have not fathomed the heart or nature of a woman, I will not consume food until I have rectified this.'

The decorum of a court can be brutal at times, even for a king.

He sat scarlet in shame till the banquet shuffled to a slow death, and set out with his servant Kai and his nephew Gawain. No food till I have understood the heart of a woman. Everyone heard his flat, humiliated vow.

And now out into a Welsh spring, into the budding, playful, bantering springtime. No snow-trancing vision, no Green Chapel, no sluice of black rain, no brooded copse of plump badger. No Grail. Everybody and everything flirting, getting together, giggling under a hedge, meeting under a tall pine in any lovers' garden. The beginning of the bloom. All loving possibility that ever was rode alongside the Bear King of all Britain. The king who now felt flattened, impotent and witless. Lacking. There was a ball and chain

to the lightheartedness of spring for Arthur. When he thought of
his wife his gut cold-churned.

But what to do now, after his big proclamation?

All three men knew of a king who was famed for thinking not as
other men did. Who could breathe in knowledge like the ocean
sucks a tide, a man not caught up with ornamentation of life,
but who took his thinking down into the black mud bottom of a
predicament. His name was Gorgol. He may know something.

What it is to ride two nights without sleep, without food in belly,
because if the king wouldn't eat, then both Kai and Gawain refused.
They cantered through hamlets, caught the smoke-rich scent of
venison on the village fires and tightened their resolution, not to let
even a slap of black beer froth their beards.

So easy to write of two nights' ride without sleep, a hell to receive
those rides.

After passing through a gloomy valley they came to a mountain,
surrounded by a sweet flowered wood and with a fortress of
polished stone visible within. For the luck of all three men, this
was the settlement of Gorgol. They passed by the outer trench and
entered the feast hall of the king, Arthur still on horseback. Gorgol
was a man most comfortable between tallow wick and shadow.
Never to be seen in full display. He kept his eye on his meat, but
spoke up nonetheless:

'Who are you, rider? Why are you barging in?'

'I am the High King. Artos. King of Britain. You are said to have
an uncommon wisdom, not an everyday kind. You see things with
a slant, Gorgol. You must tell me what you know of the heart, the
nature and the ways of women.'

'You come with saddlebags full I see. That is one of the deepest questions. There are almost none who could answer it, of any disposition, man or woman. Tomorrow I will think into what I know, but for now it is clear you and your men are exhausted, please have chops and wine with us.'

Although denying he was exhausted, Arthur saw something of a mirror in the deranged and flogged appearances of Kai and Gawain. So he broke his Pentecost vow. He sat opposite the slant king Gorgol and ate and drank to capacity.

Is Arthur asleep in his own mynde?
To make a vow and so quickly break it?
Is the dream of Arthur asleep to himself?

At breakfast the king sat down face to face with Gorgol and picked up the thread – what did Gorgol know of the heart, nature and ways of women? Gorgol sighed, then spoke.

'To be a High King I would have always presumed you intelligent, hopefully wise. But you sit here before me in full display of a grievous folly. Of naivety. In any real way, your question cannot be answered. Certainly not by me. Not this easily won. Go further into the wild country, to my older brother, Torleil, and see what he thinks. You have to travel further for such an insight.'

Arthur and his tiny retinue headed off into a darkening land; squalls of rain, grizzly woods and a good four days' ride till they came to Torleil. Again Arthur broke his vow at Torleil's request and again Torleil had nothing to tell him. Ah, but there was a third brother. Not like the other two. Deeper than them. Harder to find. Less public still. The oldest, this ancient third king.

It was a hard push to find this one, the one they called Gorlagon. Two days, two nights without sleep until they rode half-crazed into the settlement. Just as before, Gorlagon and his warriors were settling for supper when Arthur rode in, torches lit, chops on plate, bright wine in cup.

It was the strangest thing. An enchantment. Gorlagon was for all the world Torleil, he was for all the world Gorgol. They were like Babushka dolls, men within men within men. Gorlagon had some deep story in him, it was clear, some extra weight, some presence. Another man between wick and shadow. But Arthur, Kai, Gawain, all wondered if they were being spun mad in some kind of dreaming circle. Surely this was an older version of the man they had been trying to speak to all week.

Arthur made a triad of his question – tell me what you know of the heart, nature and ways of a woman. Something happens the third person you ask.

Gorlagon replied:

'Such an enormity of question is not to be tackled when you haven't eaten. And if I may say so, you and your men look half dead. Please, come down off your horse and feast with us. We will see if the morning is wiser than the evening.'

'I will not break my fast. I will not come down off my horse. I will not ask in the morning. I need you to speak to me now, tonight, in a way that brings me wisdom.'

'I will. Though this will cause me a labour, and not help you much in the long run. But you have travelled down into the well of a question, so I will try and help. But it would be good to let your hounds eat a scrap or two, yes?'

Arthur agreed and Gawain and Kai slumped onto a bench and availed themselves most readily of every condiment, meat and bottle they could find.

'Arthur, let the bear in you hear this story. Let the oldest part of you hear this story. I will speak it the most archaic way I know how:

I knew a king. I knew him well. He had pedigree, and was known for his persistence in seeking justice and seeking truth. But there was something that he cultivated for himself. It was a hidden garden.

The rumour is that it had no equal, filled with fruit trees and spices. It was something just for him.

At its centre was a slender sapling, the exact same height as the king himself. To the inch. No one claimed to have planted it, but it burst from the soil on the hour of his birth, growing diligently alongside him.

Some things waft through life randomly, others have the hoofprint of fate branded on them. This sapling was like that. So easily ignored amongst the fruit and strong spices, it held the most wisdom. The sapling was fated this way: that if it was cut down it would be a divinatory wand, it would have power. If you touched the head of someone with it you could utter the words, 'Be a wolf and understand as a wolf' and they would become a wolf and the wolf's comprehension, its understanding of the world, would flood the person.

So each man has a secret garden, and growing in the garden is a genus of wolf knowledge from the moment they are born.'

And the Great Bear leant over from his saddle, his ear open to the story.

'The king had a public life so he especially valued privacy. He built a wall around the garden, and would sit in the presence of the sapling three times daily, fasting to the evening. Growing sharp in mind by the discipline.

The man had a wife whom he adored. She him, less so. Her heart and hips were secretly for the son of a certain pagan king, and she was constantly trying to get her husband into perilous situations. So perilous she could freely take another. She monitored the time she could have away from him carefully, and of course noticed his triadic absences and his frequent fasts. She worked on him and of course got nothing as to where he went. In the end she feigned an illness, refused all food till he reluctantly (and extracting an oath of privacy) told her of his wolf sapling.

She revived then didn't she? A flush to the cheek. Kind words. Eager in bed.

Next day when the king was hunting she took an axe and went to his secret garden. She cut the sapling at the root, and slipped it under her sleeve. When her husband dismounted from his horse after the hunt, she walked towards him with her arms wide open to embrace. As he willingly reached for her, she slipped the sapling from her sleeve and struck him around the head with it, incanting:

Become a wolf.

But she slipped in the spell,

With the understanding of a man.

Not the understanding of a wolf.

Werewolf. A mix.

At that moment he became a wolf and she set her hounds on him, shriek-baying that they kill it, as the bewildered and terrified king bounded into the grey-green of the treeline.'

The king tried to call a halt to the story.

'So, Artos. Bear King. There's a little of the feminine temperament right there. Not all of it mind. Not my mother's, or my aunts', or my sisters', but this woman. So that's a teaching moment right there for you. A woman trapped in a marriage she despises may be the wolf herself, and will gnaw through any kind of damage, inflict any kind of deception to get out the trap. Now, will you get down off your horse and eat?'

'No. This is what I flogged myself through thicket and gorse to hear. This is wisdom I have had to be weak with fast to hear. Continue.'

Gorlagon spat into the fire and continued:

'For years that king watched from the cold treeline. Body of a wolf, mind of a man. He saw that young man sweep right in, take the reins of power, whore the king's marriage bed night after night, all curated by his gleeful wife.

When the new couple had two children, two boys, the wolf came across them playing by a lonely tower. Two boys for the years waiting, shivering, watching from the forest. Seemed just. He ripped them to shreds and went home to his own pups and she-wolf.

Though you don't ask for it, there's a little masculine temperament for you.

For balance.

Oh, but guards caught his pups and hung them. That's how this tit for tat goes.

He lost his mind at the death of the pups. He started after cattle, people, anything that got anywhere near him. Another nobleman set out to catch this wolf, that was of a size no one had ever seen before, vast. When the wolf was approached it behaved in many subtle manners that let the nobleman know it was no ordinary wolf. It licked him, sat by his feet, brought down a vast stag. It seemed devoted to the nobleman, and became the most treasured part of the lord's retinue. Though it was unconventional from a human perspective, the wolf was wise. It even slept at the base of the nobleman's bed.

So trusted became the wolf, so tuned to the nobleman's mood, the lord surmised this could be no conventional beast, that some kind of enchantment must be at work, and the wolf did all it could in wolfish ways to convince him that he was correct.

Over time the nobleman gathered warriors and allowed them to go wherever the wolf would lead. It led them, of course, directly to the settlement of the new king and the wolf's wife. Under confession, she admitted the enspellment, and produced the sapling, which the lord then took and touched to the head of his beloved wolf.

This time, in the reversal of the spell, his words sung true:

Become a man.
Have the understanding of a man.

And he did, he did, he did. But it was the wisdom of a wolf that hung on his shoulders now. His sagacity had come not from his time as a young king but as an exiled wolf. His Merlinness was born there. And, could it not be argued that the actions of his wife had led to a strange kind of good?

Possibly. Such a thing stayed with the king. Such things, the twists and turns of events, the moveable blame of things stay with us all as we age. Did he not become wise by betrayal? Did Odin not lose an eye for such insight?

As it was, the wolf king happily butchered the new husband but simply divorced his wife.

Now that is a story that cost me to tell you. Will you finally sit and eat?'

'Not until you answer this final question. Who is this woman at your table, far from tallow candle, who weeps when you laugh, and when you kiss your wife, kisses the head of a dead man on a golden plate in front of her?'

'Well, there we have it. I will tell you. She has committed a great injustice to her lord. Her lord is me. I am the wolf of the woods, my fur on the inside now, my wisdoms grown from a lupine state. I am the king of the wolf sapling, I am the one who lived through everything I have told you of.

I spared her life, but when she eats at my table she eats with his embalmed head.

When I kiss my wife's cheek, she slobbers the blood-crusted mouth of her long-slain king. It's just a trinket, something to keep the whole affair fresh in our minds.

That she is in perpetual exhibition, as it were.

So Artos. Will a bear break bread with a wolf?'

Finally, Arthur came down from his horse.

It was a swifter road home to Caerleon, but the wonderment of it all hung with him.

He would have no grand pronouncements about men or women. He would tarry on his fondness for oaths.

But at night, he dreamt of a secret garden,
And hidden amongst the fruit and the spices,
A wolf sapling grew.

It would take a wolf to make a bear wise.

under clay, the may

And I see tipi poles in the forest at dusk, December 29th, 4.24 p.m.
Three clacked together, rope looped,
Bound in tight by smoke-yellow canvas.
Is this a Choctaw forest now? A Seneca forest? Ojibwe?
Does Sasquatch bend his furry head at the silvery river Durius?

I ONCE SHOOK A PHOTO AND A SHAMAN APPEARED

I have a photograph of a medicine man who wasn't there when I
took the photograph.

I took a photo of an outdoor fire and there, now, twenty-five years
later, in it appears a Yuwipi man. Like a Polaroid, he developed in
slow, slow motion, and now he is a resident in the photo. Forever
looking right down the barrel of the lens.

That's what is happening now. In this experience. These beings are
appearing everywhere, like my life is the flap flap flap of a Polaroid.
What is next to appear? The Devon trees are gum-black again like
cactus in the Mojave Desert. Almost dark the dusk now. Mild, sweet
air. I think I have written something about this before. I'm sure I
have but I have forgotten what day it is. This happens over and over.
It's not a hardship, just slippery.

And in less than a month this will be over, this secret will be over.

First we domesticated fire
Then we domesticated animals
Then we domesticated myth

There's not much I can do about the first two.

Dreaming is a very deep kind of thinking. My commitment to this experience was to dream with my eyes wide open for 101 days. To un-domesticate.

I can do it to my imagining. My imagination. My imaginalis.

Little Richard did it, goddamnit. Let's gather his vinyl and spin the black magic.

Good Golly, Miss Molly.

I can't remember if I'm allowed to howl along or not. You've got to be far from a wolf if you're even debating the issue.

Life's great conundrum. When you banish Old Nick, he tends to take the salt and grease with him.

It is New Year's Eve now. It was below freezing last night in the forest, though a rain has softened this last day of the decade. I look back at this ten years past with my hands over my eyes, just peering through a crack.

They say the best way to die is to let go of everything. To lack a centre. To lack self-centre. That if you spent a life putting others first then it's easier to go. I'm not sure I qualify for that sort of ease, but I think I believe the suggestion. And that's hard for a pagan romantic. I love attachment, I adore it, I sink my fangs into the rump of attachment. I am sensualist, I am driven, I reach out to the world. And one day I will have to reverse that behaviour.

Death has tracked alongside this experience. I don't say that flippantly, and not death in its acute register, but tacit rather than explicit. It's woven through so many of these conversations, these calling songs. It's banal of me to state that, but truthfully there's nothing less banal for a human than to start feeling its presence. I think I would have presumed ten years ago I would be standing at the end of the decade, but it's not so easily stated now. That would seem overly brash. As I look at the next I am more circumspect, certainly more respectful about such things now.

Two of my very dearest, closest friends have died fairly recently. They are over there now. The Other Place. One came back as an animal and barked at my door one autumn night. But they are mainly somewhere else. Other bright friends are riven with disease. From the point of view of my ancestors' lifespans I am already in extra time. And I tell you, dear noble Gods of Fate and Destiny, I am grateful for living.

And they say if you have quietened yourself sufficiently in the weeks beforehand, departed friends and spiritual figures will come and visit your bedside. I wonder if my spiritual figures will be these stories. I tell you, I would settle for that.

And then what happens? Not blackness, not blankness, but a moment of reunion with the ones who went ahead, your angels up ahead. Then, if you've been doing your metaphysical homework, a kind of movement into the energies of the universe, free from the animal of your body. Of course, I don't like the sound of that bit much.

So not to be buried with chariot wheels, white-gold rings, hunting dogs, weeping boyfriends chucked in for good measure. All that's over. You submit. You let go. This last day of the decade, before breakfast at least, this is what I am thinking of.

The sky is slate beyond slate beyond slate grey. Through some tree fell I glimpse a tor I haven't seen before. I stop and think and think. Of course, Buckland Beacon. Clambered all over the thing. It's refreshing to see something you think you know from an entirely new angle. Suddenly it is itself in a way you don't know. I never would have glimpsed it in the full foliage of summer.

My arm is hurting my eyes close and I give my calling song.

song twelve

clack clack clack

There once was a man called Malcolm Harper. The word in
Ireland was that he was of vast disposition; generous in spirit and
in practice. You would benefit from such a neighbour. He offered
shelter and gave encouragement. His cattle had flowers woven
round their horns.

Strolling through Harper's land came a diviner, a soothsayer.
Malcolm slipped coin into hand and asked the witch to tell
him of his future. The soothsayer took himself away for magical
communing and then returned, and not with light news.

'I saw with my black backwards eye that you have a daughter
coming, and on account of her more blood will be spilt on Erin's
turf than ever before. And on this blood road, our three mightiest
heroes will lose their lives.'

Malcolm was a man of the peat and the curlew, he loved his land. So
when the daughter was born he asked an old woman to help raise
the girl, far from the kind of men that could bring such a prophecy
to fruition. She agreed, and three of Malcolm's men crafted a sweet
little bothy in the mountains where from then on the girl and the
old woman lived out of sight.

Out of sight, but not out of pleasure. For it was a gentle time they
had for sixteen years. The name of the girl was Deirdre, and she
grew sweetly and utterly true to herself. But the black backwards eye
had a point – there was a beauty to her that would make the whole
world wobble if it got more than a glimpse.

She was one of these nature girls: no hazel thicket, no passing swift, no green spring hadn't been sought out and named by her over those years. Something untangled itself from her and wrapped itself around dappled grass, broad oak, a lintel of stars. It seemed her small world was a completeness, a kind of everything. She murmured over all of it and all of it became the sweeter in the doing.

And into that mossy euphoria her guardian gifted all the intelligence she had to the silver sapling of a girl. And for sixteen years that was how it was.

But weather changes at sixteen, doesn't it? Bangs and groans, a fog comes in.

As did the weather over the bothy. More than a squall, a bubbling, black brood of a thing, a rambunctious storm. And under this nigredo of mood was a hunter, caught out by the shouting scowl of clouds. It was night, the man was exhausted, and suddenly his companions were nowhere to be seen. There was more than a smear of the prophecy over his predicament.

In sheer weariness he settled by the bothy of Deirdre and, sodden with cold, fell into a thin kind of sleep. In his slumber he thought he heard fairy music and cried out for help. Snug inside, Deirdre heard the shout and asked her guardian what it was.

'Just a bird calling to another in the storm. Through the black rain they call, but there's nothing for them here, us tucked away in this bosky den.'

'There isn't much charity in your words, grandmother. If a bird is blue with cold then we should let it flit our rafters, nibble our bread. I will open my world to the poor thing.'

It was not an ailing bird that Deirdre found at the door, but a sodden hunter – beard, cloak, brooch, blade. Exhausted.

She sat him down and fed him, and he was astonished at the glory of the girl, even more than the meat and mead he gobbled. The old woman recognised that giddy look of his and scowled in the half-light:

'It is a small price for a bed, food and rest from the storm that you will never breathe a word of this bothy and the jewel that lies at its heart.'

'I do appreciate the saving of my life. But I tell you this, with my father behind me and my grandfather behind him, that if some other men saw this woman that stands before me, they would wish to make a life with her.'

Deirdre was listening hard.

'Who would be such people?'

The hunter straightened, bright with raindrops, savouring words of power and unwittingly delivering prophecy:

'They are the three brothers: Naois, son of Uisnech, and Arden and Allen.'

Deirdre was intrigued:

'And what do these men look like?'

'Their form is often like this:

Hair black as the wintering crow,
Skin white as swan on the pool,
Cheek ruddy as the brindled red calf,
Their pace as the dappled salmon,
Their nimbleness as the deer on the grey mountain.

And with all this they have, Naois is the greatest.'

The old nurse could not ever have been less pleased to hear such a superlative description.

'Take the track away from this bothy. The rain's stopping, likely you've achieved your damage. I have no thanks for your words, or to the young woman that allowed them through this firmly locked door!'

The hunter knew he had gold from this encounter. Far more than venison or wolf fur, he had gold to bring the king. He had walked into a mountain and beheld the most blossoming branch of feminine beauty in this world. He had walked into myth. It was not to the three brothers he went, it was to the king. He spilt his tale immediately.

Of course Connacher, King of Ulster, wanted to see this all for himself.

May morning, May morning, May morning it was,
That the hunter led the king to the bothy.
Earlier than the birds they had risen, earlier than dew,
Earlier than the sun, earlier than the black bear dreaming of trout.

Earlier than everything. That's how it is when you come to steal love.

Connacher's battle-worn heart tumbled down into the dirt when he saw Deirdre.

It's an odd thing when you don't know you've been hunting for something and then suddenly there it is. He didn't notice the old nurse hopping from foot to foot with anguish, he didn't notice the cramped conditions of the bothy. What he experienced was walking into the centre of the May magic and encountering the jewelled navel of the world, drawing down all of the creamy magic of the Milky Way into the glint-black majesty of Erin's turf. Nothing, nothing in any dimension of consciousness was ever going to beat this. His heart was eviscerated by beauty.

Would it not be good for the people for the king to marry the May magic?

Beauty trumps all, then often destroys all.

Deirdre was carried out on the singing shoulders of the king's men on that May morning. Out to meet the world, out to meet the song of what is. The small was over, the vastness had begun.

Deirdre asked for a year and a day before marriage, but with the unfailing promise that she would do so. She had a life of comfort till then.

And there is wind over the mound I lie under.

I, Deirdre, speak to you from under clay.

You felt the turn in the story. I felt it too, the moment the king came to my door, opened up my hill, and me, the flower of the mountain, already betrothed to the words that hunter spoke, that hunter sheltering from the storm.

So how did I come to dying? I shall continue my story.

One day in that year and a day I summoned to give me a moment, the three brothers cantered by. When I saw Naois, a profusion of feeling came over me, all decorum was lost, I was in bloom I tell you, in bloom.

I ran after the brothers though they fiercely counselled Naois not to stop, that my call was the cry of the wave-swans of Connachar. But he heard something in my cry, he heard the woman of the mountain that is in me, and he stopped. I kissed the other brothers once, but him three times, such claiming I gave him. I was crimson with feeling, that holy giddiness. I would not be marrying the king.

He picked me up, placed me on his shoulders and we left for Scotland. It was a sweet life we had there, Naois, Allen and Arden and myself. The boys could lift the salmon from the stream with their hands they were so plentiful, could hunt the dun stag from the arrowed height of their window, so close the beast came.

But the timing came to its end, and Connacher actually invited the three brothers to the wedding, not realising, not suspecting, not soothsaying that Naois had been my firm lover for months now. The wedding in which I was meant to be his virgin bride, his marrying of the May magic.

But the May magic chooses its love, not the other way round. Land dictates its sovereign, not sovereign its land.

I felt a death in it if they went. Of course I did.
I asked Naois to read my dream,
Giving the loudest hint I could.

Naois, son of Uisnech, listen
To what has been night-revealed
Three white doves from the south
Flew over green waves
With a drop of honey in each beak
Fresh and sweet from the hive.

Naois, son of Uisnech, listen
To what has been night-revealed
Three grey hawks from the south
Flew over green waves
With a drop of red in each beak
Dearer than life, they to me.

He laughed it off, but I knew it was a formal uttering.

There was the mightiest scrap when Connacher got wind of my
lover and I.

The diviner from my birth was right, it was a blood blizzard,
an awfulness, and when brute muscle couldn't work he sent his
enchanter after us – Duanan Gacha Druid –

Who threw up a forest in which to halt us,
But we just strolled through the relentless timber.
He turned a vast meadow into a bleak sea and we
Just swam through it, but finally
Duanan turned those waves into jagged stones

As sharp as swords on one side with
An adder's poison on the other.
Though Naois scooped his brothers
And I up on his shoulders
They had brushed the poisoned stones,
And perished soon after.

And my love, my Naois, he gave up too when he saw his brothers
dead. Fell on the death fangs himself. They were the same lad, in a
way.

They dug a pit for the boys, didn't they? And the king squawked for
his triumph and the people had a gander at the three bold heroes in
the deep pit. That's where heroism gets you. Lesser men gob on your
cloak. I begged the workers to make it a big deep wide pit, and on
completion I jumped into it. I was blue dead the moment I touched
my true husband's body.

I am the woman of the mountain
Walking back into the mountain,
Naois is with me, though that is not for your eyes.
Arden and Allen are laughing with us, complete in themselves.

Above our grave, two saplings shot up and bound together, though the king had them cut at the root. They grew again, and then again, he half-mad with his cutting blade, day and night till his new wife told him to cease his work of evil.

And I tell you listener

These old stories are wretched sometimes, but we can't always see what is really going on – bindings between land and lover, sovereign and goddess.

Don't weep the cut flower when the deep root thrives.

stuck needle

And I dreamt I was moving a horse and wagon across Dartmoor in the sunlight. For a little while I was reunited with a woman I once loved to my great cost. She showed me her body that I would remember it and told me she still desired me. Not as a seduction, but a weary fact. How I loved her. When I went back to check on my horse, it started to cry loudly because it thought I was never returning. It was dark in colour and had been badly treated. The horse was singing and crying and trying to encircle me for its own sad comfort.

It's 7.32 on the morning of January 7th. Just getting light. I won't write for the rest of the day. It was the most terrible of dreams and absolute sorrow takes me.

It is now a day later and I've tossed and turned all night, finally admitting defeat and waking properly at 10 a.m. There's that sour and fuzzy feeling that you have already lost a deal of the day. Some utter wanker in a white van has parked next to the woods and is playing techno at full whack, requisite bass speakers causing a mass evacuation of any animal in the vicinity. I can hear it as I write this. Oh, perfect, the woodyard has creaked its devil roar up too, Scylla and Charybdis I am trapped between.

I woke up, ironically, with the song 'I Can See Clearly Now' in my head. Hours later as I buy leeks and hunks of beef for my tea, the very same song pumps optimistically out of the tannoy in the shop. An old woman twitches her hips as she buys up all the Pot Noodles. I swear to god I cannot see remotely clearly. It is not a lie to tell you I will encounter the song a third time before the day is out.

Well, in this mired state I will give my calling song. It is three riddles.

song thirteen

clack clack clack

riddle one

Once I was the weapon of a warrior.
Now bairns have threaded silver and gold around me.
I have had the kisses of fighting men, and have persuaded
A field of laughing men to take to their death.
That sea that is shining I have crossed by ship.
The girls of glimmering bracelets have fussed and filled me,
Then I've been left worn and dowdy on cold planks.
I've watched from a high wall as warriors boozed,
Me a bright prize, ornate with jewels.
I have called princes to feast and sent thieves
Scurrying into darkness
When they tried to steal me.

What is my name?

riddle two

I was walking and I saw a miracle.
Above me a silver beast, loping home
With stolen things between its horns.
By daring and guile and art it hoped
To craft an arbour in the soaring castle of the sky.
But another came, one we all know, shining
Scoring bright and hale both mountain and ridge
And took back the treasure and the crafty one took flight.
To the west it went, revenge on its tongue.

Who would be having such a fight?

riddle three

I can walk under waves
I hunt where you would drown
Canopy of white foam
Shriek of the pummelling flood.
Waves break on high cliffs
Seaweed, stones and sand
Hurl themselves about.
I'm trapped you see.
Weighed down by what's on my back.
Only when the wise man permits will it stop.
My guide, who draws me up from the sea's arms,
When waters are still, gentle and calm.

What am I?

little endymions

Oh for a vale of spring. Tonight, as I cooked up the beef in garlic and butter, I heard the swing-song of the songbirds through the French doors. Oh petals of the tree, spring is still months away, what's the commotion? Maybe there are orchards in bloom, and happy hogs in sunshiney mud, and horse-rides with ample girls of mischief. Maybe it is all at play.

And somewhere in the ivy is a golden owl.

I grind my thoughts around it, try and make peace with it, but it's riveted like parchment to a Lutheran church door. I hope one day, many many years from now, some kid finds the golden owl. Early this morning the owls were so loud, even the cockerel got involved, it was sonic havoc. They'll know where the golden owl is. eBay or the pocket of a poacher.

I wonder what is better for a woman than to be told she is a flower of the mountain.

I simply cannot comprehend a praise higher than that.

I wonder what is better for a man than to be told a wolf runs through his mind.

Tonight I feel like Elk Frodi. You haven't met him yet. You are about to. Out on his lonely high trail, bashing travellers over the head. Corrupted and horny, the lesser-favoured son. I'm Edmund, selling all that is good in this world for a slobber of the White Queen's Turkish delight, feeling her warm woman thigh next to my young boy thigh on the sleigh. I'm Dimitri, penniless with the clap, coming across my sleeping brother and his treasure. Chop chop chop.

These are my dark ages.

These are my dark ages, but these calling songs are lanterns.

There is a man in the snow who never stops weeping
Over a stolen photograph he keeps behind a mirror

I know I am plain like a strike to the face

I know I do not deserve what I have already stolen,
Gains far beyond my fate.

My forest holds these conclusions.
My unworthiness,
My theft of light
From people too slow to grasp it.

I need to walk the skull of the woods.

In these final fourteen days of the ceremony I will go to the forest
much more in darkness and with an empty belly.

YOU HAVE TO BRING ME SOMETHING

Yes, yes, I understand that.

FULL MOON

You Ravilious moon, you Turner moon.

I once stood in the Berlin studio of dissident Chinese artist Ai
Weiwei, and he said to me, 'Tell the west, we want the moon back.'

The Desano of the north-western Amazon say that fishing is best on
the darkest nights, within the span of new moon and first quarter,
but once brightness arrives all hunting and fishing cease. That is the
time to be with your lover. The old women say there is an element
of birth control to this arrangement.

When the moon is waxing it is a placid dog, when it is waning it is a ferocious wolf.

The Seneca say it was the wolves that sang the moon up into the sky in the first place, and that's why they howl. Prehistoric, sacred recognition.

So here, cool moon over hazel bush, here is a story for you. Hell of a story this one. I love it most when my friend Tim tells it by my fire.

close family unit

song fourteen

clack clack clack

I say here and now the name Hring, I remember here and now the name Hring.

Hring was a Norwegian king who ruled the Uppdales. He was a widower, and on the urging of his counsellors and people began the search for another wife. He sent messengers south but a mischief wind intervened and the ships were blown north to Finnmark, where they had no choice but to winter it out.

Snowflakes and blue ice. The gods brought their blizzards to choreograph destiny.

Wandering inland, messengers came to a house with two beautiful women sitting by the fire, a mother and daughter. The daughter was called Hvit, and she was daughter of the King of the Lapps. Her mother was his mistress. The messengers suggested Hvit would make a good wife for Hring. This would be a step up for her. Although it grieved her she could not ask her father's consent – it was a pressing issue – her mother agreeing:

'Out of every trouble comes some gain.'

You should know that Hring was old in the eyes of young Hvit. An old bull. Regal status but lacking vigour.

They married and he was often off at war, whilst Hvit presided, though she was not popular. The only person she was tender with was strong Bjorn, Hring's son. He didn't encourage it, but that was the direction her gentleness went.

Bjorn had a lover, Bera, and they had been close since childhood. She was the direction his gentleness went. But he loved to fight, side by side with his father, and that was where his strength went.

But Hvit got to whispering in the old bull's ear. That she needed Bjorn to not go a-viking with his father, but to stay home and help her watch over the kingdom. There was a big row between father and son, and Bjorn had to cool his boots at the homestead. His face grew berry-red and scarred fists shook when Hvit tried to calm him. He asked her to leave his sight, and for a little while she did.

One day she returned and told him plainly that she would rather be with him than his father. That in the king's absence the opportunity to play under the covers presented itself, to be bed-sharers. All he had to do was betray his father.

Bjorn rose into terrible, hot shape, slapping Hvit and throwing her out of his chamber.

Hvit rose into terrible, cold shape and made spell-speech:

'And you think it better to bed a commoner's daughter. In your stupidity and refusal to obey my bed-wishes I will punish you.'

She struck him with her wolfskin gloves.

'You will become a cave bear. A grim and deadly apparition. You will only consume your father's animals. There will be such a hunger you will consume more of his meat than ever has been taken before. This is a spell without end, you will never be released from it. I bind you Bjorn, I bind you. Permanent and terrible hunger. The ravening is upon you.'

The bang of the spell came from the northlands, from her mother, and her mother before that. Chewed upon, heated up in pan, and smoke-blown into Bjorn's undefended heart.

Bjorn disappeared. Gone. No one knew what had happened. There were search parties, torches lit through the long night and hidden places, but nothing. Of course nothing.

Because Bjorn was now a large grey bear.

He took more of the king's cattle than anyone had ever seen. He would smash them to pieces, gobble them up.

Bera, Bjorn's lover, came across the bear one day when walking alone. And she saw something of him in the bear's eyes. The bear moved away from her peacefully, and she followed after to his cave. In the cave he could take his man shape, and the two were gifted the rapture of reunion.

After a time, King Hring returned, and was informed of his son's disappearance and the huge beast devouring his cattle. The queen urged he act decisively and kill the beast. The king needed to think about the double-strangeness of all this, and delayed any action while he brooded.

At night in the cave, Bjorn spoke to Bera:

'I feel tomorrow is my death-day.

Warriors will hunt me down and trap me and kill me. This is no kind of living for me anyway, you have been my only delight in this misery. The gift I want to leave you with is the ring under my left arm. When I'm slaughtered, ask my father to give you whatever is under the bear's left shoulder. He'll give you this.

You should know that the queen has troll blood, and will sense something is up. When they feast on my flesh, she will want you to taste the meat. Don't. You, as you well know, have pups of ours in your belly. Three of them. Lads. If you consume any of my meat, it'll be clearly visible in the appearance of the boys.

You will raise the boys in the care of your father. If they prove unruly, if they prove to have a strangeness in them, take them to this cave. You will find a chest, carved with runes. Three weapons await. The runes will tell you which son should receive what. The first born will be called Elk Frodi, the second Thorir, and the third Bodvar. I think they will all be strong and their names will be long remembered.'

All night, in the darkness, Bjorn gave much prophecy to Bera.

Early in the morning he shuddered into bear shape and went to his death. Bera followed.

A huge retinue of warriors circled the mountain, each one with dogs. After a chase, the circle surrounded Bjorn and he took his fill of men and hounds, always trying to get within proximity of his father the king. When he finally got there, a blood road on the grasses behind him, he lay himself down on the ground for slaughter.

Those remaining warriors fell upon the grey bear as the king watched. Those remaining warriors fell upon Bjorn as his father watched.

Afterwards, Bera approached the king and asked for what was under the bear's left shoulder. He agreed, and no one noticed her careful hiding of the ring.

The grey bear dead, the mood of the people, especially the queen, was jubilant and a feast of his meat prepared. Bera didn't reveal her identity to either King Hring or Queen Hvit.

When Hvit noticed Bera not eating, she grew suspicious. She stood over her, and carefully cut small pieces of bear meat, insisting she eat. She ate the first, a morsel of the second, and spat the rest out. Not under torture – she said – would she eat more.

Hvit laughed lightly, like a bell:

'I think these little cuts of bear meat may have already been enough.'

Bera returned home to her father, telling him everything. It was a wretched pregnancy.

The first boy was a man above the navel, elk below – ELK FRODI

This name means he has elk-knowledge

The second boy was a man but with the feet of a dog – THORIR HOUND'S FOOT

This name means he has a four-legged disposition

The third boy was just a boy – BODVAR

This name means he has a leaning to war

(And Icelanders whisper he was born with a bear claw on his toe)

By twelve years old, Frodi was a killer. He had maimed and slaughtered warriors of the king. He had the bleak wildness in him.

Thorir and Bodvar followed in such a berserk tradition, so they were all excluded from the games of the people.

Bera took Frodi to the cave. There were three weapons protruding from the rock. A large sword, an axe, a shorter sword. Of course Frodi wanted the grand sword but it wouldn't budge, then the axe, and then finally, angrily, he reached for the small sword. Oh the rock it crumbled and it fitted sweetly in his fist. He tried to smash it against the stone, but so sharp it was it slid straight in. He agreed the thing knew how to bite.

Elk Frodi took his father's gift and left his mother's side. Not even a farewell. He took a road into high mountains and robbed travellers with his blade. Building a hut, he settled in up there.

Bera took Thorir to the cave. The axe crumbled from the rock and into his strong paw. He travelled to Elk Frodi's hut, where Frodi told him of the people of Gautland, and how their king had died and sought another. Frodi told his brother the king's throne was big enough for two men, and whoever could fill it would likely become king. Following his brother's advice, Thorir went to the people, fitted the throne beautifully, and became King Thorir Hound's Foot of Gautland. He was respected and led from the front in battle. There are many sagas told of King Thorir Hound's Foot.

Bera took Bodvar to the cave. Crumbled from the rock came the bright sword meant for him. Bodvar was not meant to rob travellers on high lonely passes, he was not meant to be King of Gautland. He was meant to make good on the death of his father.

When King Hring saw the ring Bera and Bodvar produced, he agreed it must be his wife's magic. In fact, he had long suspected it so. But due to his softness of heart towards her, he begged for no vengeance. Bodvar spoke:

'Banish her and there will be no vengeance.'

Hring could not do this, and offered all sorts of treasure and even sovereignty, but his grandson was not for any of it. In a righteous fury he pushed past the old king and went to the queen's chambers. He carried a rough leather bag and tough string. He wrestled her to the ground of her chamber, covering her head in the pouch. He paraded her through the streets, whilst pulling the string tighter, finally strangling her.

And those that were there say that was only half of what she deserved.

But the king could not recover, and soon died of grief.

Bera married again, to a man named Valsleyt, already an influential man, a jarl. Bodvar was present at the celebrations and then rode away, looking for his brothers.

He would wander the high lonely trails and find Frodi. The Elk-Man would take a blade to his own calf and make Bodvar drink the blood for extra strength. It turned out that whilst Frodi would butcher the wealthy, he gave shelter to the vulnerable in his hall. Bodvar would also be reunited with Thorir, and finally would earn the name Golden Hilt from King Hrolf Kraki.

At the time of these adventures, Bodvar was eighteen years old.

These are things to speak of
When we bang our cups together
And the snow falls.

How the fuck do you earn a name like Golden Hilt?
I want to live in that world. I DO live in that world.

soul creeps out of your mouth

It is in the hours before dawn now, Sunday, January 12th.

This time just before light seems to have a deep sacredness to it. Something, against all the odds, wipes some murk away in the slow hours of the night, and then by morning everything is ready to begin again. It's that word again, freshness. Even for me, a middle-aged man.

I pour coffee on the roots of the hazel tree. It's grown somehow more aplomb the more I gaze at it, just by consistent, delighted attention. But it's also a bit cheeky, a bit anarchic, the way its pale branches spring waywardly out. I do care for it very much. My eyes go up to the mycelium of branches above my head, jet black, interlocking, lacing above me and the sky. I enjoy the drag of my boots over half a foot of leaf mulch as I wearily walk back to the cottage and the secretive warmth of my bed.

And now it is pitch-black night and I am out and about.

Cold and the drip drip drip. The moon's etheric halo, and odd flashes of light that flood the whole circle. A plane far away and up high. A little tube filled with high hopes and crazy breathless oxygen. Every bud and twig on every tree in mad clarity against the moonlight.

Walking by the roaring river, for the second night running I have walked past a stationary white van with the driver's pale light on, no one home. There's a strange feeling coming from it.

Big bad wolf moon.

The next afternoon now, and Storm Brendan is coming in. The shed doors have flown open, leaving agape my much-coveted dry wood store. I've leant heavy rocks against the doors. My car has been moved from the treeline and the rain has the tang of salt in it. Wind rattles the wood burner, the cottage hunkers down for the flogging to come.

It's always a moment, when you are waiting for a storm. In the woods I can see further around than ever before. The bracken is fully stomped down and my eye ranges its longest lupine distance. I drop a little silver in the moss and the bucketing rain-wind picks up.

Buckle down

Raven Tor
Combe Wood
Greypark Wood
Hardridge Wood
Eagle Rock
Cleft Rock
Lovers' Leap

The big spit approacheth

And now I can't stop thinking about the abandoned white van by the roaring river. I brave a mad squall to walk the brimming banks, an eye out for something I would not want to see. For once I pray for a diminishing of the moon, of its lunatic aspect, its twisted-headness. All day my phone has been buzzing with people in pain. The rain is so slanting hard I end up sheltering in my car. When I look at the scrawled words I was writing, it reads, 'sheltering in God'.

I sit in the half-dark with the smell of eucalyptus air freshener and wish that we all shelter in God tonight.

It's been an odd day. I receive a message from my mother for the benefit of someone else.

This is it, exactly:

'My son Martin is distantly related to Ken Kiff but I believe is unaware.'

This is the Kiff I TOLD YOU ABOUT. He's a painter. I trapped a painting behind a radiator, remember? It was somewhere around there. And my mum, out of nowhere, with no conversation leading up to it, drops the fact that he's a relative. This is how this went, no spin. This is how it went.

So as I stand in the forest in the middle of Storm Brendan with my lantern and its scent of paraffin, I'm thinking about Ken and the book I mentioned, *Folk Tales of the British Isles*.

Ken Kiff, good god. I have a calling song for you. A song that is a story that you made a painting from. Ken Kiff is my ancestor. I can say it, I can say it twice, but my head spins to conceive it. In months of haughty ritual weirdness, this is another floaty swipe from the side.

song fifteen

clack clack clack

It was two men wading across a glen looking for sheep. They were knackered, but it was a sweet, warm night, so they settled themselves by a stream. One immediately fell asleep, the other lay awake.

It was a shocking thing when the sleeper's mouth slowly opened and a white butterfly flew out. It trailed along the body of the sleeper, then flew down a rough stone pathway and under a broad flagstone under which the stream flowed. The waking man followed, agape. The butterfly flew through some sedge a couple of times, then settled on an ancient, bleached horse skull. It flew through the eye socket and gave a deep search of the skull before flying back around the sedge, under the broad stone where the river flowed, up the rough path, along the sleeper's body and into his mouth, and then the man opened his eyes:

'It must be getting on now.'

The other responded:

'Whether the day is beginning or ending, I've just seen wonders while you slept.'

'You wouldn't beat mine! I wandered a fine broad road, with trees and flowers on either side, till I came to a vast river. There was a bridge, ornamental and strong that I crossed, best I ever saw. After the bridge I made my way through a fragrant forest until I came to an extraordinary castle. Gleaming pale walls, so elegant, but no one about. I wandered from room to room, overwhelmed by the beauty. I started to grow tired so eventually left, walking back the way I came. It was just incredible to behold, I've never been so enraptured. I was just getting peckish when I woke up and you were staring at me.'

'It seems the soul is a butterfly that wanders while the sleeper dreams. Let me show you your route.'

And the sleeper saw his fine broad road was a rough path, the exquisite bridge was a flagstone, the fragrant forest a lump of sedge, and the majestic castle a bleached horse skull.

And so it is when the butterfly that is your soul beholds your life.

The rain is crazy now so I retreat to the lights of the cottage. That tiny story seems to be telling me everything about this ceremony.

The problem with dreaming, says Patti Smith, is that we eventually wake up.

It is strange for me that you will never quite know the cottage and the hazel bush and the shed with the bearskin in it. At least not mine. But that your imagination will furnish you quite wonderfully with another cottage, bush, shed. From this rambling skeleton of a tale, you will construct an animal to give you warmth or advice.

And later in the continuing storm a rider turns up at my door with a parcel from Minneapolis. In it is a book that I had mainly worked on eight years ago. Publishing can be slow. It took so long that my partner on the project has actually died in the meantime. But I knew this day would come. I gather up a small parcel of his ashes and walk to the river in full, outrageous flood. I crouch by the truly manic torrent and fucking bellow, I swear bellow, some of the words from the book over the crash and watch the book fly for a second into the spray as if my buddy wants it himself. I did nip in and get it but it has a great curve to it now. I felt the grind of bone and saw the grey dust on the whorls of my fingers then let my dear, true, magical friend fly.

It was so great it was so loud, I could shout and shout and shout. I wasn't angry, wasn't quite sad, but mad as a box of frogs.

The moon has fallen into the water and everywhere I can hear it. Not from the direction of the river but above me on the incline, left and right, rumbling through the earth beneath me, moon-water. It's not something I have ever heard before.

The moon is a blast. I heard tell that the Breton women used to cover their bodies so as not to get touched by its rays. If they did, the concern was they would birth a 'moon-calf', get 'mooned' and birth a lunatic child, a deformed child. That's not a sacred way of viewing the moon, it's a spooked way. But it's not all nonsense either, not really. It's just another aspect. I've felt queasy under its power more than once.

But my favourite moon is Keith Moon. There, I said it.

If ever there was a drummer that lived up to his surname it's Keith. Not a bull slamming his hooves to the floor on the two and four, but a skittish, volatile brilliance, decoder of lunar patterns, tidal-sweeper, no one like him before, no one like him after. Keith. His drums spit and swoop over Who records, rarely keep daylight kind of time. And the restlessness of Peter Townshend has been looking for his buddy ever since his death. Pete needs night rhythms, moon rhythms, not day rhythms.

I go to my record player and carefully take off my Little Walter album and put on the Who single 'The Kids Are Alright'. And suddenly I'm crying my eyes out. The sweetness of it, memories of west London, memories of girls, Richmond Park at night and all my kiddish hopes and dreams. Music gets us straight there, no pussyfooting.

And old Vainamoinen sweeps by the window on his blue elk, he shouts over the sound:

—Fucking love the Who.

When I was about five, my dad and I tipped all the furniture over in the front room, so I could run around and around on it like an assault course. He put on 'Summertime Blues' from *Live at Leeds*, and I swear to god my tiny head exploded with joy. It's just the bloody greatest. It's Little Richard great, it's Billie Holiday great, this is Mount Olympus pedigree I swear it.

Years later, as a drummer I rehearsed in the same studios as the Who. I remember Paul Weller sipping on a Becks chatting up the receptionist at a distinctly early hour in the day, Robert Plant and Jimmy Page banging out some tunes next door. I thought it would always be like that.

In less than a year I would be fasting on a mountain and I would have to give it all up.

But dear Keith I do not, for a second, forget you.

Keith sadly is not in today's painting. As I scrawl my hands are

abattoir-red with cadmium oil. I'm making these tiny paintings of
Mayo boats and scenery. Boats that become hills and sometimes
fish. I think I'm a little crazed by the woods at this point.
Mad for the sea.

A week tomorrow this is over.

It's a joy to paint. No one buys them anymore, so storage is the issue.
Every painter everywhere has cupboards stuffed to repletion with
missteps, solid-gold masterpieces and a hundred agonising gradients
between the two. You end up cracking one day and driving ten years
of work to Newton Abbot dump and pulping it between 1970s
shelving systems and woodwormed tables. True story.

Weep no more, pilgrim, it is a great victory just to make your nutty
little paintings.

You are an Irish beekeeper gazing at the mountains.
You are a half-penny lost in the lining.
You are a legal document nailed to the door of the squat.

I feel I have brought nothing back from the forest of any worth to
anyone else.

The January sun is coming in through the window onto my dining
table. In a couple of hours I will pick my kid up from school and we
will walk around our favourite freezing-cold supermarket and fill
the trolley with sensate delight. I can't wait. When she's not here
I start making a low growling sound after a couple of days. Other
people alert me to it. I love putting her sheets through the wash and
plumping up the pillows when I know she's coming home. I will
never love anything more completely and utterly than her.

Blue sky and corvid honks. Ravens overhead. Here, these are for
you, light-bringers:

song sixteen

clack clack clack

A hunter found a run of seal holes. Good news.
He looked around for where to make camp.
Above him flew a black raven who pointed out a spot.
'Below the mountain is where all the hunters camp.'
Pleased by this he settled in. In the night a boulder
Rolled down the hill and killed him, completely crushed.
Raven flew down.
'Why on earth do these hunters believe me?'
It said, pecking out the dead man's eyes.

clack clack clack

There was a kid in the snow whose mother was making him
Raven-skin trousers. Just one more raven needed,
Which the kid found and killed.

At that moment, an old man came past with a big pile of
Dead ravens humped on his back.

'That's mine. I'm the raven man. Please give it to me.'
'No, I need it for my trousers!'

And the boy started to skin the raven. Old man spoke:

'It's over. You're doomed.'

As the boy walked home with his skin he felt drained and tired. He
collapsed, crawling and shouting for his mother.

'Who are you?'
'I'm your son!'
'I don't recognise you. You are an exhausted old man.'

Out of sympathy she took him in and he told her his story.
As he did so, he grew white-haired and covered in lines.
At its completion, he died of old age, there and then.

I've been thinking about old man raven warning you not to start flirting with black feathers until it's really your time. That you have to keep your Hermian wits about you, when the entrancement of croak tells you where to build your camp. Many camps, many boulders, that's me. I always preferred a croak over a trill.

Johnny Cash was a crow to most, but I bet his wife could coax a nightingale.

When Isolde would no longer visit the orchard in the moonlight, Tristan learnt about the opposite passage. Caw caw caw as she finally beckons King Mark to her bed and Tristan sees shadows by candlelight up in the high room, and him down in the scrub. Don't feel like playing your fucking harp now, do you pretty boy? As Mark grinds his unimaginative weight down on your soulmate, and she knowing that you crooned from under the apple bough. She knowing you know what is going on and still she is spreading her legs for the whole ancient world.

Shit hits the fan when the mythological and the acutely personal get cosy. As it always does.

Joseph Campbell used to wax on about the noble agonies of love. I wonder if Joe really, truly burned for it. If he really knew what he was saying. If he stopped his slideshow of comparative mythology for just a moment, undid his necktie and just howled at the whole university crowd who had gathered to see him. I wonder.

Tonight I'm working under eternity's wick at my oak desk, sober and late for bed. I'm thinking about some of the other lunatics, wrapped in their furs, alive and dead, doing the same.

There's George Mackay Brown
Pissed on Orkney, keen for a pretty student,
Germaine Greer giving her canon to Oxfam
Not giving a hoot about what she wrote.
There's a hundred Emily Dickinsons out there
Keen for discovery at the exact moment of their death
Cramming all their life into tight secret journals
But please don't read it now, not when they could actually
Benefit from it. That would be unpoetic.
Know a thousand of that breed.
These are all crazies really, usually AWOL from raising kids,
Inconstant fuckers walking back and forth in front of the newsstand
In case their name is mentioned.
And you wonder how I know such things.

Of course they dangle their dicks, female or male,
These wounded and deranged mammoths, aurochs,
Basically extinct bastard art people. Follow the orgasm
To the end of the line. To the end of the bus route.
To the end of pleasure. To the end of the deer track.
Let the fantasy live. Stand by it. Own it. Be your freak self.
And when you are briefly empty you can zip your skirt up,
Make coffee and go back to the table to write.

He left some time ago, he
Knows the drill. No one is offended.
He doesn't feel unloved.

And the moon-rain came and washed the forest away. Washed
away the hazel bush, washed away the golden owl, washed away
Vainamoinen and Hamer and all the calling songs, washed away any
memory of summer.

My Navy peacoat is pulp in the squall. Always wanted one of those double-breasted captain jackets and here it is, on stage today, centre light on it, take the terrible-beautiful pummelling of the never-ending arse-end of Storm Brendan. Brendan seems to have doubled back in case he didn't truly establish himself the first time round.

Oh Brendan,
Water Giant.
Big Celtic Bastard,
A calling song for you.

song seventeen

clack clack clack

A Cretan king once went to a soothsayer, who delivered him the prophecy that he would one day be decapitated, his head cut off by a man with immense strength. That this man would come from the womb of a sixty-year-old woman. The king absorbed this great anguish and through further enquiry found out that the woman lived on the island.

A great wash of insincere generosity came over the king, and he decreed that all babies should be christened at the palace on his coin. A blessing for all. Well, the sixty-year-old woman turned up with her bairn and the little sweetheart was wrested from his mother and taken to the forest to be slaughtered by two warriors.

Good men, they couldn't face the task, so left the boy wrapped in swaddling and warm in sweet scented leaves, hoping for the best. The best came in the form of a mother bear who adopted the little one, brought him into her warm cave, and weaned him on delicious bear milk. Because of the milk, dark curly hair appeared all over his strong little body. His eyes gleamed happy and brown as he suckled.

This milk coursed through him, giving him unexpected gifts.

Bear milk gave him the capacity to decipher the bird gossip of the forest and the general murmurs of nature; he had a scent about him that the wild recognised. Odd wisdoms hung about him.

Around the same time he was born, the queen had given birth. The young prince grew fast and over the years developed a fondness for hunting. He was allowed to hunt on the arrangement that whatever he caught he brought back in a bag to present to his father the king.

One day he went up into the blue mountains as all young men must, and met the lad we will call Hairy Grylos. The bear-milk boy.

The prince brought back an especially heavy bag that day. He spoke to his curious father:

'My king, I've given you all I've ever caught, but today I ask you let me keep what's in the bag. This is for me.'

And with that out leapt Hairy Grylos, filled with exuberance and mischief.

The king, for now, let his son have his catch from the blue mountains.

Hairy Grylos was fascinated by the palace, and as he grew he haunted every corridor, tried every lock, down into the belly of the castle. It surprised him that the king had so many locked doors.

After persuasion, the prince gained loan of a key. When they finally got in, everything changed. Behind that door was an empty room with a small portrait of a woman on the far wall.

Many years before, the king had longed to marry that woman and she had refused. The depth of his grief was such that the king had kept the door locked ever since. And maybe for good reason, for the moment his son beheld the portrait he too was sick with love for her.

He petitioned his sad-eyed father that he be allowed to set out to
find her.

And she was on an island.
On the island there was a tower
And at the base of the tower
Forty doors with a dragon
At every door.

They told the dragons they
Were looking for the woman
Who refused a king.

These forty dragons were distracted
By the young men's confidence
And told them of another
Tower where there were dragons
That ground their teeth
And sent out fiery terrible sparks.

She may be there.

At the tower the men repeated
The question and darted around the sparks.
The dragons were thrown by this
And spoke of another tower
With even more terrible dragons.

I have to tell you that none of the dragons, nor any number
of serpents, proved too terrible for the boys. Hairy Grylos's
inventiveness always saved them. When they came to the final
tower, the woman who refused a king was there. And this time,
it seemed that she would not refuse a prince. There was some
openness in him, some contact with spirit that attracted her.

As they left, the prince heard a desperate cry from the dungeon of the tower. It was a man begging for bread and water, having been placed there by the serpents. In the full flush of his joy, the prince fed bread and water to the emaciated man, who in a second took the shape of a monster and made off with the woman.

The prince was beside himself. If I had the rest of the winter to tell you, I could only begin to do justice to the search for the maiden. The prince was brought into the care of the dragons and Hairy Grylos searched until he found her, about to be reluctantly married. Using a magical carpet he'd found on the way, he and she managed to escape. After a time, Hairy Grylos, the woman and the prince arrived at the king's castle.

When the old king gazed at the radiance, the once-in-a-lifetime radiance of his son's betrothed, the ancient, anguished longing lurched up in him, blacking out all goodness.

He sent Hairy Grylos out collecting taxes from a people that had never been taxed before, and the king invited his son to his chambers. Once there he committed to the unholy – he wrestled his boy to the ground and gouged his eyes out, stuffing them in the blind boy's pockets and shoving him down a dry well.

Poor Grylos survived many assassination attempts in his tax gathering. He learnt never to sleep in the bed offered that night, but on the roof. For in the morning it would be riven with arrows and knives. When he would then calmly reappear, the villagers would pay up swiftly. But it was a task he hated and questioned to himself.

When he returned, he went searching for the prince, though the king swore him dead, dabbing an eye. Hairy Grylos let his mind uncurl till he had an idea. He took the prince's dog for a walk with a little dry bread. He gave the dog the bread and followed it, until the dog dropped the crust down the dry well.

'Help me Grylos!

Help me!'

But what to do with an eyeless man?

For a second time Hairy Grylos uncurled his mind, and moved out into bird-energies that spoke to him:

'Pull the root out of a tree and grind it till thick juice runs. Wash the prince's eyes in the juice and he will regain his sight.'

Hairy Grylos dug the root up with aching hands in baking heat and then ground it. When the liquid poured he washed the eyes in it and gently placed them in the prince's sockets.

Grylos returned to the possessed king.

'Where is my master?'

'I told you, he's dead!'

'I will walk him into this room alive and without blindness, and I will lay you over my knee and end your life.'

Into the room walked his son, seeing afresh, saved by wild counsel. Of a sudden the king understood the whole story, the prophecy, the sixty-year-old mother, all of it. He knelt and his end was decisive.

And as far as I hear it, as far as I know, the king and queen reign in contentment, with Hairy Grylos by their side, and not a single door locked in the palace.

Two local thoughts tonight:

1. Never eat a fish from the head down, it will scare the fish from

Devon coasts. When you eat from tail up this brings them to our shore.

2. To be wisht is to fall into an odd melancholy which is more than personal. Places have wisht. The forest has its wisht spots, and I was careful not to end up in one these last 101 days.

And last night I dreamt that it was happening, that I was becoming some kind of wolf. First my breathing went crazy, then eruption after eruption of skin and bone, like an earthquake of the body, mad cracking its migration to a new shape.

I woke and was glad to wake. The window was flung open and curtain flapping, the last of Brendan flogging the room with spray. I left it so, pulled another pillow under my neck and commenced night-drifting.

I find I am a Spaniard dreaming the New World.

I find I am a Viking dreaming the Green World.

I find I am a Cornishman dreaming the Gold World.

I scurry by horse and cart over the Tamar to Plymouth docks. Wait weeks for the next ship west.

It took one slave with smallpox to kill off half the Aztecs. Cortés was a sorcerer or so it would have seemed.

Such a plague seemed a form of magic in the hands of Pizarro when he arrived in Peru. A steamboat comes down the river with one nip of smallpox and there goes the village. We're the miracle workers: sea compass, fire-spitting iron, mirrors, sprung clocks. Goddamn it, we'd even learnt to trap time. The Aztecs weren't even sure the whites were human, such was their lust for gold. The Spaniards weren't sure the Aztecs were human due to them worshipping the devil in the form of Huitzilopochtli, the war god.

So, back to the drift.

The Spaniard will die at sea.

The Viking will stay, though his gods will get thinned and depleted.

The Cornishman will stay and help make New England, though his daughter will return. We try and make what we don't know what we do know – all the Yorks, Granthams, Lincolns and Stamfords on the shifting shell of Turtle Island. Despite all the damage we did, despite how magical/terrible we may have appeared, we must have been scared shitless.

This takes me through till dawn. Makes me a zombie for the morning after, though. I prepare a sandwich of tiger bread, peanut butter and honey for my little one, and drive through the floodplains to school.

Sometimes it all feels like such a mess.

It is dark when I get to the forest. The worst of the rains are over and there is a stillness to the place. Murky, but a lively scatteration of stars above. Tonight's calling song is for the oldest inhabitants of the woods. The ones who pixillate.

song eighteen

clack clack clack

I, a young widow, lived at Berth Gron, a lonesome farm in the ancient parish of Llanfabon. After I lost my husband, my last little candle flame of happiness was my son. I'd named him Pryderi, and he was a snug bundle of life.

Llanfabon was overrun with fairy. Everyone knew it, was tangled up with the Otherworld one way or another. The moment night fell, their music would strike up, fiddle and flute from the forest and fields until the cockerel crowed and BANG, all would fall silent. On a dark moon they'd get you strayed in the swamp, and they played any number of tricks if your wits weren't on full display.

One day, of a sudden, all the cows in the top field started to fret. I ran up, but by the time I got there they were munching gobfuls of grass as if they'd never uttered a sound. I felt a deep-down terrible anguish and ran back to Pryderi in his cot. He would have been about three at the time.

Well, there was my boy, but there wasn't my boy. He smiled and reached his arms up for me. Same tuft of hair, baby teeth, but there was shadowing on him somehow. And he spoke clearer than he did before, more words, more measure.

Christ, it was a dizzyingly awful moment.

In the next year, Pryderi stopped growing completely. I'd sometimes look into his cot and it was a little old man angrily staring up at me. Then the features would soften and he'd be young again. I asked him over and over if he was my son, and he always said he was, sickly little smile.

But I knew my boy had been strayed away. This was a changeling.

I had a little angry man as a son
His mood like a caged bull
A weepy cloud longing for the sea
A toddler with his mug in the cider

In the parish we had a man of high degree, a cunning man, and I knew I had to go and see him. He had particular pedigree for making a home in a place called the Castle of Night. This castle had been built from the stones of the old Llanfabon chapel, and was cursed, blighted and utterly haunted. Many had moved in and swiftly moved out. But the man had quietly entered and calmed the place and made his den there. I tell you, that is what you call an achieved position.

So I told him all about my angry-old-man-child. He was quiet and patient and had advice for me:

'This is not as desolate as you may think. If you follow my directive, I can help you. At noon exactly tomorrow, take an eggshell and organise yourself to brew a little beer in it. He will watch but pay him no attention. When he asks you what you are doing, say you are brewing beer for the harvestmen. He will mutter something, but pretend not to hear it. When you are finished and the little old man is in his cradle, come see me and tell me what he said.'

I did all the man from the Castle of Night told me to do, then went to see him later. The changeling had muttered something. When I told him I was making beer he said:

I am ancient this day
I was alive before my birth
I remember that younger oak
A tiny acorn in the earth
But I've never seen the egg of a hen
Brewing black beer for harvestmen

I remember something moved across the pedigreed man's face when I told him.

Next the man told me to wait four days for the full moon. At midnight to go to the place where four roads meet, above the Ford of the Bell. That I was to hide and report back what I saw. That if I was glimpsed his own life would be in danger.

So I waited. Waited at the lonely junction of four roads above the Ford of the Bell. Waited under the baleful, bloated moon as a melancholy swept through and around me. I sat in deep silence and for a long time absolutely nothing happened.

It was only when the moon was obscured by long, dreamy clouds that the distant music began. It was silver and beauteous and a rapture all of itself, that music. I was spell-whacked by it. A procession of fairy made its way past me. A vanguard, hundreds of them singing. And just as I could barely take any more beauty, the cloud cleared and the moon shone down directly on the face of my son at their centre, my true Pryderi.

I had to grip a thorn bush not to leap out amongst them and claim my lad, my dear, dear boy.

Even though it was dawn, the man was waiting at the Castle of Night when I got to him. I told him about waiting at the crossroads, the music, the procession, my son amongst them.

He took out a calfskin book, huge it was, and took his time reading through it. After a while he gave me strange instruction:

'Track down a black hen, absolutely night-black, not one with a white feather or any other colour. Understand?

Kill it, but keep it intact. Light a fire and bake the hen before it, feathers and all. Block every passage, crack or holes in your wall, just the chimney open. Stay absolutely transfixed on the black hen, don't look at the changeling, just the hen, until the last black feather has fallen off.'

I had to troop the length and breadth of the parish with the angry-old-boy-man strapped to my back, gurgling, 'Mother... mother...' down into my chilled ear. Made me gag. I searched farmyards, bothies, even neighbours' fields whilst they snored until I finally located one of this rare breed without a single coloured feather. Black as coal, as rook, as night. Nigredo black.

And it baked
The black hen baked
And the boy-man stared
As the black hen baked
And slowly shed its iridescent
Feathers

He called to me and I'd reply
But no way would I look at him.
Not when he groaned or cackled
Or crooned would I look in his agitated direction.
But the trance of the thing took me

I was enswooned, I went under
As I watched the delicate feathers fall
I fell into the darkness of the feathers
I fell into the mind of the black-feathered hen
And I heard the music, that crossroads music
And when I awoke the little angry goblin was gone
And I heard my boy's voice from the procession outside
The fairy had come even in my black-feathered swoon
I heard them I saw them

And my boy grew strong from the wan, elfin shape they left him in.
He recovered, but always with an ear for music, and the moon.
And a friendship with the cunning man.

I sit in the forest shivering in a Castle of Night and the stars brook celebration over my head. For all the children walking back out of fairy.

Denizens, that is my story to you on this night of 17th January.

*

The morning brings a crust of frost. I break crusty bread, lather it with butter, two eggs and salmon. A great mug of tea. I sit on the porch and am thoughtful.

The tree wants feeding again, gifting again. Once the particular contact is made, be ready for maintenance, my friend, be ready. No one wants a hazel bush with hurt feelings.

I am aware that I am almost out of time, that the ceremony only has a few days left. There are bags under my eyes that were not there when this began. I wake up every day not where I fell asleep. I am run through with dreaming. And still I'm sad. It will be important not to go back to the hazel bush for a while when this is done, otherwise I suspect it – this – may never stop.

keep looking till you see the story appear on the walls of the cave

Higher up in the woods this afternoon kicking at a woodpile. It's utterly unusable but sweet to find the pile nestled between oak and hazel, as if ready for any passing wayfarer. It'll be here I'll be coming to for the last night of the ceremony. I want to be deep in the skull of the woods for the last push.

Y'know it's here I fell into the belly of a horse. Do you remember that? I wonder if I can get out from a wolf this time. It's a rookie move to outstay your welcome. The trees are crooked and bald, and have bushwhacker Oz magic against this sudden blue bank of sky we've been having. My imagining of the deep old Australia I have never met.

And under my boots: bodies, bones, arrows, swords of the Britons. It'll be here at the hill fort I shake my horse-rattles and make my songs.

Bucca / Dyer

Big fellows both

I wouldn't want to interrupt your peregrinations, but I'll be there
perched in the centre of the Bard Skull this coming Tuesday night.
I'm just a scruffy little poacher, not worth noticing. But I wouldn't
want you coming across me out of the blue, so to speak.

Hereward the Wake are you out there in the dark this night?

When you were dangerously lost in midnight Rockingham woods
on the way to attack the Lincolnshire town of Stamford, a vast wolf
appeared and guided you to safety, a candle flaring up on every
branch and shield to lead you safely through the darkness.

Will such holy candles light up the wood for me? Illuminate the chase?

Jack of Batsaddle, you who killed the last English wolf, are you
skulking out in the dark this night?

But be it 1375 or this very night, I wonder if the Wake's wolf is
stalking you tonight.

St Brannoc of the Beasts, the one who can make cattle leap from
the centre of the pot, serve you fresh milk after their death, have
wild deer draw your plough, maybe you will join me for a spot of
breakfast if I return from the great, the unsmashable Holne Chase,
this Devonian Yggdrasil.

It is colder than a witch's tit today, and the radio whistles a Siberian
sweep is coming in. Minus six tonight and dropping. I need to keep
my energy for tomorrow night and as I jump over the water creek
to my spot, this time, for the first time, I notice it is silent and slick
with black ice. There's a lot of energy up on the branches, birds
everywhere frantic for food as the world turns itself finally to iron.

There's a surprise when I come down by the hazel bush.

There's a bunch of lads standing there, with a dog. They don't have phones, and their clothes are odd for modern kids.

They've walked across Wolferland to tell me something.

One of them looks impassively at me and speaks.

—They said it was the end of the world. What was happening in 1940. To be in France in 1940 felt like the end of the world.

Our names are Marcel – that's me – Simon, George and Jim.

(He gestures to the other kids.)

Simon had a dog we loved to walk, a little fox terrier with ears black as lumps of coal. We'd wander the hills nearby, strolling through the pine trees. It was late September.

The hound bounded ahead and seemed to disappear into a hole. Being young and up for anything, we cleared the moss round the hole and climbed in after him. We couldn't hear him bark you see, and he always barked when we called, always.

We climbed down, into the dark, held our nerve.

And what we found was the mighty underneath.

It was the horses we saw first.

Mane, tail, full-bellied horses, processing in front of our torch light. Under the ground there were horses. There are HORSES under the ground.

With time's benefit, this all sounds exciting. But at the time it was shit scary. Because we saw more down there, huge cows and ponies, bison, even characters that seemed partially human. Animal sorcerers.

We touched the paintings, scared they would tremble and snort. We smelt oil ochre on our hands. There is a magical rumour that we could only find the cave because we looked on it with young eyes. We saw as children saw. That adults could come and not see anything until we made them look again, and again. Our eyes being young, the images came slowly up through the rock. I mean the rocks rearranged in front of our eyes and the paintings appeared.

We had found Lascaux.

Our lives were never as they were after that. Never.

And they say now, in your time, that it is the end of the world.

Underneath every single person in the world is a cave filled with unimaginable wonder.

And I walked with them awhile, chucking sticks for their dog.

Last day. I am assembling the kit for the final long sit. Up in the Celtic fort. Lanterns, bearskin. Freeze or not, I'm not making a fire. It'll dissuade the very beings I'm talking to. No food no drink. No sudden moves. But I'll take my old Hopi night owl blanket. I will need my owl eyes.

I will need the old face behind my everyday face to push forward.
I will need mud from the bottom of the Durius.
I will need two rocks so my clack is louder still from rocks a thousand thousand years old.

It is bright, euphorically bright, and stone, stone cold. This abrupt change of weather at the end of this seems almost curated, and I'm grateful. I walk along the Durius, past an eviscerated woodpigeon, hundreds of tiny feathers everywhere, white and grey, delicate. Like it exploded. I pick my way down the bank to the freezing waters. I slip my hands into a tributary and pick out two rocks for the midnight sit. The thrill of winter water over my fist.

The rocks have a wonderful coppery sheen, and scent of sweetness about them. Both feel fabulous in the hand, oddly warm, and one clear jagged edge each, like a runic mark. Later when I will gaze at them on the kitchen table I will see that they actually slot together.

I am approaching the time I need to bypass language.

The sky before dusk this last night is the palest pink and grey. As I say words of fondness to the hazel bush, the woodyard even now is in full goose-step thud to match the headache that's come on. I look to my left and see endless holly bushes squatting triumphantly up the hillside. Fit as bloody fiddles, butter wouldn't melt, impervious to the cold, the rain, the bearded man standing in the gloom looking at them. As I look at the mulch of oak leaves around their base, I see the Holly King has triumphed over the Oak King again. But the times they are a-changing, dear spiky god.

The whole wood is sepia now, and minutes from utter darkness, and some mad fucker in the woodyard is still feeding logs into the grinder. Why not get football lights in so the business can go 24/7? Someone with bills to pay, just like the rest of us.

As I walk out of the wood I am transfixed for several minutes by a star, the first star I see. Sirius, you old dog, let's bound back to the cottage together, woof woof.

Early evening, the phone rings. Only three people ring on the landline: my father, a diviner of the runes, an Irish comedian. That's it. It's always good to pick up that phone. Tonight it's the old man.

He tells me, with no preamble or enquiry, that I am a descendent of the infamous Christian martyr John Porter, a man who was literally left to rot in a prison cell for daring to read the Bible out loud, bringing people closer, not further away from the words. Of course I think of Hamer and his life work in defiance of priestcraft.

As I scrawl this, down to my left is a stack of books by the famed mystical Christian martyr Giordano Bruno. I didn't know I had a kindred in my blood. Porter's heresies seem far milder than Bruno's, and the punishment enforced Luciferic. Digging around a little, I find that he seems to have queried the notion of communion as the literal body of Christ, and that, alongside a propensity for outdoor preaching, did for him.

Kiff and now Porter. It appears I must have been calling for ancestors all this time. I hope this gives Hamer a little less to carry. If the news had arrived tomorrow I wouldn't have been able to add it here, but my dad, unknowingly, just got it in under the remit of the 101 days.

And now it is time. The trudge up to the fort is sobering as the night rapidly descends past freezing. There is fox bark and owl call as I lay a crescent moon of creamy milk on the oak-leaved mud, then a crescent of good whisky.

It is really, murkily dark and my eyes haven't adjusted yet. There are miles of trees and hill drops and slumbering stags on every side. No quick escape. I settle in the *temenos* of the hill fort – a place literally set apart by ridged banks – and sit down amongst the hundreds of thousands of fallen leaves on my owl blanket. Underneath the mulch the ground has a terrifying iron freeze to it. And is filled with the pale bones of the Celtic dead.

I settle under my blanket and find I have nothing, just nothing to say. There are no more songs left.

For a little while my back is high-alert straight and when I hear a nearby thwack of wood in the pitch black of my front and centre vision, I am utterly flooded with adrenalin. I just sit and sit and sit. I had thought there would be words of gratitude or barter but I'm dumbed by it all. The deep darkness of the wood, the dazzling brocade of stars, the clear blue hoot of the owls.

There is no need for words of complaint or even deference.

Time passes in the pure experience of it all.

I find I am experiencing something unexpected: happiness. I am enjoying this. I think an odd thing in this condition:

I love Flann O'Brien more than Plato
I love Brendan Behan more than Socrates

This gives me an extraordinary sense of resolution. Of pleasure in fact. A settling.

I watch the Plough overhead and I think about John Porter, my third ancestor of this journey, my Giordano Bruno, starved, mangled and rotted for daring to riff on holy words. I can't feel him yet in the darkness, but I wish him well.

Then I am concentrated, focused and utterly there,
And I remember I have river stones in my pocket

I beat them together and / and /
And / something else happened.
This is exactly what happened.

I glanced to my right in the darkness and I see it

I see a huge, falling arrow of light descending through the air into the forest earth. The effect is like a reverse firework, it narrows as it hits the ground, but it was far wider up till then, bands of emerald green, pearly white and gold. Really like an upside-down firework, or a kite shape with the point near the ground. There is no sound.

It isn't high up in the sky, it is much lower. Just a ways to my right. It's big.

The tip of an arrow. A piercing of everything. An entry to the impossible.

I see it. I see it like I see the washing up, school reports, and flat tyres. With my ordinary eyes. But I don't know if my eyes are ordinary anymore.

It is the deepest uncanny, sustained for maybe four seconds and then everything is plunged back into black. It is coming down, not going up. It is as if the light descends into the fontanelle of Holne Chase, into the Bard Skull.

An impossible, beautiful arrow.

clack clack clack

It was the most wonderful of all the calling songs.

I stand from here on in, moving from foot to foot it's so cold. Again, real, clear, uncomplicated happiness. I am soaked in wonder.

I am shuffling from foot to foot with the Lascaux kids and mother wolf, daughter wolf, old Vainamoinen, crane women, cripple storytellers, all the stories are shuffling together, Hamer is with me, and Ken and John, the ancestor boys with frost on their shoulders, hooting away.

And then, somewhere deep after midnight I fell

I fell into the darkness of the hen feathers
as the white crane flew away and the black hen baked
I fell into the sleep
that would make bear fat drip lovely from my paws
I fell into the mountain flowers
like all of summer in one day.

And I am again the man riding his horse and cart in the Dartmoor
sun to his old love and she is wearily shaking her head but sadly
beckoning and my horse the black horse forever is crying loud and
turning in circles in its distress.

I fell into the warmth of curling by the wood stove I gripped the blue
elk's reins as some young twat threw a bolt of malice and I was that
idiot at war with everyone bigger and wiser than me and I screamed
I screamed when I saw the man with the ravens hitched up in a great
black mass on his back and I am screaming now as he grins his pale
face at me and raises one thin shhhhhhhhh finger to his mouth.

Wolferland bangs and crashes around me, cuts and pastes the stories
in maddening shapes and I on my knees in the pitch-black Pict-black
night in the very centre of the world. And above is and could only
ever be the Milky Way and I watch this as Putu the hole the woman
who is pulled apart by horny northern men and constellates into
another woman and then another woman and then another woman
fucking and maddening and brillianting their way through the ages
and the lonely kirk has the red candles lit and I cry in the snow.

It is only my wolf my soul trusts enough to talk to.

I said that a hundred years back and it is here now in this sharp and
marvellous night.

I still have not ventured back with Elana to the court. No one I
loved has made the call naming the husband that stops time and
space. I am flying over the Hebrides with the waters of life and

death to save the second or third or fourth mashed-up version of myself.

honk honk honk

And the trees are talking ravenese to each other.

And the trees are no longer leaved but feathered, there is not bracken but fur underneath me. And the leaves are up off the January floor and under my fingernails, and vines unwrap and come in through the mouth and ears. Such a humming. My blood is green. And everything is beating like Drake's drum, bringing down the magical children of the Milky Way. The trees are bones now and are thinking big thoughts like spasms through me. Some trees are covered in owl feathers some rook and some sparrowhawk. Their tree roots are now big, scaled claws.

And then, over time, they are roots again. Gradually the choreography settles.

At some point in the outstanding weirdness of the night it is finished, and I wend my way over the ridged mud tracks and low-lying fog back to the lights of my cottage.

This extraordinary contortion of a night is over. I am coming out of the wolf-womb now. As I walk through the woodyard at 6 a.m., everything is finally silent, the tractors and machinery glitter-white with frost.

In the early morning, I find I have something in me that wasn't there before. Something is in me like a mineral or splint of bison bone or a spirit light.

It is these words:

Inhabit the Time and Genesis of Your Original Home

I'd heard old Vainamoinen refer to his songs a little like that, but at the end of this I realise our calling songs are trying to call us back to *ourselves*, to our naturalness. They are a spell to break spells, they are a great returning. This is a great returning.

They are a beautiful arrow piercing our body to help us remember.

When I get up and walk from this ceremony, I am to be my original home. When I speak, I speak the music of that place, when I call, I call in the time signature of that place. Not a distortion, or facsimile, but real time, real home. Ultimate naturalness, a den of beautiful learning.

It's how the gods intended us to live.

The salmon moves through deep waters to its source. The wolf howl is the most pristine sound in all creation.

That howl is morning has broken, night has crested, we exist, we live.

Maybe this is what Hamer was looking for in his travels, maybe this is what Ken Kiff was painting, maybe this is what Vainamoinen made at the beginning of things. Maybe he is my old grandfather. Maybe this is the fat in the bear's paw that helps us remember, maybe this is where riding the back of the wolf is taking us, maybe this is crane-woman knowledge, maybe this is flower-of-the-mountain knowledge.

These nine words were worth 101 days.

Inhabit the Time and Genesis of Your Original Home.

We lie down in the tail of our name
& we are ourselves at last.

part four

unriddling

I rub out the trail behind me:
Double-back, obscuration,
Disappearance, chicanery,
And when you least expect,

Attack

I seen you nibble on seaweed and conifer leaves, lie still like a
sun-browned plank all afternoon in the meadow, yet would not be
dragged by your ears into a field sullied by rabbits. There can be a
foulness to them, a brutishness many don't spot. The buck rabbit
cracking the skulls of a baby hare with its teeth, slaughtering a whole
strew of little ones within minutes. Don't see that on the Easter
cards, bloody tarts.

Hare.

I seen you out the corner of my eye, gathering your familiars in
a circle on my lawn, under the roses. Seconds of chat, then one
odd, high call, like a human in distress. Then out, onto the moors,
stopping only to breed and eat and sleep. Every time there is a clap
of lightning a hare has taken seed; when hare sleeps in heather, the
next morning it leaves the shape of a weeping girl. Hare, you are as
social as a punch in the face. And I think there is little magic greater
than yours.

I seen you swim out into the Atlantic squall when I was seven years
of age, I seen you keep pace with William Pollexfen's ship, the
Dasher, as he sailed out of Brixham and into the arms of Sligo. He,
Yeats's grandfather, the sail bearing your rough insignia.

You were on deck sheltering in the shade of a barrel when Tristan
and Isolde drank their potion. You snoozed as they fucked like
pagans in the sun. You are fortunate, in the way that you are. You are
a lucky coin.

People say you are cold, but I heard the shriek as the kestrel hovered over your babies. The hawk will always win – so swift in bashing air – but I saw you punch one sideways as it lifted your wriggling kin. I seen you box to your death, skull caved and spit-chewed, upright and moon-drunk as the bigger bastard kills you but can't murder your spirit. Can't be done, to kill the spirit of the hare. I seen three Welsh farmers stuff the barrels of their guns with the root Black Bryony and still you stayed stock as the air trilled with the deadly twigs. Not one hit you, just withered like their cocks as you showed them pandemonium.

It's not cold to fight like that, not cold at all.

A hare tooth has a terrible magic. They never stop growing. Frightening. I have six under my pillow. It magics the fucking, keeps a man hard. I've seen you crawl up from the river into the forest edge at dusk to shorten your teeth on the trunks of trees. God help an orchard if you get your hands on it. Ring-barking the apple trees, round and round, up on your hind legs like a god. A shit you could not give. But I've never seen you breed in the woods, only out under a thorn bush, facing the sun. Shameless. Even when pregnant you can take another seed, start growing another, and another, and another.

I told you before but you didn't listen: under my cloak there is a hare that is telling me things.

When I sit on Big Rock I can see all the way to Dawlish. I can see the sea. It's that vast, what Hare can spot. Hazy things, far distant, in and out of focus.

Rationalists call what I see mirage,
Mystics call it prophecy.

I never go to Big Rock at night anymore, my legs get strayed from under me. Well, I *will* go, just when I need to rattle someone. With my hot little pan of herbs to blow. To dissuade an enemy from a bad decision, and to never, ever take aim in my direction. The pan smokes up, and I will blow and say three words. The message locates its owner in a fraction of a second. Less than that maybe. That is all and only that will get me up to Big Rock in the dark.

Solemnity has come to the world. A sickness. Everyone, prepared or no, is journeying the deep interior. Most of us without compass, sobriety or even much enthusiasm.

But Hare can see on my behalf, here under my cloak. I can see for miles. Around every forbidden corner.

We are the last seer on Dartmoor. The rest are whimsical bluffers or nasty bastards.

So what should a human do when they get out of solitude?

Make new stuff. Not like the old stuff. A time to recreate the earth. No more pussyfooting.

So with hare-eye I am looking over the hills at my old manor, Torbay.

There is a crescent moon of concrete that covers Torquay. I think I will be lifting it up. Tearing it off. Why not? Just cranking the thing up on its crumbling elbows with the dark-dog-strength of Cú Chulainn. In this time where everyone is sheltering, I can get away with this kind of shenanigans.

Let's rip the plaster off this constipated county. If I wrench the concrete up, all the exiled giants can grimace their way into the light. The ones that Brutus of Troy scattered. A brute, that Brutus. The old ones can scramble up out of a three-thousand-year-old dark, big and shouty, ablaze in their jubilance. They will do all that hollering because – above Cockington Primary School and Torbay Hospital and the new ring road to Newton Abbot – they will glimpse the distant ridge of the Dartmoor tors, their ancient, solitary, pugnacious home.

Up you come, you famished originals, you smashed-up, moon-faced indigenous. Shuffle that ring road, arms above your heads like you've gobbled ecstasy, weeping and vowing never to fight again now all this May morning freedom is upon you.

RIP RIP RIP

Goes the concrete and the burger van and the bowling lawn. It's a right proper smash-up. I can't stop now. I am amok in the mosh.

RIP RIP RIP

Goes the Imperial Hotel, the kebab shop, even the Princess Theatre where Max Bygraves shuffled his song and dance act. The lot, down, in under a minute.

And fook! bang! crash! Here comes the tremulous wallop:

Up burst lost knyghts of Camelot, centaurs, Pooka, naiads, dryads, Dylan Thomas with a pie-ad, clutching his sloshing pint of Best. Up you glorious Fianna, sweep the beach clean of needles and kiddie-fiddlers, stove them, swipe them and banish them into the beetle-black sea.

This is the punk rock move. Jesus and the moneylenders.

Here come the culture-makers, ready or not.

This is my rocky little Ithaca, what I am describing to you.

I am always thinking about this bay. It's my earliest prickles of consciousness, you see. There is a cove in which, one summer's day, my father lost his wedding ring. Slipped off into the blue. And he dives, he dives, he dives to find it. In and out of the centuries he will dive. In and out of friendships, love songs, religious texts, he will dive for the union of him and my mother. And I say that is a worthy splash. He will never stop diving.

And I am diving now, like him, into the deepest recesses I can. Another kind of union.

Newsflash! It's happened. The concrete is upended, and out charge the unruly guard of arcane Britannia. It's fucking brilliant. I love this kind of thing.

I note that myself, as a smaller me, has crawled out too. Something young and buck-wild has erupted in me as well.

Me as kid. Hidden in my face is my old face, but I have a young face too. This one the giants stick on their shoulders as they pass his house on Pilmuir Avenue, and I glimpse the gleeful scamp. Boy-me is shouting something but I can't hear him yet.

It's odd to see 'little you' on the shoulders of a giant.

I don't know how changeable the mood of a giant is, I hope they don't eat him. There's not much flesh on your inner child, anyway. Hare is whispering he may, indeed, be gobbled.

But Martin's been gobbled before. Gobbled at ten, twenty-three, twenty-eight, forty-two, terrible gobble, gobble, gobble. As I say, wasn't much to gobble. He wasn't full-fat then. Auditioning for the role. Takes so long to become a man worthy of a clinked glass, there has to be so much slaughter before he can even say a single word with any swing to it, have any pistol-powder in his saddlebags. We don't trust a man that was never clobbered.

And now earth is clobbering us. And we need to stay down and take the kicking. But even when we are battered, we are imagining. Even when there's blood in our piss, our frivolous little mind is working on stuff, skipping around as the blows cobble our skull, posting and zooming.

Our deepest cultural infection is imagination.

The poison AND the remedy, the great queasy lurch of mind-magic. Imagining. We can't stop doing it.

As I mash up Torquay seafront, I rip up all psychic tidiness. All the wires and lights are gone, the angels are back in the fields. It's all coming back, because I say it's coming back. I say it in a certain, particular way, and the god that lives in the idea crawls out of my mouth and is amok in the world.

I can still see Martin from the seventies, wobbling about on the shoulders of Goemagog. I will colour the kid in for you a little, sketch him.

In his House of Origin he knew that some stories gave off light, some smells, others colours. He knew he didn't have to decide a favourite, but could be dumbstruck by the fragrant stupor of them all.

He loved highwaymen very much. Enormous and unexpected acts of gallantry. True vengeance. Journeys north in the middle of the night, secret societies, wild horses in the fields, witchy girls in abandoned castles.

A good movie would literally blow him off his feet. He would always walk different out of the cinema, like he was just trying out his body for the first time. He would make little changes to his personality, but no one would notice. A little Zorro here, a little Doctor Zhivago there. He didn't want an anorak, he wanted furs; he didn't want the bus, he wanted a chariot. Life was going to try to slap that shit out of him, but it would fail. He was always bursting into rooms, just in case something terrible was happening that only he could address. He prowled about, certain that he was under observation by Cossacks who were about to fix him up with a sabre, horse, and a little gold. That was the tempo, the register, the pitch of what crawled around under the kid's skin. He was all set for disaster. And he got it. And here we are now.

When everything blows up, whatever's just-about-left gets another petition at a good story.

If we are freshening the joint up, then we need a gabble of stories to do it. The new-old wonder. Let the strangeness of Dartmoor speak to the strangeness of other worlds back and forth.

So up from the ripped-up seafront, and our ripped-up schedules and our ripped-up souls, come stories. And it is the young part of ourselves that will tell them.

These stories you will hear through the high winds of my rant are to steady us.

They are a back and forth between the very far away and the awfully close. That's a dangerous thing to do in these times, can be misunderstood. It's a wild seeking of echolocation I'm after, a banging up against a warm body in this time of chilly distance.

Martin from the seventies speaks with the voice of a Siberian woman on the back of a moon-pale giant. I can't know if we are back with him forty-five years ago, or he with us.

But sometimes you need something from far away.
To tell you exactly what you stand upon.

Instruct us, please.

❧

There is always a moment when a daughter becomes a bird.

This was my time.

I lived on the taiga with my mother and father and two sisters. When we went to collect berries, we would turn shape into wild geese, and fly out over open water. It was in this bird shape that we got to visit far sea-islands. One day we saw something very odd on a lonely outpost, we saw a man with only one side to him. As he breathed you could see his lungs and heart move. This scared us and we would swiftly fly away. But food was scarce and soon mad hunger would drive us back out to the far sea-islands.

One afternoon, everywhere we landed, the Half Man would scamper after us and we would take wing. He hadn't learnt to hide his heart, we could see it there, banging away, and it terrified us.

We came to a place of so many berries we could barely carry them, overjoyed we were. So focused on our gathering, we didn't notice the dusk sweeping the afternoon under her arm, and a pale hand steal my wings from where I had left them.

I panicked but my sisters mocked me, claimed I'd set it up, that I had a fancy for the Half Man. I did not. By now it was almost dark but my sisters refused to help me search for my wings and flew as geese back to our parents. I was alone, wingless, on a far sea-island.

Of course he came from the darkness with my wings, of course he did.

He asked to be my husband, of course he did. I jutted my chin and spat, but as hours were swallowed into the blue time of night I was even more afraid of being alone than being with him. So I agreed, I would have died otherwise.

He took me back to his hut and we began our life together. Just like that.

But I never got used to his halfness. I would lie with him, but I did not want to see his jumping heart, jumping lungs. But at night that was how I learnt of sex, with Half Man.

Soon he had seeded me, soon I had a pup in me.

I'll say this: he could hunt.

Once the baby was born all he did was hunt. He brought home more meat than ever we could eat: reindeer, elk. He stuffed all storage with hunks of flesh. He hunted by foot, not horse or reindeer.

But there was something strange about it, it would turn to rot if we weren't careful. Maybe all young husbands are like it. He was fanatical about it.

One day when he was hunting, my sisters burst into our camp and swept me and our son away.

As we flew over the head of Half Man our kid shouted out to his dad, said we were being taken to my old home. Below, he just about lost his mind. I was scared, even high above him. He aimed an arrow at my sisters but it hit the hand of our son, taking a finger clean off. I heard Half Man moaning and crying at this, and gathering up the arrow and finger into his hunting pouch.

I knew this would not be the end of it. God no.

Half Man came looking. Not for one day or two, not for a week, but for a full year he looked for us.

He would die before he quit. I knew this about him already. I admired it.

He came to our settlement, and looked at the kids playing stick games. He saw a boy who was in worse shape than the others, battered and scrawny, bruised head and thick scars. This was our boy. We did not live in a peaceful tent. We did not live in harmony.

He sat with the mangy boy and produced the finger from his hunting pouch, and it did indeed fit the stump on our lad's hand. The boy wept, said he had no father, and that he was knocked about by my sisters if he tried to enter the hut by the main doors. That they would set about him with big, heavy sticks. It was true, this awful thing my son said. Half Man told him he was his father, but the mangy boy struggled to believe him. He spoke to his son:

'Let's go into your hut.'

The boy walked in first and my sister had at him with her staff. When she saw his father behind him, she threw herself at his feet. Oh forgiveness, she asked. Be sweet, be sweet. The sisters made a huge feast and brewed tea. They ate in silence till it was time to sleep. In the morning, Half Man invited the husbands of my sisters to see who was the best shot with the arrows. They readily agreed, desperate to kill him.

First the eldest shot, then the second, but with the skill he had at jumping – jumping heart, jumping lungs – he was able to leap faster than they could aim. His turn.

He killed them both – arrows to the chest – then walked into the hut and killed both my sisters.

I watched. Then he took me and our son home to the far sea-island with him.

I began to understand the hunting the Half Man did was not quite as simple as just killing animals. One day when he was far from me, he took off the half skin that disguised who he really was. He hung the skin at the top of a pale larch tree and returned to me.

When I saw this handsome man taking his boots off at the end of my bed, I shouted at him!

I told him my husband was not as other men, he was Half Man.
He seemed to like this, and gave me the directions to the larch tree.
Where I saw the skin of disguise hanging from the pale branches.

It is a moment when you see your man finally in his fullness. I have
never kissed anything as much as I kissed this new shape he was in.

Now I live with my Full Man and our kid, on a far sea-island.

We squirm when people get killed in the old stories, even the bad
ones. But it usually gives me a sense of tremendous relief. I love it
when something that wishes you harm gets wiped out. No talking
circle, no counselling, just sharp arrows. Makes me relax, reach for
the cigars. Lightens the mood. Kids understand this kind of dynamic
truth. They can detect a pulled punch in a fraction of a second.

Our souls are appalled by us.

It's taken months of aloneness to even lift that fragile thought
to parchment. I think what I've been writing circles around that
statement; it's like a rotten plank that keeps bobbing up to the surface.
For me at least, it's good to know my approval ratings are down.

All these half men and half women wandering about, what a
sustaining image, so good to know. Remember to warn them on
Tinder: *there's currently only half of me available, and you really may
want to check if your sisters warm to me first.*

And how much do I hunt down and kill that I don't even have the time
to consume. What rots and buzzes and hisses in piles around me?

It's now I see something. Martin from the seventies is waving at me.

He's missing a finger.

I lost one as a kid, and many years later my father would recognise me by that damage. He carries it in a bag round his neck.

I pity the children with a full set of pinkies.

We will collect other ones with damaged hands now. The story is telling me to do so. When you smash the concrete you'll find giants and mangled, beautiful kids. Lads and lassies the like I worked with for years.

The Giant Procession can be seen at the Penn Inn roundabout, at the entrance to Newton Abbot, still heading toward the old homestead, Dartmoor. There's no one around, but the giants are slobbering all over the hot cross buns at Sainsbury's. There's more now, gathered with them. A few kids in shell suits have slipped in with them, keen for another life, nicked a few tinnies. They have the heads of feathery hawks, stabbing their grimoires with long enthusiastic fingers. Gangly youths lift a shingle of hungry eyes up to the moor. Half of them noble men and women in some other life. Some very distant other life. They need a lightning strike, or something close.

Hare knows some of the faces, from those ages back. Long before Newton stood.

So now, dear Hare, a story for the story Martin from the seventies told us.
Give them something of what you know.

—No, fuck you. I'm not an ATM. Not a jukebox. Talk to me proper first. Say my many names. I need something from them first. They are sick to the back teeth of being given things for free. The artfulness of theft is better for them than handout. But this will be neither.

So, against some wicked odds the Newton Abbot Road Men and Women intone, scrolling down an iPad:

Old Bouchart who makes the way,
Acre-flogger, lurker of the ditch,
Magician of the growing tooth,
Night stag of the cabbages,
Breaker of covenants, dew-hopper,
Boxer, beater, circle-maker,
Slink back, gobbler of the dark,
Heretic, dusk-junkie, god of bracken,
Black blood of the many jugs,
Scoundrel of the lambs, back-stepper,
Shy girl, skittish runner,
Eyes-wide sleeper
Of the hawking moon.

Ah, a key that fits the lock. *Respect.*

♣

A Dartmoor story.

A new moon in a mist is worth gold in a kist.

Moon woke me, touched my scrawny bones, scuttled me up from
libellous dreams. Moon played a trick. Fibbed to me. Borrowed the
brightness of her lover, the Sun. Had me up, kettle on trivet, belly
lurching for grub. Oh the first slap of strong tea. But there was no
yolk in the air, but pale, vast moonlight. Well I would have a good
start on Tavistock market, and I filled my basket with many good
things for the flogging.

Down the West Dart valley I took my small-hours processional,
with nag and goods, over the wet gorse.

Hi ho and slow we go
Hi ho and slow we go

Moon kept up her end as candle, the contract for waking me in the first place. And an old woman sees things under a freshening moon. And I did my seeing, I did. A pounding streak come at me, over tussocks and wet, grey slate:

A witch moving
A swift-paced hare

Jumps up and into my lap, all muscle twitch and wet fur scent of bracken and smoke. Just time to push hare down into my basket and cover with a scarf, as thrum of hoof announces the incredible, the full arriving, the living field of wild that is Dyer.

Dyer: a-thatch his darkling horse and thigh-deep in the swirling of his darkling hounds, thrashing his darkling whip of dried black tongues; speaking is bone and boom, shuddering adders in the glinting grass.

'Lady have you seen the hare?'

An old woman's guile: my guts broadened by many years, many husbands, I croaked up, chin jutting like a Spanish dancer:

'Take the bracken over Standon towards Hare Tor
The old stronghold
The longhouse

The ale-hut
Of those
March-mad runners

You could still catch her sir.'

A nod.

The terrible court shifts, departs at pace
Over the brow of Cudlipp Down.

Old woman she ambles off.

Hi ho and slow we go
Hi ho and slow we go

Hare emerges from the basket
And is a young woman.

Young woman that is a-dreaming of the moors.

I am of the Other People
And I will walk back
Into the hill singing.

I am nightjar singing,
Horseshoe bat flying,
I am spring water moving,
Old beech sitting.
I gift you:

Hens that lay two eggs for one,
Cows that twofold the milk
And a tongue
That can never be bested.

Young woman that is a-dreaming
Walked into the dawn and was gone.

Now old woman's life is rich: fried egg on the plate,
Cake risen in the oven, wealth of speech;
At the goose fair the tellers' tent shakes
With her language.

Hi ho and slow we go
Hi ho and slow we go

❖

Hare incants the story as we stroll, and kids watching start to slip down and join us from the Newton estates. This new bunch I know. The wonderful freakiness of Ancient Giants and Road Men is a mesmeric proposition. A Road Man is a particular sort of young gentlemen, often selling weed or pills, inevitably in cheap black or grey sportswear from the absolute-slap-down-arse-end of the economic food chain. Even Devonian Road Men speak as if they have just arrived off the boat from Jamaica, via a little stop-off in south London. When I was eight I briefly produced a Jamaican accent and was something called a Rude Boy, which my mother found the most appropriate name there ever was. Ironically by the time you get old enough to be regarded as an adult, you can't be a Road Man or Road Woman.

Ned Kellys, Jessie Jameses, the Laughing Gang of Robin's Greenwood. They are walking with us from a virtual reality to a living reality. They'd likely never step in with me but the sight of giants and a talking hare has its persuasions, its odd charisma.

Come now! *John Wesley Hardings, Black Beards, Hounds of Ulster,* bang bang you sabre rattlers, *Attilas, Genghises,* the fur-minded lot of them.

If you are going to be a fucking outlaw, you may as well be grandiose about it.

But these are titles that should really be given by older men and women. After steady, walkabout observation of the kid.

Youth like that long to be *unriddled* you see.

Unriddle them and they will walk with you through anything.

To unriddle a youth you have to *see* the youth.

And just that, that three-second X-ray, is what they long for. There's a reason there's no colour in their clothing.

Dis-a-fucking-point-ment.

But when giants walk the earth, and Hare spins them round and round with their stories, when kids are walking up into the mouth of God, well, the unriddling is at play.

There are many roads to sovereignty, and the one I see leaving Newton towards the moors has a hundred kids from the shit-kickingly worst parts of Torquay, Paignton, and Brixham scudding along it. The gobby ones get scooped up on the giants' shoulders, and mutter something about a 'cheeky Nando's' into the ears of their vast and terrible mentors. No Nando's, no KFC, no Maccy D's. It's all closed. I could do with a little junk myself. The hippies forget just how GOOD it all tastes. Yum baby, give me a face full of that.

We trail out past the entrance to Seale-Hayne Agricultural College and keep step alongside the Rising Sun pub, then up past Stormsdown and then hang a left and wind down the green lanes to my place. We can stay there a little while, spread out over the riverbank of the Durius. It's hot, like summer, not early spring. Little water spirits gaze out at this processional.

And now we are at my place. This first station of the cross, this Camino. I don't know where this is going exactly. My place is an owl court next to the river Durius. This is where I live and work. I once knew an old Indian, who would have winced if I'd handed him an owl feather. He was my teacher, and wiser than me, but I love owls, and where I live is little short of rammed with them.

Long-Eared Owl, Little Owl, Tengmalm's Owl, Boreal Owl, Short-Eared Owl, Pygmy Owl, Hawk Owl, White-Faced Scops Owl, Laughing Owl, Eagle Owl, Screech Owl, Great Horned Owl, Elf Owl, Bay Owl, Saw-Whet Owl.

They gaze down on the kids, wishing them good. They won't hoot till dusk, but they're up there in the branches.

Like the kids, owls get a bad rap.

To take the owl – *be in a rage*

To walk by owl-light – *to be hiding from the police*

To owl – *to smuggle*

They say in the New World, if you hear an owl cry you have to take your shoe off and turn it over onto the ground. They say in the Old World, if you hear an owl cry you have to turn your jacket inside out. I tell you, if I did that, I would be shoeless and weirdly clothed about half a dozen times a night. That doesn't mean these things are not good advice.

The kids are scattered on the bank of the river, making tents out of shopping bags and twigs, and I lean back under a beech and drift. It's time to disappear a little from their adjustment, see what they can start to figure out on their own.

But one of the Road Men comes up and sits beside me, starts talking quietly, as if to himself, but really for me. And he speaks from the old prehistoric man inside himself, and says things he should not be able to know.

—At the beginning were three women whose hair was all tangled together. They told us about this place. They came to our camp on the seashore and told us. There was a face of God inland, Bright Owl. We could walk into it, onto it. There were many holy beings up there. The women with twisted hair told us this.

We came as shadows up the Tavy, Plym, Erme, Dart, Teign and Yealm in our canoes. Knowing our footfall was weaker than steamy animals that watched from the oakey, we pushed on till we were in higher land. Up on the moor we saw that there had already been a great battle, there were teeth sticking out of the ground. We were in God's mouth. You call them 'tor', but that is from the older name, *twr*. The word has been combed through till it became known as *tower*. Your tors are our towers that are really God's teeth. There are so many teeth in the mouth of God:

Gutter Tor, Rippon Tor, Thornworthy Tor, Great Kneeset Tor, Branscombe Loaf Tor, Leather Tor, Bagga Tor, Kitty Tor, Hunters Tor, Ingra Tor, Rattlebrook Tor, Sittaford Tor, Trowelsworthy Tor, Vixen Tor, Bearsdown Tor, Crockern Tor, Shavercombe Tor, Little Hound Tor, Laughter Tor, Honey Bag Tor, Gidleigh Tor, and these just a handful of your gnashers. And each one a spirit, requiring libation. Each a cantankerous postcode embedded with specific libational instructions.

And then God let us range around hunting and scattering bead and bone, but would have us fuck off to the coast pretty soon after. If you stay in God's mouth for too long it will start to grind on you. We buried our dead up there, so God could chew them free of all life's nonsense. Masticate them to heaven.

That's why we didn't overstay time in the high moor.
Not complicated. We knew it was God.

And you Martin, you sleep by the big tongue of God.
You sleep where the two tongues meet.

SWINCOMBE MEET   STANNON BROOK

HEXWORTHY STREAM   WALLA BROOK

DURIUS MEET

East and west Durius meet and charge through the valley your very head rests in. Where the kiddies make their camp.

It is no surprise a hare is your instructor.

The deep bog is the heart of God and seven life-giving rivers rush from it.

Who else is so generous?

Our canoes are Elk Bone, paddling up dark river to find Bright Owl.

Then the lad becomes nice and normal, starts wittering on about Stanley knives and anal sex and lottery cards.

Hare tells me that the giants stomping back home like this is nothing new. That Hare was there when they arrived the first time.

He says they don't know it, but they are called Road Men because they are trying to find the road home.

They are on a quest. They only know this when they are sleeping; it's all wiped clean with weed and porn in the morning. But Hare knows these kids' faces, through the sourness of time he knows them, from the freshness of time he knows them.

Hare talks to me...

—It's not a vine you are crafting, not a tree you are growing, it's a path you are walking. That's it. Come back down to earth and look right in front of you, Elon Musk. What you see is two lumps, south and north moor. Few rivers, few tracks.

Elk Bone people encountered stories. And not stories necessarily in their tongue. They were going to have to hang back, get quiet, catch the gossip. There was the imprint of the big people everywhere. At night I would go to the edge of the river where they slept by their canoes and tell them of what was to come.

I clacked deep dark Durius rocks under the vine-wrapped oaks next to Blacka Brook, Lymenstream, Sherburn, Ockment, Tavus, Bovi, Teng, and yelped courage into their adventuring hearts. To keep paddling against the current, up through the places your people of the deep future will name.

Mewy country, Plym country, Yealm country, solitary Erme country, Avon country, Swincombe country, Blacka Brook country, Cowsic country, West Dart country, East Dart country, Double Dart country, the South-East desolate, the Eastern Highlands, West Webburn country, East Webburn country, Ashburn country, Lemon country, Bovey country, South Teign country, North Teign country, Taw country, East Ockment country, West Ockment country, Lyd country, Tavy country, Waltham country, and the wildest, roughest-glory country of all: Metheral brook, Maish Hill brook, Great Mire stream, Cheriton Coombe water.

But there's something all woven up inside those names.

Before all of that naming there would have been a goddess at every turn of the river, every beat of a fishing pool, and the very survival of the shadowy people was them learning the particular libations of the particular denizen. You gulp Ockment water, you better know the holy tit from which it pours. Elk Bone people would have navigated from deity to deity, not by grid direction, their canoe laden down with gifts. Road Men remember this time of being low-key, keeping their heads down, going with stealth. But in those days it was not to rob a pound shop but to court a deity.

In some of these place-namings, all crushed and upside down, are the gods, calling to get out. The better you understand the naming, the more breathing holes in the words, the more spaciousness. Crack the egg of a place-name, free the yolk of its power.

I choose my people carefully, but over the years I whisper to them.

I relished my time with Amos Shillibeer of Headweir cottage, a good Mewy man. He'd puff his pipe sitting on the base of Sheepstor cross, and I'd speak my backwards stuff into his head. History lessons in a kind of Devonian Braille if you were March-mad enough to commit to deciphering.

I had a crack at Dinah Tuckett, last keeper of the Dunnabridge Pound if you even know what that is. They'd bring wandering cattle – those illegal to a legal eye – and get paid in cake. Dinah would sit on the Judge's Chair with staff and long coat, every inch a Darty Cunning Man. He'd have some of the apple booze later in the day and I'd tuck up through the heather and talk through him for an hour or two. Seance him in the summering glory. Three thousand years before that I'd played with kids when it was settlement. They'd bet on whether I'd run straight or crooked through the grasses.

And I loved Frederick William Symes of Huntingdon Warren maybe most of all. Bush man, poet, philosopher, maker of tea singed dark orange and so strong when I slurped it I shuddered. Great snowflake of hair on his head, rough jacket, every day grabbing a fry-up in Buckfastleigh then dragging half an oak home for the fire, if Tony from Scorriton didn't catch him sawing first. Any of those three could have been here a thousand years ago, or a thousand years before that.

They say what makes a moor man is how they handle cattle, ponies or sheep but that's not it. A moor man can be dropped in the scald-dark up near Dead Lake or Crazywell Pool and not lose their mind. Can be back at table for breakfast, hard on the bacon, mopping his toast in his sugary tea. You be on the moor on a dark moon it will derange your senses if it chooses. Not one single step you take will you feel you ever taken before, even in your own hut.

The moor is changeable, look at it funny, and it'll follow you out into the car park.

Hare is not talking and now it's me, or him through me:

You need different identifications up here, a tufty passport not
to have your tyres slashed and petrol drained. It was the ruffian
reputation that kept the place fairly clear of plague whilst Exeter,
Totnes, even Ashburton and North Bovey shuddered with its dead.

And three women with their hair all tangled together. I can't stop
thinking about that.

All moor women are half-hare, really. The church in Widdicombe
that my aunt Met's grandfather presided over has a trine of hares in
its rafters, all circled, mid-leap – the Tinners' Hares.

They are the leap all artists wait for, contorting or disciplining their
consciousness in hope of contact.

Artists are waiting to Get Leapt.

When Dermot was placed under magical bonds to elope with
Grainne, he became Hare when he leapt the walls of the compound.
He knew the ground he launched himself from, but where he would
land he could not tell. He leapt a hero, and landed an outlaw.

Every island Odysseus came to was a leap; in consciousness,
character, substance. And he needed hare-tongue to twist and turn
his way through whatever he may encounter. He bragged once
to blinded Cyclops and that did him damage for years. He rarely
blurted after that. He learnt to go from somebody to nobody. Hare
knows about that kind of camouflage.

In the quiet, restless now, some are glimpsing the fires of Ithaca,
maybe for the first time. They are going to need sea legs, old
captains, scrappy maps and strange intent.

Will you tell us a story of magic birthing, oh fellow in the rain?

Will you thump a story out on my knee so the people can hear? The batty-brained, weed-addled lads who sang to you just then, the Adidas-shod, hammer-wielding nutjobs just dreaming of Camelot and Stormzy in the minstrels' gallery. Will you out-weird them, Hare? Like all kids need?

I think you will. The kids are quieter now, and the giants are listening now, for a faraway story. I think Martin from the seventies has walked back into me, but I can't be sure.

You have your audience, Hare.

For a mad long time I was a blade of yellow grass.

I can't remember it in a way I can describe to you, but I know it happened, I know I was one.

My mother tells me I was taller than the rest, which is why she picked me. She went home and slipped me under her sleeping mat and all night I felt her warmth seep into me. By the morning, as she went to open the smoke hole, I was a bawling, red-cheeked girl.

Things happen like that sometimes, they just do.

I grew up with her and was so very happy. I think I knew I was different. From my right sleeve would come sables and martens; from my left sleeve, red foxes. My tears would become pearls, when I smiled it was a smile of precious jewels. I was like you or your sister and I was absolutely not like you or your sister. Once I was of marrying age, word was out, and a young man came to see if the rumours were true.

I liked him, liked his eyes and his strength, and agreed to be his wife. We were married and I left with him to go to his settlement.

On the way to my man's place I got thirsty, suddenly thirsty. I could barely swallow. We were just passing the great witch Yaghishna's place. If the thirst hadn't come on me I would never have suggested we stop there. But I asked my husband to walk out on the ice lake with his pick, and fetch me some water. So off he went. He cut here and there but the bottom was always dry. But he was determined, he got right out to the middle of the lake, and finally out of sight.

The moment he was out of view our dogs went strange and pulled the sledge right up to the witch's door. I had no strength over them, they seemed possessed. I was scared but the door opened and Yaghishna came out, took me by the hand and offered me tea. I sat on a resplendent new reindeer skin as she prepared me meat and drink. It was grand in its way.

As I took my very first sip of tea, the witch pulled the reindeer skin from under me and I fell into a dark cave.

I should never have let my guard down. I should never have crossed her threshold.

I landed on many rotting bodies, blue in the half light, many bones. It was so awful. I called up for help and she said she'd only help if I gave her my clothes. I took off everything but my undershirt and she dangled a rope and I tied them as a bundle. Idiot. She then left me to wither. The bitch changed into my shape, put on my clothes and skipped off to be with my husband.

HUSBAND

She looked just like her. I didn't see it. Maybe I was so exhausted at hacking all over the ice. And she didn't even want the water when I brought it! That should have been a clue. I'd cut maybe twenty holes for her, my shoulder ached. I'd heard that women could be changeable, so I left it.

But there were no pearls, sables or foxes when she arrived at my place. She spat and snot flew from her nose, that was about it, just a little broken glass to cut your skin on. As I say, there were clues.

I did not like my new wife, and spent most of my time hunting swan, elk, reindeer and geese, anything to stay out the house. I loitered on the taiga.

Over time we just about squeezed out a pup together, and one evening the lad was crying for tit.

My wife did something odd, she turned to the wall so I couldn't see what she was doing. The boy continued to wail and so I peered over. There was no milky nipple in his mouth, but the hard tip of her filthy boot. It could have been days since he had received any real nourishment. Suddenly I was both terrified and furious – I shot words at her bitterly, that she had savage blood, savage mind, that she was unclean to raise our boy in this unhallowed fashion, that our marriage was through. If we thought we had argued before, it was nothing like the blue fury of this one, and in the morning I persisted in taking her back to her mother.

And there waiting, was my real wife.

GRASS BLADE WOMAN

So there I was left, slipping and sliding over the bodies of the foul dead. I was to be the next chunk of stink in the dark. But my mind gleams you see. It persists. I heaped the bodies up with my strong peasant arms so I was able to crawl up on my pile of bones. Skull shards in my feet. I started to run back to my mother, but the bitch-witch knew I was out and sent black bear and hungry wolf to surround and kill me.

And dead I would still be, had not one drop of my blood stained a tall grass blade.

A blade that my mother found, laid her warm weight on, and made me again.

So I was back, safe in the hut with her, when my husband and Yaghishna turned up.

This is what you call a situation.

My mother invited them in for tea, as my husband just stared at me. He knew.

My mother claimed I was a storyteller to the guests, and asked me to tell a tale. So I did:

About an old woman who found a tall grass blade, about a woman that grew from it, about a man that loved her, about the two of them passing a witch's house and a terrible thirst coming over the grass blade woman—

At this the witch leapt up and shrieked that I was prattling, and that she and her husband wished to sleep.

Ah, but you can't tell a story that it's prattle. Especially when it's true.

The story took hold of my husband, took residence. Told him what to do. He marched the bitch out of my home and shot her dead with twelve new arrows. It was quite wonderful. Justice.

I have raised their kid like my own, and feed it on the milky pap of story.

The giants, the kids, me, we all sit in the quiet of the story.

Seems there's no escaping the shitty stick when you show up in this life. No dispensation even for a girl created from tall grass and the heat of an old woman. You are still going to get chucked onto a pile of corpses and try and figure your way out. Still get gobbled up and have to start all over again. And there's hubby, dutifully cutting a hundred ice holes. And so many of us sucking on the tip of a dirty boot and wondering why there's no nourishment. Presidents will lift a boot to a thirsty nation. But this is genius. A few lines of an old story and you've got the whole thing mapped out. And yes, a nice, lip-smacking bit of annihilation at the end. I wonder what it means that the arrows were new? Sharper, I suppose.

The kids by the river need to hear that story. And a hard thought: Am I Grass Blade Woman or am I a sorcerer disguised as Grass Blade Woman?

OK, Hare, here's one I know, right back at you.

I live on the anvil of God. Dartmoor.

My grandson is with me. Robin, an old English magic name: coven leader, hedgerow rustler, ruddy-embered bird just when we need a pick-me-up.

I, me, is his grandmother.

I'm no sweetheart of the county fair. I tell you that much. Rough-knuckled from digging my patch between the reaves – more bog and stone than soil. But I have the olde gift: can turn my feet to paws, fur-backed, I can

Become a hare
Just like that
Just like my mother could

And witchiness runs with canniness.

I sends the boy to the squire with news of a hare
In his Longacre fields,

I knows he'll pay well for that.

And he does –
Six silver coins through the air.

So I commits to changing, taking to the fields, become a fetish for
the slobbering dogs. Soon I am pursued by the grunt of man with a
saddle-bashed groin, the high whinge of the hounds, the sleek sweat
bead of a horse too long in stable.

I as Hare runs a thin moon crest round the field then darts under
hedge and back to the cottage.

easy easy easy

At table the squire is distracted, too much black beer that evening,
when he mounts his wife he sees a hare over grass under moonlight.
He's rough that night, terrible.
Needs no persuasions when the boy brings news again.

Six silver coins.

Again the merry dance and the sudden turn to the invisible.

Again and again I slips away, and always at the same moment. Daft
squire. My boy has a jangling purse now, has been seen buying geese
at the fair. The squire shivers at that kind of thing – a plump native.

Final time boy arrives, this time they are waiting, the dogs, more
men, a parson. They've twigged. They bloody know. They've seen
this kind of thing before.

So they dog me back to the cottage, keep step. I nips through a hole in the kitchen wall but is seen, as are heard the shrieks of my boy.

Run granny run

The last line is broken, a sweaty surge through the doors: hound, hunter, holy man, and up the stairs till the door is booted.

A woman in nightdress, combing the sins of a village out of her thin, grey hair with a shard of bone.

But there is the truth of the thing. A pitted range of snapping dog bites on my shins and ankle. They sees me bitch marks. They knows I witchy.

Consequence rains down.

The parson girds himself for a devil's confession,

The squire recalls a choice cell perfect for such a villain as me.

Then the bells start.
Across the grey waves of hate
The bells start.

Surroundingbeguilingenchantingconfirming

Everything calms,
Slow dust in the sunlight,
The parson lowers his cross.

Could there still be a path to the Door of Mercy?

I love the Dartmoor bells, I've ranted about this before. And now I tell the Road Men about it.

That now nobody believes in anything they can't weigh in the hand, the God of the Bells and the Gods of the Moors have teamed up. They bang their charm all gooseskin great and spinney wise, the old, melodious sway that rustles the delirium of this blessed moor into full heathen charge.

Some parts of the moor just will you to quit. There's no shame in admitting it.

Do you know of Grippers Pound, Waterfoot Clatter, Ryders Ring, Zeal Hill? Have you daubed their red mud into your eyes, so your grubbiness was finally blinded? Not easy up there, not for any dweller. Testy, very testy.

On 21st March 1859, the moorsman Michael Aden wrote to the Duchy of Cornwall's secretary from the loneliness of Fox Tor:

Dear Sir,

FOX TOR FARM

I beg to inform you that it is my intention to quit the farm at Michaelmas next 1859, on account of my family being so afflicted. I have a family of six children, three of them quite helpless they cannot help themselves to nothing or are ever likely they ever will be able to. One ten years old, one three years old, and one two years old.

I am Sir,
Your obedient servant,
Michael Aden.

(Hemery, 1983, p. 356)

Little broken children, hidden away up in Fox Tor Farm. Good for a dad to get them out of there. Bad things could happen.

Fox Tor is where Childe the Hunter came to his end:

In vain – for swift the bleak wind piled
The snow drift round the course;
And Death his victim struck within
The gutted, dreadful horse

Hundreds of years later, the Hunter would place me in that blood-ribbed cathedral and I would learn something.

These fuzzy shadows keep gabbling to me. They burble and cackle like the river. It's like this when you talk to people sometimes, you get weather reports from different lives, one flaking onion skin after another. Usually they, there, standing in front of you, are oblivious to their psychic multi-talking.

But I get shakes when I hear the kids shadow-speak, goosebumps.

Know what they are? Goosebumps? A remnant of when we had fur covering us, fur that we could make stiff to catch air when we were cold.

I lie on a rock in the centre of the Durius and hear them chatter these things from the bank. These shadows have no idea it is not thousands of years ago. They accept things.

They bend newness into oldness. I've slipped in and out of this warming dark for so long I am spotted black and white like a magpie.

After a bit Hare tells me I'm going bonkers and has me walk upriver a bit. Leave the kids alone.

As we walk up to Spitchwick, Hare tells me that the world is to turn silver, and to expect less from it. Hare has a point; there's a mizzly cloak over the sun, and the river is low, with big-bollocked rocks splayed out over the banks, a few bluebells starting to peep. It's a limited palette. I like it. Even with the swathe of Arthurian fog and three-inch moss on everything it's glorious, utterly fresh. I can still hear the whine of a chainsaw some way off, cutting down the rotten birch before it pinions some poor eco-hipster to their death.

I enjoy watching a duck valiantly swim against the flow. I look for the river beats that actor Michael Hordern used to fish. He's not here today, for the simple reason that he's dead as dead is, but I carry his quavering warhorse of a voice with me. There's a lovely lack of drama in this moment. After all the concrete smashing and giant marching. There is a quiet thrill to the ordinary. I wonder if this is about as much God as I can take. This unadorned depth.

If the furry shadows were right, then the higher I climb, the further I am climbing into the mouth of God. A god riven with other gods, goddesses, as many as there are tributaries to this bloody river I spend my life trooping up and down. Please don't bring those teeth down on me just yet. I feel ground down enough.

And then suddenly we see them, Hare and I see them.

Outlaws. Curfew-breakers.

Three lamps lit in a copse,
Nine women,
Out and about.

A loopy delegation shaking off the day, expanding like dark concertinas from the compression of Buckfastleigh, or Little Tremulous, Arkansas, or Odetta, Nebraska. Settling in the chalk circle with their Nick Cave stories and their cakes for sharing, thoughtful always, even when in exile.

They seem delighted with each other, drinking Irish coffee from thin white china made from the bones of useless ex-lovers, too sophisticated to bitch, but swift with a sharp knife.

With their Ouija ears they hear voices from burial chambers, not the recently croaked, but the whispery ones, far back, so far back that when they speak you can't be sure you're not talking to an owl.

Hare tells me we are secretly watching other hares, in their womanly shape.

There's a great flood of love in me as I glimpse them. I know I shouldn't look anymore, but think of an old question:

Do women have a secret, original wedding their husbands know nothing about?

And not so long ago down in Bucky such men guzzled bad booze through the dodgy pipes of the Kings Arms, and the White Hart, and the Globe. Enthusiasm – breath of God – isn't that what it means?

They are barely breathing save when a goal is scored on a screen as big as a church, and the bastard-flat, toffee-warm good stuff is guzzled by the thirsty old man inside them, endlessly scratching his crotch.

The men do their epileptic dance to the very last ritual they have left. When a ball roars into an enemy goal it is a pinprick of magic, a white-leathered angelic emissary, rupturing this knackered, erectile disfunction of a day.

Yes.

And we are young again, and it is summer.

We are the Iceni,
Outnumbered,

And we charge the Roman flank,
We will earn our name here today.

Later, both husband and wife will wheeze and furtively screw in
their Devon beds and wonder at the million worlds they can't touch
together anymore.

Their kids wander drowsily about the landing looking to pee, and
the stars overhead arc and wheel, arc and wheel –

Already dead,
Long dead,
Magnificent.

That is a lot for Hare to show me. I don't want to see anymore. We
pick our way back from the gathering, and just as we are about to
leave, Hare pisses on our prints.

It was good to catch a glimpse of the women. There was a power
to it, even if they were drinking Irish coffee, not spruce beer spiked
with honey and ivy like the maenads of old. But today these sibyls
work their Hecate ways calmly, like the life of corn: from unripe to
ripe and harvested. A witch knows when to comb and when to cut,
that is the way of things.

Some things I have learnt about Hare.

She's not a bridge, not a guarantee, but a collapsing ladder, a
scalding pan, something brilliant you heard and eternally misquote.
He places his paw on your pen as you think up your spiritual
franchise and scats on the publishing contract. He waits patiently
for his master in the shadows of Gethsemane, and was the first out
of Eden with a tinny and toothbrush. Those big teeth, you see. Hare
understands his prescribed ordainment in the witty fever of life, she
knows her gig, delights in his obscuration, changes the story, the
record, the mantra, his name. She is sweating away in a bubbling

pot to give flavour to the meal that is his life. She's not afraid to get cooked. But you're going to get the melancholy if you try and eat him, regardless of the red onions and a river of wine, you're going to know you're eating some deep down, strange and abundant holiness. I don't think you'll get through more than a bowlful. And then the deep sighs and the baby blues. Cry me a river.

If we chivvy open the coffins of half of our heroes we're going to find hares.

Don't make them queen, but get them close to the queen. You kill Hare when you make Hare the sovereign. That kind of weight is a debasement for them, iron boots, nails in the guts. They need to fuck and run, ignite and retreat, sleep in snowdrifts, call up your conscience when you've forgotten its pin number.

Allow Hare closer and she will run your pen faster than your mind can catch, little's more thrilling for a writer than the strange midnight gallop over parchment as you see his paws smearing magic all over your neurotic piddling.

Tonight there are a hundred thousand hares between here and Ashburton – roughly two dozen fields bristle with their lovely stink, but there is only one Hare and he, like Elvis, or Strummer, or Simone is here, doing Vegas high-kicks in the rat-a-tat-tat of these blue-streak words. When there are no more hares the world will end – Hare is telling me this and I am her buck-toothed secretary – world ends not in a gradual decline, not in a roar of fire, but just one simple little poof of smoke. It will be just too fucking painful for the universe to look down on us anymore without the shagger in the bracken, the drunk in the ditch, the holy boxer of hopeless causes.

She's not a tablet of stone, a manifesto, even a pamphlet, but he nags, and pulls and bites until something vast is happening to us. We are dragged into the presence of strange angels and so pathetically grateful we can only weep in this Chapel Perilous.

For Hare, the Chapel Perilous is that changeable dimension we call our heart. Perilous it is, when the animal presences are absent, when there's no sweet stink of the low-bellied spirits. Hare will clamp his buck teeth straight into that squirming organ, swinging back and forth like a dervish in the rigging. He agitates till we are out the door, into the night, into the storm, into the rain.

I swear Hare is in the hay at Bethlehem silent knyghting the whole thing from somewhere back in the stable. In her calm, weird eyes, she looks at the baby born in the glow of animals and knows peace.

Hare officially approves this message.

As we walk back to the river and the kids we keep an eye for the little gateways en route, the mossy tolls that require a tale as we go. Takes a while. Both of us chime up, here and there, here and there.

And now it is later, a cool, magnificent spring evening. I've been watching the Road People, down by the river. They have something approximating a camp sorted, even a couple of big fires. They seem taller, broader, and seem, in this moment of the unexpected, newly kind to each other. Their voices seem stronger, breaths deeper. Maybe I'm imagining it.

Rilke knew that wherever we were breathless, that was the source of a lie. That our cramped, squashed selves were a result of some politic fiction that was itself a result of some past trauma. And that's why I listen to Hare: no foldedness, utterly itself, teeth that never stop growing.

I've been breathless for years. My body attempting suicide over and over again the moment I close my eyes. Utter constriction of the throat. The death terror of crawling around the bedroom floor in the dark trying to reboot breath-memory. The deepest thing I've seen in this long stretch of listening is that we all need to unfold. It's got grotesque. Everything I write is an attempt to learn how to breathe, to be my naturalness. To be like Hare. Fuck, sleep, scrap, breed, inhabit darkness, whatever shows up. Here's my wingspan, deal with it.

Because I have suffered, I have spent a long time with the moon. And the moon is a place that Hare lives, they have trackways up and down through the stars, you see. The moon is not a place that an astronaut has stood upon, not really. Not when you get down to the yellow gleaming bones of the thing. But I am not Hare, and I cannot get down from the moon, I can't. And because of this I watch what Hare does, how Hare does, why Hare does.

In my scribblings this last year, I have circled more than once around the damage of love, and underneath that damage, a kind of immovable and mysterious sorrow.

At the very end of his life Ted Hughes deeply regretted not saying bolder, more personal things earlier on the nature of love. He was unimpressed by the temporary rewards of concealment. I know some sorrowing is not meant to be vanquished, but saying stuff has its balm.

When Aztecs gaze at the woman they love
Giving birth
They say old magic:

That she is birthing a pearl
Or a beautiful feather

That she dwells in
The House of
The Tortoise Chair

The words blow
The yellow teeth
Of the wolf away

The words construct the
House of the Tortoise Chair
That which protects the most-precious-thing:

That the Moon will not be killed

❖

And that is all I have for the moon right now.

Hare says it's OK, a little bleak, I may have to have another crack.

I chivvy that heart-clobbered processional out to the dingly danger
of Hangershiel Rock, Dreshelcum, Braitor, Vurtor, Lether. I pick
over the names. What folks created such pungent names? They
gleam in my mind. At the end of prehistory the high moor emptied
of people, changes in weather made crop-growing impossible, and
it became the kingdom of wolf, osprey, polecat, badger, fox, adder,
pine marten, boar, lynx, white-tailed eagle, a flood of wild ponies.

When did these names crawl into use? Were they muttered in the
old Celtic forts, before the roofs became mulch, lodge poles rotted,
and children no longer collected water from our streams? Before the
relentless fucking rain and bleak cold swathed the moor? Before the
great eviction, was a word or two collected, to make a sound-house
for a goddess? A resting hut? I suspect not, say the linguists.

But some hid Celtic goddesses from the Saxons in their jaw. I know
they did. The deities crawled up all fragrenty into our mouth and
we nod and say nothing of the paradise between our teeth.

Every story I've ever told is done to keep her company. True fact.

We appear to have a conjunction down by the river now.

The old Ravilious moon strums its blue note down on us as the owls shudder a-bliss in its hunting light. Our future is huddled in their sports-gear by the fire. I am hoping the nine women will wander further down the river tomorrow and speak with them awhile. The owls of bad reputation hoot for the girls and boys of bad reputation and we quietly brood on what it could take to make a life of a *true* reputation.

Blue Moon of O'Keeffe can see me and Hare are tuckered out tonight, so it watches down on the man with a goddess hidden on his tongue, and decides to tell him a story. The moon is bringing the weird.

It is a busy life for my neighbour the Sun: he burns out his servants if he's not careful.

At dawn his sledge is driven by Polar Bear

At noon his sledge is driven by Buck Reindeer

At dusk his sledge is driven by Doe Reindeer

At the end of a day bringing warmth to people and animals, his son Peivalke bounded up and announced he wanted to marry. The problem was none of the women on earth could bear wearing his golden boots, maybe they were too hot, but whatever the reason, earthly women were unable to walk up into the heavens with Peivalke. He was lonely.

So his father promised him my daughter, the daughter of the Moon, already to be married to a son of the Northern Lights. When the Sun found out he cooked up a thunder that shook everything. Nothing has more poke than the Sun, more power. But my daughter the Moon Maiden brought another kind of light when the Sun rested, a different glow. She could be spotted.

For safety, I gently placed her in the bough of a tree for humans to find, and an old, kind couple soon did, calling her Niekia, the very word she had called to catch their attention.

And so my daughter the Moon Maiden grew in the orbit of the couple, becoming as sweet as a blueberry, skilled at tanning reindeer hides and ornamenting them with bright beads. But she had a silver glow to her, her braids silver too. It was a kind of beauty people gossip about, and sure enough, it got into the ear of hot-fingered Peivalke, who thought he should meet her, try his golden boots on her.

Well he did meet my girl, and force those boots onto her delicate feet, but she immediately became an iridescent mist and disappeared. She hid out in the forest till he had gone, and then she started to walk under my moonlight. In time she came to a great sea, and an empty hut.

The place was a tip, so she took a pail of seawater and cleaned it, to make it fit for her. When she heard voices she turned herself into a spindle as men entered. Ah. The place belonged to the being she was always meant to marry, Nainas of the Northern Lights.

He and his brothers ate and then performed a mock battle that sparked up vivid splashes of colour: sparks of white and gold, great eruptions of purple and greens that flooded the sky above them.

When all that was done, and the other brothers had gone to their homes, Nainas spoke:

'Please show yourself:

If you are old, you could be our mother.

If you are in middle years, you could be our sister.

If you are young, you could be my wife.'

And with that my daughter the Moon Maiden appeared, and quietly but happily agreed to be his wife.

She missed him when he would leave in the mornings, and begged him to stay, but he refused, saying the Sun would incinerate him if he remained, that he could only be with her at night. She made up songs about him in his absence:

Hair like the bright bush of a squirrel's tail,
Tall as an ash of the mountain,
When he leaves, I have no energy
And the day drags long,
But at dusk he comes through
The smoke hole
And my heart softens
Like snow in the spring.

A strange idea took roost in her: she would make a quilt filled with stars and the Milky Way. She did so and hung it from the roof of the hut. That night she slept with Nainas, and every time he opened his eyes he thought he had longer to rest, as the stars glinted above him.

Ah, trouble in the order of things.

When he saw the Moon Maiden leave the hut for a moment he glimpsed daylight, and to his horror saw the simple trap of it. He leapt from the furs but was flogged by the Sun the moment he left the hut, eviscerated, becoming nothing.

The Sun grabbed the Moon Maiden and brutally tugged her up into the sky by her braids, but she refused under any circumstance to marry his son. So the Sun threw her back into my arms where she shelters to this day. They say when you look at my face, the face of her mother, the Moon, you will see the Maiden gazing over to the distant shimmer of the Northern Lights, longing for her Nainas.

✣

Hare likes this story, because it is hard to hold onto. The youth like the story because its strangeness feels real to them. This is not a tale arranged to make them feel good, but one to puzzle over, to fathom then unfathom, to be bent and provoked by.

Maybe to be owled by. Bright Owled by.

Moon never gives a straightforward story.

Who knew of all this trouble in the heavens? This ardent commotion? My hands twitch at the mention of secretive quiltmaking, and binding lovers to my bidding beyond the correct movement of things. Of the heavens. These stories push a strange integrity into my conscience. Maybe I have been loving a constellation of stars as if they were rivers and trees. Wrong approach.

It's hard to love the long-distance runner.

I keep thinking of the furry shadows in their Elk Bone canoes, pushing higher and higher into the mouth of God. That they now, again, mythless, are lying sleeping around me. Eighties Martin is with them, having forgotten everything he knew in the seventies. Nineties Martin will have to find an old door in a Welsh hill and walk through it to start remembering again.

I told you of the women whose hair was all tangled up together. They were dark and were the ones who put the amber beads in the cairn. They loved white horses very much, and a stretch of grass up the top of what we now call Ivybridge. No one took a seal-bone comb to the tangle, everyone knew what they were.

They were the ones who roamed through the minds of their people and said:

—Higher! Higher!

Unblock the energy points of Merlin's Enclosure with your ley-line words, pull taut the bark of the World Tree with your tough thumbs so it may stretch to hold the weight of these baby roady-owls in its fresh branches. Scatify their dreams, make them freshlings to themselves again.

I look around this loopy hoot of a valley. I've told many stories from Dartmoor. They often don't travel well. I go more than thirty miles from their origin and I am struck silent. Like I never had a thought in mind. Silent in Topanga Canyon, Los Angeles, silent in Mound, Minnesota, silent in Burlington, Vermont. Not a peep.

The stories have burnt their passports, screwed up the release forms.

They want you to come to them to hear the tales. In the place.

But Hare is not really interested in such restrictions, and lists a glimpse of his many shenanigans.

She's pleased to show me she's travelled, that's she's seen stuff: I have been stuffed with hay and used as a scarecrow.

I have been the cover of a book and sailed to the New World.

I have cut my teeth on one hundred and sixty trees in one night.

I have been a hieroglyph on a coffin to sing you to the dead.

I have gripped the wrist of Eros, made him miss with his arrows.

I have been white as winter, blue as a Mayo mountain

And now I urge you on, as a culture, as a shadow people

To higher ground.

Elk Bone Canoe will turn to Bright Owl Flight.

part five

the falcon hath borne my love away

Lully, lully, lully, lulley,
The falcon hath borne my love away!

He bears him up, he bears him down,
He bears him into an orchard brown.

In the orchard there is a hall,
That is hanging with purple and pall.

And in that hall there is a bed,
It is hanging with gold so red.

And in that bed there lyeth a knyght,
His wound is bleeding day and night.

And by that bedside kneels a maid,
And she weeps both night and day.

And by that bedside there stands a stone,
'Corpus Christi' written thereon.

Lully, lully, lully, lulley!
The falcon hath borne my love away.

It was early morning outside Troy, as Paris, son of a king, was
moving a herd up Mount Ada. He expected nothing on his path
but maybe swaying grass and a little sunlight. Certainly dirt and
cattle-grunt. But in a moment Lord Hermes stood in front of him,
all a-jingle-jangle with his storytelling magic. And behind him,
three of the great goddesses of all imagining and beyond imagining:
Hera, Athena and Aphrodite. Paris was levelled by the scene, agape,
gasping like two punches to the guts.

Hermes needed something from him. He needed a judgement. The gods knew that Paris was a fair man when it came to assessment, if a little green. Hermes explained that there'd been a wedding on Olympus, and to encourage harmony, the goddess of discord, Eris, had not been invited. She had found out and rolled a golden apple into the party, an apple with a phrase on it guaranteed to create utter mayhem:

To the fairest.

Fresh from bathing in the spring on Ada stood the three deities, all with an offer for the young man.

Hera offered to make him a king.

Athena offered to make him invincible in battle.

Aphrodite offered him the most beautiful woman in the world.

Ambition, power, beauty.

What would you choose?

But what if Paris had chosen Eris?

She came anyway, in the consequence to the answer he gave. She came anyway in the mayhem of the Trojan war. She came anyway in misinformation, betrayal, sheer awfulness and bludgeon.

But what if she arrived as invitation, not imposition? What if we had formalised the arrangement a little, less of the hurt feelings?

A vital patterning can be caught from the dark rhythms of her chaos, a loosening, a rugged potential, a dastardly seat in the wider arc of the spirit of creation. Listen to my caution. Like everything, she can have utterly ghastly aspects. If you stay there forever then it's hell, a useless, dog-chewed anarchy, but we learn again and again: no chaos, no eros. No life force. No duende. No spark. I wonder if Paris could have made another choice. Maybe not, in the presence of those three.

If we submit to the moment – our moment – and don't repair the sails too early, allow the whirlpool to swallow us, then maybe we honour the witch that never received her invitation. Easy to speculate, hard when it comes. Knowing types say things like this and look spiritually smug, but alas, this thought of the apple is staying with me.

Is this where we are? What Eris brings is the disruption of the Underworld, of difficult dreams, of hay bales untethered. She's here anyway. Maybe we need to name her. Maybe she needs to hear the naming.

A young Parzival met her when he left his forest home to seek Camelot. It was not the Aphroditic rapture of a young woman that told him his true name (he doesn't know it at this point), but contact with a widow pawing the stiffened corpse of her dead husband. In the deep unravelling of her circumstance, in the sheer bloody mess of it all, a young man is gifted his name, and then challenged to go out and earn the thing. Parzival would not have learnt his name at Zeus' wedding, he learnt it on the Baghdad road, he learnt it through a virus, he learnt it through his abject failure to save someone else from pain – the Grail King.

He learnt it from all the questions he had failed to ask.
I wonder to myself yet again, in this moment: what is the question we are failing to ask?

—All of them, mostly.

That's Hare. And he's bored and wants to rub the track of this conversation out. It's him speaking now.

—I'll tell you three things I've lived through that show you what you should think about. Ready? Three stories. Maybe four.

1. There was lion that could gobble up all the other animals. He would throw a ball around, and whoever it landed on had to walk up and be consumed. This was ghastly – he'd eaten almost everything, there was no end to his appetite. Finally the ball landed on little me. Thin, stringy, wild-eyed Hare. I was horrified and he was unimpressed, I was little more than a toothpick for him. But he yawned and told me to present myself. I said that before he consumed me, I needed to show him he had a rival.

That's how you get a lion's attention. Another Lord of the Animals.

I walked alongside him to a well. I told him the magnificent beast was down in its depths. That I'd never seen anything as terrible-great as this other lion. Well, my walking companion just about ground his fangs down with rage. But it was true, when we gazed down the well, he saw a lion looking furiously up at him. The lion-in-the-well even snarled at him.

He roared at this and jumped right into the darkness.

I laughed as I watched him drown, and invited all the other little animals to come watch.

Good times.

If you can unbalance someone with a blow to their vanity, there's almost nothing you can't pull off. Hare teaching.

2. I had this bag of beans that was too heavy for me to carry without help. Camels tried, horses, cows, even a lion. Nothing, they buckled. In the end I asked a scruffy little cock, in exchange for some of the beans. Plucky fellow agreed, and though he wobbled here and there, he got my bag of beans home.

Cock had a sore and bruised back from the carrying, so I crushed some healing leaves and rubbed them where it hurt, and immediately sprung up a beautiful tree. He didn't seem to mind the weight. Some tree seeds must have got tangled into his wound with the leaves. The tree sheltered him from the heat of the sun.

It bore the loveliest fruit, which I would throw stones at to bring them down. The stones landed in a river and became an island from which I could grow melons. There would come a day I would travel into the soul of that fruit and see all the beings that dwelt in its vast succulence.

A lot can come from asking for help, and not judging what turns up. You can make a whole world. Hare teaching.

3. Once a swallow came to my place for dinner – I served it vegetables garnished with almonds. He said it was good, but not as good as when it was cooked up not in water, but in his own sweat. That he actually got in the pot and provided the moisture. Weirdest thing I ever heard.

Next day I went round to his home and he proved it. I chewed on maize outside till I heard the flapping of wings and he landed in front of me, dripping and steaming. I have to say it was better than mine. I was impressed. Lovely little detail to the cooking, great addition.

Next day I made my wife squeeze me into the pot with the vegetables and put the lid on.

Swallow came round and asked where I was, wife said I was in the pot. Swallow was upset. It was a joke! He had hidden in a crack in his wall and just flown through the steam flapping his wings before I went to meet him. Swallow was very agitated and begged for the lid to be taken off.

I was dead. Hilarious.

Don't take things so seriously. Hare teaching.

And finally this:

Once I climbed on the back of an elephant who asked me not to eat the pot of honey that rested there. Well I tucked in, until he felt a few drops on his shoulder, sticky in the heat. He asked what it was, and I told him it was blood from a wound. He was happy with that and we continued on.

Don't be so sure that your wound isn't your honeypot, baby.
Hare teaching.

But this is a Grail time, you wise old smart arse. You know it is. That we ask the *earth*, 'What ails thee?' rather than some encrusted old white king whose ballsack hurts. Hare laughs at this with me, but tells me I should absolutely know better. That he was there (of course), and that the Hawk of May, *Gwalchmai* – Gawain himself, doesn't get enough credit in the old stories.

Gawain saw a castle
And at every window
A woman standing
With a candle
And a castrate as a keeper.

He paid the ferryman
And crossed the waters.

A royal hawk
Of the apple-blossom
Month.

A lion in battle.
A lamb in court.

Gawain,
Are you still with us?

And how could we find you again?

In some distant copse
At the edge of a Lincolnshire farm,
The edge of a Heathrow runway
Sheltering under plastic,
Pissed on mead, playing on your phone?
Do you make camp with Gringolet,
Your ever-faithful steed?

Gawain,
Could I find you still,
Lingering with Tristan,
In a dark Tintagel pub,
For just one word about Isolde?

Gawain, don't you want to go home yet? To quit? Perpetually questing
through the centuries, through world wars and plagues. Someone just
saw him, saddle over beech bow on the green lane out of Bruton.

I can't even begin to tell you how alive Gawain is for me, far more
than any factory I worked in, or school endured.

I handle my memory in such a way that the old stories are the
foreground, and calendar time has to settle into the background. It has
to audition in relevance to the bigger stories I'm witnessing. It spins too
many fictions otherwise. Febrile and cheap. Lowers your standards.

Fuck it. I'm glad you are out there, Gawain. For my heart to
understand, for my heart to lean towards. But I wish you the fires on
the beaches of rocky Ithaca. I wish you a Penelope and a strong bed.
I wish you a hound like Argos, a son like Telemachus, I wish you a
place you carry your oar to and no one knows what it is.

I think the most frightening island that Odysseus came to was not full of Cyclops, or the sun god's cattle, or the long-outstayed-its-hospitality run at somewhat stalkery Calypso's.

It was the Island of the Lotus Eaters.

That is the place of the rabbit hop, not the hare's leap. Comfort but no shelter. Where cherub to warrior sucked on the fruit that kept them stultified, malleable, drunk, stoned. Kept them weak. Easy to colonise. For a second we have had the fruit pulled from our mouths.

There was a time that Arthur of Britannia was waylaid by a giant, a lord of the animals. Furious that Arthur had offered portions of the forest off here and there to his most gallant, the giant was planning to take his head. Using that head of his, he asked the giant if there was something more productive he could offer in exchange for his life. As it was, he was dressed for hunting, not combat, so there would be no honour in the kill. The giant caught the moment like a feather in the wind, and asked gently, with true curiosity:

'What do women really want?'

In the year-and-a-day that passed, Arthur and Gawain asked every woman they could find. Towards the end of the enquiry Arthur ended up alone in the forest, knowing he had not heard the deep bell of truth in any of the responses. In this melancholy he came across a great and ferocious being, Lady Ragnell.

Hair a boar's mane down her back, rusty tusks from her jaw, eyes that rolled in ten directions, lion's paws for hands. She strummed a mandolin and rode a donkey and Arthur knew with every twitch of his eyelid that this being did indeed know exactly what women wanted. And she did, but she wanted suitable payment for such a life-saving answer: Gawain's hand in marriage.

Gawain of course did not hesitate to agree.

The response was given and Arthur's life saved. On the night of the wedding the couple retired to the chambers to consummate their vows. If anything, Ragnell had grown during the day, she spilled over the sides of the bed, rooks flew from her, volcanoes bubbled, vipers writhed and spat in her lap, she was her own queendom, utterly.

She asked for a kiss and he gave it.

Of a sudden there was another woman standing there, in all her ordinary beauty.

'That was a brave thing you did. Now, I can only be in this shape half the time. Do you want me like this privately, or publicly?'

Gawain had the words calmly in his heart.

'Today I gave you everything I have. My name, my lands. The choice, of course, is yours.'

She spoke:

'Sovereignty offered, sovereignty accepted, sovereignty given back.'

That is what women want.

And whatever spell needed to be broken was somehow broken by the two of them.

It turned out that the giant was her brother, so it may be they also gained a little forest back in the arrangement after all.

I'll say it again as a Sicilian storyteller said it to me:

Sovereignty offered, sovereignty accepted, sovereignty given back.

Hare stretches happily:

—Any king, any queen, has to wed the wily, dangerous, exacting spirit of the land.

No primary relationship to all of this, and you, and everyone you know, has run their race.

You are a sucker without it, a lotus eater.

That's why Gawain matters.

Christians and pagans have far more in common than they do with atheists. I've even seen Pan listening in the moonlight to Midnight Mass, I saw it I tell you. Moon on snow, and there he was, Christmas Eve, 1873, Hexworthy chapel.

Hare stands and boxes, ducks and weaves.

—I gave you three knock-out punches when I gave you those three stories earlier, remember them?

1. Lose your arrogance. (Lion)

2. Even knowing one seed well can build a new earth. (Cock)

3. Loosen up, stop being so serious. (Bird)

I say it again, know your patch and proceed deity by deity, not by grid reference or postcode.

That one thing could save you. Completely.

Gawain would understand, you see. Let me tell you another story about him. I was in his saddlebags for this one, hitching a lift with his great steed Gringolet.

Christmas, Camelot. Arthur's merry and declares an adventure must take place before they all settle down to chops and cupfuls of brimming beer. This is to be a two-week-and-one-day banquet, of high carousing and the pleasure of the splurge and gobble. The very thought of it has kept a saddle-sore warrior going on a long, rain-daubed tour of the north. As you are detecting, there is a keenness in the hall for the story, adventure or event to speedily reveal itself.

Bursting into the hall – green horse, bridle, saddle, body – is a primordial, an old, old one. His hair and beard are shorn no higher than his massive, green elbows.

The Green Knyght.

A power as old as even the dream of Merlin. He imagined himself for five hundred thousand years before he actually took form. Worked on the design plans. This is a remnant, an energy source so far back in the mist of things it's almost as old as me.

In his vast and ancient fist a sprig of holly.

Green Knyght wants to play a game, an ancient, pagan game. Mayans like this kind of thing. Looking for someone to decapitate him, to loosen all logic from his body and just let the animal surge take over. Now my Green Knyght is properly frightful, and gives everyone the willies. In the end Gawain gets embroiled – what a star – to save Arthur's reputation. One blow, off goes the giant's head. It rolls around the floor and the body calmly rises and gathers it under his arm.

Oh shit.

Turns out Gawain has to meet him at something called the Green Chapel in a year-and-a-day's time, to receive an equivalent blow. Should really have studied the contract. The Green Knyght rides away, terrifying – I mean terrifying – and the party attempts to continue. The queen is ashen and the boys try to make light of it, but everyone knows a drive-by shooting has just occurred. Gawain, flower of the court, is a dead man. Moribund, posthumous. That was it, his bell just chimed, all jumbled up within the rules of the 'game'.

The day we leave there is much keening in the gallery, and whispered advice from Lucan the Good, Ywain, Lancelot, even Sir Dodinal the dreaded is heard by patient Gawain.

Ah, but we are leaving in that wintering light, flaming orangey light, crisp snow underfoot. Me tucked up in Gringolet's saddlebags, warm in hay. It is a huge thing to set out into the wilds of Olde Britannia, portals to other worlds are cranked even wider in them days. Every bothy, copse, rain-wrung moor contained fairy, brigand, spirit. Every tump is encoded with ghostly script if you know how to read it. Spirit-Braille on every dyke and branch.

After the mysteries of Anglesey it is up and around the Wirral we go, ducking in and out of forest, hamlet, settlement, always asking for information. From scald crow to swinekeep, everyone's silent on the matter. The goosiest of goose chase.

A grimy and sullen trip it is, low on laughs, advice and hot water. How we are suffering for one moment of glamour.

When the year is almost up we come to a castle of mistiness and crow call, tucked away in a sullen wood. Gawain is welcomed in by a large fellow, Bertilak, who tells him that the Green Chapel is only a few miles away. This is both good and bad news for our man, as he doesn't expect to survive the encounter. Bertilak invites Gawain to stay, the chapel being so near, and introduces his wife Lady Hautdeser, and an old woman who stays back in the mix, but always peering at him, proper creepy. It is Christmas again, and Gawain cautiously welcomes the shelter, and the chance to build his strength up.

Big ol' beardy Bertilak had a weird game he wanted to play. That as Gawain rested and he hunted, they would swap whatever they had received throughout the day at supper. That morning, as Bertilak hunted the woods, Gawain received a visit from Lady Hautdeser, who was gently inviting. She received nothing but a chaste kiss from Gawain. On the return from the hunt, Bertilak gives him deer, Gawain returns with a little peck. Bertilak roars with laughter.

Second day Lady Hautdeser visits again, only receives two pecks. Bertilak returns with a boar, and gains two pecks. Again he laughs, but I have to tell you, his laugh is alarming. Like the bell of a stag.

Third time Bertilak's wife turns up the heat. Offers him a gold ring which he refuses, then a belt which, if worn, will keep him safe from harm at the Green Chapel. Ah, now that's all of our sweet spots, isn't it? *Life.* Survival. He grinds his teeth, wrestles in the depths, but quietly takes the belt and slips it on.

On his return Bertilak hurls the rancid carcass of a fox at Gawain's feet.

Three kisses. No laughter.

Next day Gawain leaves smarting, but with the belt still tucked away till he gets to the chapel. A lonely but a more sacred place you can barely imagine. Our minds barely have the stretch to conjure such a holy place anymore.

As he bends for the blow he can't help but flinch a little.

'Stay still man!'

He flushes with shame, especially when the next blow is held a quarter-inch above his neck.

Now Gawain roars:

'Fucking strike! Don't you dare hold back.'

Third blow just nicks Gawain's neck with a shot of blood. He doesn't waste a single second but grabs his warrior kit to face the Green Knyght –

And finds Bertilak standing there, laughing softly, his arms extended in peace.

'You truly are a great one.

It is no shame to value your life.

I am the Green Knyght, and this whole test was devised by the old woman of my keep, the great Morgana.

Go with honour, and a lesson learnt, dear man.'

Gawain, Gringolet and I travel home much swifter than we set out, as if our way was lit by bright torches. Gawain confesses all in court, no spin, held nothing back. I saw him do it, takes guts. To reveal his imperfectness.

But you know what?

From that day forth, once a year, all the knyghts of the Round Table would wear green belts in solidarity with Gawain.

It is no shame to value your life.

♣

Hare says:

—It is good for people to hold themselves to a high standard, but to understand their humanity. To be humbled.

Otherwise you are a lion drowning in a well roaring at your own reflection. Otherwise you don't understand the value of dirt to a seed. Otherwise you don't understand the value of getting killed every so often.

Tell me this:

Was the strike of the Green Knyght not a kind of honey for Gawain?

Can you not see the bees gathered around the chopping block?

Each drop of blood was honey by the time it hit the dirt.

Tor-Teeth-Tower.

Chomp chomp chomp

Grail still carries the dream that Elk Bone could become a Bright Owl, that we raise the red dirt of human experience so it smears the underside of the moon. That we have a cosmos again worthy of the name. That you yourself could become a moon ladder.

There is a teaching that we are falcons whose eyes have been sewn shut.

We don't know our nature and have no sense of our wingspan. There are guards of distraction surrounding us. But there is an angel up ahead if we can just break free, a spiritual companion.

That friend's maybe Cundrie, maybe Gawain, maybe a Hare whose teeth never stop growing.

Not every wound is filled with flies, some are a ritual cut. It can be such a blow that scatters the guards of distraction.

Samson tore a lion to pieces as if it was a young goat, and when he returned there was a hive of bees making honey in its body.

The Fisher King could be offered honeycomb from the body of Samson's lion.

What ails thee?

The Fisher King became dangerous to the church because when he fished in deep water he encountered relief from his pain. It wasn't a dove from above, it wasn't transcendental relief, it was soul knowledge. That God could speak to you like that, alone in the wilderness, from below not above, was taboo for a while. That Godpower could fly through a cave as well as a cathedral. Like a bat.

It's up to those little Elk Bone canoes to fish in the great waters of ourselves.

Throw the hook out into the blue ripples of Corpus Christi.

I have to be fifty to be able to dare to hold that thought in mind for even a moment. It is a massive thing: it slips from me like a trout and is gone into far water.

It is finally coming to the end now, this March madness of mine. These three immersions into the fontanelle of Holne Chase. This year of deep-drop divine foolishness. This mercurial triad of smashcrash magic that has so thrummed me askance.

Tomorrow I will break all police guard and take myself to Crockern Tor with this roving tribe of giant, Road Man, nymph and satyr. The third station since I started smashing up Torquay. I will climb Crockern Tor and announce in the Old World, formal way of things:

A call to Bright Owl for our people, our beloved antiquities sucking sweets by the fire, our gnashing housebound pups. I will libate every single bottle of whisky I have left and leave a dry cottage. I will implore, entreat, stab the air, wave my staff of words at the utterly uninterested sheep, and see with my steely eye, canoe become feather.

It is a line of song I can see from Big Rock with my hare-eye. I can see Torquay seafront before the heroin, I can see Lee and Dave, Danny, Tim, Becky, Christine, Alec, Rob, Sal, Anna and Tom. I can smell the sting-hot pavement of 1977 and hear the churn of bells on a Chelston Christmas Eve. I have all of this in me, and a thousand more days, and a thousand more days after that.

In the house of my birth, books are flying off shelves and the waves are licking the door, the trees behind are pushing my sleeping baby body between their dark branches, I slip from beech to beech. I have hewn my incompleteness into the finest shape I can, scallywag I am, and am weeping at the bottom of the garden where the Heavenly Woman will not visit again, no matter how much kindness I leave.

And then I walked out, one spring morning.

The gorse was out the whole way, like torches I swear, yellow blaze from my door to the foot of a god. I'd never seen crows so happy, sweeping around on breezes so warm you'd swear you were wandering the hills of old Crete. The wild ponies were happy, crunching tall dry grasses, bellies fat with foal, the coal-black cows were happy, their young tottering the greening humps of the moor.

And as I walked, I walked with all the stories I had ever told up there in the mouth of God. Round every fire I had lit since the year 1971 to this very moment, up there in outlaw country.

Red Bead Woman walked with me

Parzival walked with me

How Daylight Came walked with me

The Listener walked with me

The Half Girl walked with me

Tristan and Isolde walked with me

Wild Cat-Man and Emu-Woman walked with me

Dermot and Grainne walked with me

Grey Wethers Stones walked with me

Birth of Hermes walked with me

The Benji and the Mid-Wife walked with me

Fenist Bright Falcon walked with me

Pleiades and the Wild Bee-Man walked with me

Goose Girl walked with me

Handless Maiden walked with me

Psyche and Eros walked with me

Ivan and the Grey Wolf walked with me

Bird Men and the Fight by the Lake walked with me

Ivan the Bear's Son walked with me

The Birth of Taliesin walked with me

The Odyssey walked with me

Tatterhood walked with me

Six Swans walked with me

Gawain and the Green Knyght walked with me

Faithful John walked with me

The Moon Palace walked with me

The Rudiments of Time walked with me

Wolverine Makes the World walked with me

The Fox Woman walked with me

The Serpent and the Bear walked with me

Akanida, Daughter of the Sun walked with me

The Two Brothers walked with me

The Earth Gnome walked with me

The Marriage of Gawain and Lady Ragnell walked with me

The Birth of Shoshlan walked with me

The Whale Boy walked with me

The Birth of Ossian walked with me

Old Kytna walked with me

Deirdre of the Sorrows walked with me

The Firebird walked with me

Elfrida of the Flowers walked with me

Chaw Gully Raven walked with me

Brutus of Troy walked with me

Blind Tarvaa walked with me

Twelfth Night Wassail walked with me

The Woman Who Became a Fox walked with me

The Lindworm walked with me

Deer Woman walked with me

The Red King and the Witch walked with me

Valamon and the Wild Third Daughter walked with me

Sedna's Comb walked with me

The Huntress walked with me

Cinderbiter walked with me

Taligvak walked with me

Vasya Whitefeet walked with me

Bleak Shore walked with me

Mayaki at the Smokehole walked with me

Clorinda, Queen of the Shepherds walked with me

Pwyll and Rhiannon walked with me

Blodeuedd of the Flowers walked with me

The Holy Couple walked with me

The Boyhood of Finn walked with me

A Drum Used for Magic walked with me

Connall Crovi walked with me

The Seal-Woman walked with me

The Woman who Married a Bear walked with me

Briar Rose walked with me

The Singing Man walked with me

The Six Cranes walked with me

Arthur and Gorlagon walked with me

The Making of Bodvar walked with me

Iron Hans walked with me

Bearskin walked with me

The Judgement of Paris walked with me

The Wanderer walked with me

Hairy Grylos walked with me

Spirit of Sickness walked with me

Daughter of the Moon and Son of the Sun walked with me

Wudu-Wasa walked with me

Half Man walked with me

Raven walked with me

Childe the Hunter walked with me

Culhwch and Olwen walked with me

Merlin walked with me

Dafydd ap Gwilym walked with me

Lorca walked with me

Finegas walked with me

Odin walked with me

Horse walked with me

Wolf walked with me

Hare walked with me

And I walked to a god of Dartmoor with my people.

Below me –

The roads are empty, the lanes are empty, the cities are empty, the towns are empty, the villages are empty, but underneath it all, hoofprints are breaking through the concrete. In each house, hidden-away families hubble bubble toil and trouble in the appointed strangeness of it all. This ghosting, that is also a wombing.

Behind every door, Jacob wrestles with an angel. The keeper of keys is throwing one to every household, the Maker of the Way.

And the Road Men and the Road Women are becoming the tyke cherubs they always were. The crumpled exits, the unworthy, and wingspan enters. Let these rascals lead us on. Three steps it took, just three stations to becoming a true human being, a moon ladder for others.

And where is that grief I have gnawed so fervently? I cannot locate it in my shape today. It would appear I have walked down from the moon.

And walking on earth I found heaven. I saw that drystone walls were in fact loaves of fresh bread piled high for the sick of heart, I saw that the reaves of the fields were in fact the tracks of Elk Bone canoes skimming the grasses. I bang on the door of the Tower of Song. It opens.

I bring a sachet of myrrh
A cluster of henna blossoms
A vineyard in bloom

Dear God of
Mercy and kindness,
I am refreshed.
The Bright Owl is here.

Let us leap as a people,

Burst from the skirt of Boudicca into the greenness of things.

And I saw a great gathering of humans and animals, even nightjar and curlew and cirl bunting in their swooping hymns. I found Belus the Sun so large and kind I could have wept, you could have made wine up there. Come all the originals of this place: lion, hyena, wolf, bear, eagle.

Five years ago, I clung to the face of Crockern as the wind butchered me, slaughtered me, hanged, drew and quartered me, now it cradled me.

In those five years of punishment that followed, I would not cut a hair on my head or wipe a tear from my eye.

And today I gave my plait, a foot of hair cut away and left as offering to this slate-grey denizen.

And suddenly, there he is. The rider. My teacher. The one who has stalked me this whole time. And he speaks and finally I understand. What was dark sound has become new wine.

I kneel before him.

This place is Grail Castle,

This place is Green Chapel,

This place is Living Vine.

I buckle in my happiness;

I, who crawled into a Hare

Who crawled into a Wolf

Who crawled into a Horse

Am crawling into God

And it is blissfully too late

❧

Is þes middangeard missenlicum

Wonder is the world, without compare

SOURCES

BARDSKULL

Vita Merlini (Arthurian)
Boyhood of Finn (Irish)
Blodeuedd (Welsh)
Rhiannon of the Horses (Welsh)
Culhwch and Olwen (Welsh)

PIXILLATION

Ivan and the Grey Wolf (Russian)
Briar Rose (British)
The Woman Who Married a Bear (Siberian)

WOLFERLAND

The Hunters Who Slept All Winter (Siberian)
The Singing Man (Siberian)
The Six Cranes (Siberian)
Old Kytna, Wolf Woman (Siberian)
The Wanderer (Anglo-Saxon)
Odin's Sayings (Scandinavian)
Maxims (Anglo-Saxon)
Arthur and Gorlagon (Arthurian)
Flower of the Mountain (Irish)
Three Riddles (Anglo-Saxon)
The Making of Bodvar (Scandinavian)
The Butterfly Soul (British)
Raven Tales (Inuit)
Hairy Grylos (Cretan)
The Changeling of Llanfabon (Welsh)

UNRIDDLING

The Half Man (Siberian)
Dyer and the Hare (Devonian)
Grass Blade Woman (Siberian)
Silver and the Hare (Devonian)
Moon Daughter and the Son of the Sun (Siberian)

THE FALCON HATH BORNE MY LOVE AWAY

The Judgement of Paris (Greek)
Hare's Stories (African)
The Marriage of Gawain and Lady Ragnell (Arthurian)
Gawain and the Green Knyght (Arthurian)

References
Hemery, E., *High Dartmoor: Land and People* (Robert Hale
Limited, 1983)

A NOTE ON THE AUTHOR

Martin Shaw is an award-winning writer who lives on Dartmoor in the far west of Britain. He is the author of many books, including the Mythteller trilogy, *The Night Wages*, *Courting the Wild Twin* and *Smoke Hole*. A deeply respected oral storyteller, Dr Shaw created the Oral Tradition and Mythic Life courses at Stanford University, and is director of the Westcountry School of Myth as well as a long-time wilderness rites of passage guide. His work has been published in *Orion*, *Emergence*, *Poetry International* and *Mississippi Review* among others. A Reader in Poetics at Dartington Arts School, he contributes regular essays and audio at his Substack *The House of Beasts & Vines*.

Unbound is the world's first crowdfunding publisher, established in 2011.

We believe that wonderful things can happen when you clear a path for people who share a passion. That's why we've built a platform that brings together readers and authors to crowdfund books they believe in – and give fresh ideas that don't fit the traditional mould the chance they deserve.

This book is in your hands because readers made it possible. Everyone who pledged their support is listed below. Join them by visiting unbound.com and supporting a book today.

With special thanks to
Justin Adams

Supporters
Nicholas Adamski
Shona Alexander
Rob Ammerman
Valerie Androvette
Mark Armen
Nigel A Ball
Giles Barrow
Francis Barton
Delia (Bear) Beadle
Tom Belcher
Arwen Bennett
Astra Bergmane
Robert Berry
Carolyn Biletziclis
Heather Binsch
Heather Anne Blankenship
Joanna Blundell
Kurtis "River" Bonholzer
Francine Bonjour-Carter
Justin Bonnet
Bart Bourdeaux
David Brazier
Stephanie Bretherton
Robert Brock
Jerilyn Brownstein
Erica Bullivant
Dan Burgess
Jacob Bush
Ben Campbell
Victoria Capps

Jordan Christine Carmichael
Daniel Carmody
Holly Cartlidge
Louise Chalice
Laura Chatain
Beth Childs
Tracy Chipman
Judy Clark
Peter Clark
Amabel Clarke
Tyler Clemens
Lucy Coats
Myranda Cole
Emma Collins
Michael 'marked for death'
   Collins
Tracey Collins
Maryjane Conroy
Douglas Contreras
Flick Cook
Lucy Cooper
Jennifer Corcoran
Anna Corsini
Tessa Cowley
Aoife Cragg
Adam Craig
Daniela Crawford
Suzi Crockford
Sam Crosby
Audra Crutchfield
Nic Dafis
Michael Dallin
Michael & Kim Davies
Kelly Davis
Stephanie Davis
Fiona de Wolfe

Miki Dedijer
Audrey di Mola
Tracey Dillon
Sarah Doffman
Tanya Dorrington
Coe Douglas
Jen Drake
Nathaniel Dyas
Erin Elizabeth
Julian Ellerby
Taylor Ellis
Casey Ellison
Cherie Elm
Eddy Elsey
Elizabeth Saxon Erikson
Phoebe Evans
Sally Evans
Katariina Fagering
Logan Donovan Fahey
Penny Fellbrich
Jennifer Ferraro
Anthony Fisher
Sarah Flinn
Erin Flood
Kristin Flyntz
For Osian Wren Hulse-Toghill
Jan Fortune
Charles Foster
Shaggy Fox
Esther Frankort
Anna Freud
Jason Frey
Monique Gaboury
Rachel Galan
Miguel Gallo
Amanda Yates Garcia

Elizabeth Garner
Ann Garrett
Rina Gill
Zach Gill
Edward Gillespie
Barbara Gittes
Mallory Glaser and Robert Lee
Tiffany Gordon
Kathy Gower
Emma Gray
Jez Green
Barbara Greenstein
Mike Griffiths
Leslie Gumbrecht
David Guy
Suellen Hammer
Jeremy Hanks
Brid Hanlon
Ethan Hanna
Jan Aksel Harder Klitgaard
John Harrigan
Neil Harrison
Andrew Hartwell
James Harvey
KJ Hawkwood
John Hawley
Justyn Hegreberg
Donnachadh Hehir
Amy Heneveld
Lucy Henzell-Thomas
Kate Hewett
Jeremy Hill
Barbara Hockley
J.M. Hofer
Kelly Hollen
Lucy Hounsom

Eric Hudson
Rob Hughes
Joshi Hume
Sarah Hundley
Hillary Hunter
Ruby Huzel
Khaver Idrees
Derek Irwin
Troy Ivey
Sophia Jackson
Laura Jacobs
Ashley Gates Jansen
Dave Jeffords
Prescott Jennifer
Candace Jensen
William Johnson
Brian B Jones
Jacob Jones
Kathy Jones
Phill Jones
Siân Jones
Mary Jordan-Smith
Gabriele Joy
Andy Jukes
Alex Kahler
Aya Natalia Karpińska
Jared Z. Karr
Anatolia Karteras
KC KC
Alexis Kennedy
Ros Kennedy
Suzanne Kennelly
Catherine Keough
Kidthunder
Dan Kieran
Karen Kimmett

Linda Kingsnorth
Charlotte Knaggs
Michael Koenen
Chris La Tray
Nigel Ladkin
Laura Lamb & Dave Miatt
Riversteadt LaMoreaux
Clayton Lancaster
Angela Lane
Sue Lansbury
Sienna Latham
Patrick Laurie
Scott Lawrance
Christy Lee-Engel
Hilary Leighton
Fiona Lensvelt
Roxy Lenzo Douthit
Alana Levandoski
Joshua Levine
Levontines
Chaise Levy
Jennifer Lighty
Tor-Egil Lilleholmen Braaten
Sylvia Linsteadt
Kevin Longrie
Lotni & Desirae
Oakley Loudon
Ganin Lovell
Sarah Lowes
Brigitte Colleen Luckett
Dalrymple MacAlpin
Paige MacKenzie
Fiona Mackintosh
Demne Máel
Antonette Magnatta
Liane Maitland

Oileàn Mara
Knicki Markolf
Frances Marshall
Adam Martin
Paula Marx Rush
Eszter Matrai
Rory Matthews
Amanda Mayflower
Maryann C. Mays
J. L. M. McAuley
Sharon McCarthy
Dan McDonagh
Carey McDonald
Ruth McKay
Lynn McMillan
Pam McWethy
Joel Meador
Simon Medhurst
Marcia Mercadante
Kristina Meschi
Anna Maria Michalska
Helen Miller
Virginia Miranda
George Mitchinson
John Mitchinson
Ioan Mitrea
anna molitor
Erin Molitor
Tonya Molnar
Taymara Montague
Adrian Moonwood
Jonathan Moore
Sharon Moreno
Lee Morrell
Selena Morresi
Jackie Morris

Laura Mosteller
Care Motika
Jaya Penelope Mullumby
Claire Murphy
Carlo Navato
Nick Neame
Hilary Neilson
Melissa Nelson
Nigel Newell
Viryapuspa Nolan
Burgess Norrgard
Joseph Nutman
Laura Joan O'Neill
Jennifer Obbard
Samuel Griffiths Osborn
Angela Osborne
Susie Osler
Al Overton
Jeremy P
Roderick Packe
Asher Packman
Jes Padgett
Sara Parker-Fuller
Emily Paskevics
Duncan Passmore
Lauren Patridge
Justin Patterson
Priscilla Pena
George Pendle
Hugo Perks
Andrew Perrin
Sarah Coleman Peters
Autumn Peterson
Robert Phillips
Tanis Poole Phillips
Jennifer Pilgrim

Shannon Plummer
Justin Pollard
Hannah Pope
Karla Pringle
Thea Prothero
Nicky Quint
JS Rafaeli
John Ralph
Paul Rankin
Katie Rauk
Victoria Reddick
Catherine Reyes
Kate Greenough Richardson
Silvatiicus Riddle
Deborah Rim Moiso
Reggie Riverbear
Mark Robinson
Anne-Sophie Roos
James Roper
Chris Rosenau
Amaya Rourke
Diana Rowan
Patrick Ryan
Yuka Saito
Justin Scarelli
Terrie Schultz
Cristiane Scolfaro
Matt Scott
Neil Scott
Gemma Sealey
Jonathan Seaman
Seanchas
Seven Fables Dulverton
Rachael Shanahan
Alison Shapiro
Faye Sharpe

Linda Shaw
Alexandra Shore
Bob Sima
Mike Simmonds
Emily Simpson
Krys Sipple
Joe Skade
Peter Smith
Anna Southgate
June Hilles Staal Robles
Charlotte Stark
Tristan Stark
Robert Steadman
Noah Sterba
Brandt Stickley
Matthew Stillman
Gavin Francis Stoneystreet
Stacey Sullivan
Penelope Swan
Linda Swanberg
Celene Syntax
Will Szal & Kyra Kristof
T & K
Sandy Tabin
Itai Natan Tahori
Anne Tame
Annabel Tarrant
Katarina Tavčar Možina
James Piers Taylor
Susan Taylor
David Taylor-Jones
Jillian Tees
The Bard of Tysoe
The Oak and Bone School
The Storytelling Circle
Nick Theisen

Esther Thomas
Brewer Thompson
Grant Thompson
Helen Thompson
Liz Thompson
Tim
Justine Toms
Leon Trice
David Trillo
Michaeleen Trimarchi
Ben Trollinger
Ian Tromp
Jade Tseng
Alan Twiddy
Ben Tye
Kenia Umphrey
Jo Valentine
Stuart Voaden
Jody Vyner
Celia Walden
Jamie Wallace
Eleanor Walsh
Bert Wander
Lee Ward
Tama Leigh Ward
Dave Warren
Olivia Watchman
Muriel Watson
Liana Woods Weiland
Karen C White
Rachael Wildman
Reg Wilford
Julia Williamson
Alison Witham
Katherine and Katie Witteman
Richard Wolfströme

James K Wood
Tom Woodhead
Mark Woodsford-Dean
Cecilia Wootz
Maggie Burbank Yenoki
Susan Zasikowski